HIGH PRAISE FOR BRIAN KEENE!

CITY OF THE DEAD

"In the carnival funhouse of horror fiction, Brian Keene runs the rollercoaster! The novel is a never-ending chase down a long funneling tunnel...stretching the reader's nerves banjo tight and then gleefully plucking each nerve with an off-key razorblade... There aren't stars enough in the rating system to hang over this one-two punch."

—*Cemetery Dance*

"Breathtaking. Absolutely breathtaking. Keene manages to build characters that jump off the page and bite into you."

—Horror Web

"[*City of the Dead*] will force even the most sluggish readers to become speed demons in the quest to reach the resolution. The pacing is relentless, the action fast and furious."

—Horror Reader

"Keene reminds us that horror fiction can deal with fear, not just indulge it."

—Ramsey Campbell

"Keene has revitalized the horror genre."

—*The Suffolk Journal*

"A headlong, unflinching rush."

—F. Paul Wilson, Author of *The Keep*

MORE PRAISE FOR BRIAN KEENE!

THE RISING

"[Brian Keene's] first novel, *The Rising*, is a postapocalyptic narrative that revels in its blunt and visceral descriptions of the undead."

—*The New York Times Book Review*

"[*The Rising* is] the most brilliant and scariest book ever written. Brian Keene is the next Stephen King."

—*The Horror Review*

"*The Rising* is more terrifying than anything currently on the shelf or screen."

—*Rue Morgue*

"*The Rising* is chock-full of gore and violence…an apocalyptic epic."

—*Fangoria*

"Hoping for a good night's sleep? Stay away from *The Rising*. It'll keep you awake, then fill your dreams with lurching, hungry corpses wanting to eat you."

—Richard Laymon, author of *After Midnight*

"Quite simply, the first great horror novel of the new millennium!"

—Dark Fluidity

"With Keene at the wheel, horror will never be the same."

—Hellnotes

"Stephen King meets Brian Lumley. Keene will keep you turning the pages to the very end."

—*Terror Tales*

A LIVING NIGHTMARE

Out of breath and panicking, I ran around the side of the building and slid to a halt. The thing that had been underneath the shed was definitely not an oversized groundhog. It had crawled back outside, reopening the tunnel beside the woodpile. Half of it jutted from the hole, thrashing in pain. Stinking fluid sprayed from the knife wounds in its side.

I couldn't believe my eyes.

It was a worm. A giant earthworm, the size of a big dog—like a German Shepherd or Saint Bernard—but much longer. It undulated back and forth in the mud and grass, covering the ground with slime. Watery brown blood pulsed from the gash in its hide.

More of its length pushed out of the hole, and the creature whipped toward me like an out-of-control fire hose. The worm's tip (what I guess must have been its head, though I couldn't see any eyes) hung in the air in front of me, only an arm's reach away. Then the flesh split, revealing a toothless maw. It convulsed again, and then that horrible, yawning mouth shot toward me. Shrieking, I stumbled backward to the shed door. The worm followed....

Other *Leisure* books by Brian Keene:

CITY OF THE DEAD
THE RISING

THE
CONQUEROR
WORMS

BRIAN KEENE

LEISURE BOOKS NEW YORK CITY

For my grandparents,
Ward and Anna Ruth Crowley,
because part of this is their story.

A LEISURE BOOK®

May 2006

Published by

Dorchester Publishing Co., Inc.
200 Madison Avenue
New York, NY 10016

Copyright © 2005 by Brian Keene
Previously published as *Earthworm Gods*

ISBN 0-8439-5416-7

The name "Leisure Books" and the stylized "L" with design are trademarks of Dorchester Publishing Co., Inc.

Printed in the United States of America.

Visit us on the web at www.dorchesterpub.com.

ACKNOWLEDGMENTS

Thanks to Cassandra and Sam for weathering the storms and bringing sunshine on a cloudy day; Shane Ryan Staley and Don D'Auria for giving me shelter from the rain; the Cabal for up-to-the-minute weather reports; Tim Lebbon for backyard bourbon under the stars on a clear, cloudless night; Tracy, Mom, and Dad for *The Rime of the Ancient Mariner* during dinner; Mark Lancaster, Matt Warner, John Urbancik, and Tod Clark for providing rain gear; and to you, my readers, for waiting at the end of the rainbow.

AUTHOR'S NOTE

Although Renick, Lewisburg, Baltimore, White Sulphur Springs, and many of the other places mentioned in this novel are real, I have taken certain fictional liberties with them. So if you live there, don't look for your house. The forecast calls for rain.

PART I

THE EARLY WORM
GETS THE BIRD

There were giants in the earth in those days . . .

—Genesis
Chapter 6, Verse 4

CHAPTER ONE

It was raining on the morning that the earthworms invaded my carport. The rain was something that I'd expected. The worms were a surprise, and what came after them was pure hell, plain and simple. But the rain—that was normal. It was just another rainy day.

Day Forty-one, in fact.

My name is Teddy Garnett, and I guess I should tell you right now, before we go any further, that I'm no writer. I'm educated, sure, and a lot more than most of the good old boys in this part of West Virginia. I never made it past grade school because my father needed my brothers and me to help him with the farm. But what I didn't learn in grade school, I picked up during my thirty-five years as a radioman in the Air Force. That's pretty easy to do when you've been stationed everywhere from Guam to Germany. Seeing the world gives you knowledge—the kind of knowledge you just can't get in a classroom. During World War Two, and in the years that followed, I saw most of the world. And I always loved to read, so between my travels and my

3

books, I've learned everything I ever needed to know.

I can read and write and multiply and discuss in German, French and even a little bit of Italian, the ramifications of Nietzsche's *Beyond Good and Evil* and the poetry of Stephen Crane. Not that there's anybody around these parts to discuss Nietzsche or Crane with—even before the rain started. If you mentioned Nietzsche in Punkin' Center, folks would think you'd sneezed and offer you a tissue. And poetry? Shoot. Poetry was just something they'd heard tell of, but had never actually experienced for themselves. Kind of like visiting Egypt or Iraq or some other faraway land. Not that most of our residents could have found either one of those places on a map. When it came to current events, if it hadn't happened here in our county, or maybe over in towns like Beckley or White Sulphur Springs, then it didn't matter. Most folks in these parts didn't know about Vietnam or Iraq until their sons and daughters got sent there to die, and even then, they couldn't find them on a map.

I'm not trying to sound smug, but I was smarter than most folks around here, probably because I'd seen the world beyond the mountains and hollows of this great state. But I never once let it go to my head, not even after my eightieth birthday, which is when a person is allowed to sound like a wise old man. I never bragged, never belittled someone less smart than me. Some nights, after my wife died and before the rain started, I'd go down to the Ponderosa in neighboring Renick, or the American Legion over in Frankford, and beat Otis Whitt's boy Ernie at chess (Ernie Whitt was the only other one in Punkin' Center or Renick that could play). Or I'd explain current events to my neighbors, or write letters to the paper and try to put things into perspective for folks.

But writing books and stories? No sir. I'd always left that up to Mark Twain, Zane Grey, Jack London, and Louis L'Amour—the four greatest writers of all time.

I'm not a writer, but I can tell you it must be a tough business. I'm doing this by hand, here in the dark—cramming words into this little spiral notebook, and my arthritis is acting up something fierce. I've been lying here on my side, gripping this pen for the past couple of hours and now my fingers have blisters on them and my hand is twisted up like some kind of deformed claw. I don't know if it's the dampness in the air or just the act of writing itself that's doing it, but it hurts. It hurts really bad.

So why waste time writing about how much it hurts me to write? Because I've got to get this done. Because it's important for you to know what happened. It might save your life, should you ever find this.

I'm just glad that everything below my waist has gone numb, so I don't have to deal with *that* pain anymore. I looked down there once, at my legs.

And I haven't looked since.

I am afraid. I can feel something sharp inside me, grating and rubbing up against a soft part. There's no pain, but there is a strange, queasy sensation. I don't know what it is, but I certainly don't imagine it's anything good. My stomach has a big purple and red splotch on it, and it's spreading.

I'm still coughing up blood. I can feel it in the back of my throat, and my mouth tastes horrible.

For what's easily the thousandth time since the rain

5

started, I find myself wishing that the electricity were still on. Then I could go down into the basement and write this properly, on the old word processor my grandson and his wife gave me after they bought their computer. It sat down there on a little particleboard desk I got at the Wal-Mart in Lewisburg.

But the power isn't on, and it's never coming back. It went off the same day the chubby weatherman on the *Today Show* shot himself live on national television in the middle of a forecast. One minute, he was joking around with that pretty anchorwoman with the nice smile and vacant eyes who's always after people to get their prostate checked, and a moment later his brains were splattered all over that big map of the United States behind him. Seems like years ago, but it really hasn't been that long. Apparently, he'd been getting death threats.

Death threats. All because of the damn weather . . .

He got off easy. Those poor folks at the Weather Channel never had a chance. Fellow drove a box truck loaded with explosives right up to the building and blew it all up. They never did catch the people behind it, but I guess that doesn't really matter now. Maybe there wasn't anybody masterminding it at all. Maybe the suicide bomber was just fed up with the weather reports. Today—a one hundred percent chance of rain. Tonight, rain continues. Tomorrow? More of the same.

Even if the power *was* still on, I couldn't go down into the basement. Not now. Not after what happened. The desk and the word processor and everything else in the basement are gone now. The only things in the basement are bodies, floating around in the darkness, along with the remains of that—*thing*. Once in a while,

I hear its carcass bumping into what's left of the stairs. I'm sure the water level is getting higher, too. Pretty soon, it will start seeping under the door, and I don't know what I'll do then. I can't go outside.

Who am I kidding? I can't even move my legs, so why worry about going outside?

There's an old generator out on the back porch, but I don't think it works. I haven't used it since the blizzard back in 2001. Even if it did still work, I'd have to go down into the basement to hook it up to the power box, and then go outside to start it. And like I just told you, I can't do either of those things.

So I'm lying here in a puddle, wishing I had electricity, but what I really want is a dip. My last can of Skoal was empty on Day Thirty. I had to lick the shreds of tobacco off the lid just to get any at all. I've been sweating through nicotine withdrawal ever since. A chew would set things right. Wouldn't matter what kind at this point: Skoal, Kodiak, Copenhagen, Hawken—maybe even a cigarette or a cigar (though I never much cared for smoking) or some leaf like Mail Pouch. Just a little bit of nicotine would be finer than my wife's blueberry pie right about now. And her blueberry pie was mighty fine. Mighty fine indeed.

Maybe you're wondering how an old man like me, an old man who's injured, is finding the strength and energy to write something like this down. Well let me tell you—I'm doing it to take my mind off the nicotine cravings.

I've lived through a lot in my eighty-odd years. I survived a rattlesnake bite when I was seven, the smallpox when I was nine, and a thirty-foot tumble out of a big oak tree when I was twelve. I made it through the Great Depression with a half-full belly. I fought in World War Two. Lied about my age and went to boot camp when I was fourteen. A few months later, I was over in Europe, right after the invasion at Normandy. After that, I got sent to the Pacific as well. I couldn't tell you the number of bombing runs I participated in. I killed other people's sons in the war and never thought twice about it. I made it back home, only to have Vietnam claim a son of my own in return. I always figured that was God's way of making things equal. I've watched the baby boomer politicians and the ex-hippie Wall Street tycoons destroy what my generation worked so hard to build. We gave them a nice country, and they destroyed it with their greed and their lobbyists and their Internet-capable cappuccino bars and their rap music. I've seen my good friends get old and die. Most of them are gone now, except for Carl. One by one, they've succumbed to Alzheimer's, cancer, loneliness, and just plain old age. Like a Ford or a Chevy, eventually our parts wear out, no matter how well we're built. A few years ago, I watched Washington's World War Two Memorial dedication ceremony on television and was shocked by how few of us are actually left. Felt like a mule had kicked me in the stomach. On top of everything else, I've outlived my wife, Rose. Let me tell you, that's something no husband should ever have to go through. It may sound selfish, but I wish that I'd gone before her. Rose's death was just about more than I could bear.

But despite these trials and tribulations, the hardest thing I've ever had to suffer through was sitting here listening to the constant patter of big, fat raindrops beating against the windows and the roof, hearing it non-stop, all day and all night, without a pinch of tobacco between my false teeth and my gums for comfort.

My apologies. I'm an old man, and look here what I've done. I've gone and gotten off track. I started out writing about Day Forty-one, and then I went on a tangent, ranting about my life story and the damn weather.

Of course, I reckon this is the end of my life story. And I suppose that somewhere deep down inside, I've known that since my trip to Renick.

Renick. That was on Day Thirty. Maybe I should start there instead.

Oh Lord, do I need some nicotine! This must be how those heroin junkies feel. I never understood how these young people could get hooked on dope, but of course, I was hooked on a drug, too. Only difference is mine was legal. I miss it. Didn't know how bad I'd come to rely on it until it was gone.

It was that same insistent craving that woke me up on Day Thirty. My body was pleading with me, promising that if I'd just give it a dip, it would make the headaches, insomnia, toothaches (because even when you wear false teeth, you can still get phantom toothaches), sore throat, chest pains, diarrhea, night sweats, and bad dreams go away. I knew that was a lie. Those things didn't just come with nicotine withdrawal. They came with old age, as well.

I don't know that a nicotine fix could have done much about the nightmares, anyway. I dreamed of Rose at least once a week after she was gone. It was also that way when my boy, Doug, died in Vietnam, though it passed with the years. As terrible as it sounds, there are times now when I have to stare at his picture just to remember what he really looked like. I can't remember how his voice sounded anymore, either. I guess that's all a result of old age. But it didn't matter, anyhow. Even if the nicotine could have chased the dreams away, the closest place to buy a can of chew was at the Ponderosa gas station over in Renick.

Renick is the next town after Punkin' Center. It was a forty-five minute drive down the side of the mountain on a wet and slippery road. I'd avoided making the trip ever since the rain started. But on Day Thirty, caught in the grip of some really nasty nicotine withdrawal symptoms, I walked out into the downpour. It took me a whole minute to reach my Ford pickup truck (I haven't driven the Taurus since Rose died), and I was soaked to the bone by the time I got inside. I dried my glasses off with a napkin from the glove compartment. Then I fumbled with my keys, crossed my fingers, said a prayer, and started it. The truck came to life, sputtering and coughing and not at all happy about the situation, but running just the same. I checked the gauge and saw that I had three quarters of a tank left. That would get me to town and back.

Most of the stones in our gravel lane had been washed away by then, leaving only mud and ruts. Even after I put the transmission into four-wheel drive, the tires churned and spun. I didn't think I'd make it out to the main road, but eventually I did.

Sighing with relief, I started down the mountain road to Renick. I experimented with the radio, hoping to hear another voice or even some music, but there was only static. I'd wondered for several weeks what was going on, ever since the power and the phone lines went out. It had been some time since I'd heard someone else speaking, and I was lonely. I'd taken to wandering around the house and talking to myself just to ease the emptiness, and I was sick of the sound of my own voice. Even one of the talk-show nuts that seemed to have taken over the radio these days would have been welcome. Instead, the only sounds keeping me company other than the radio's static were the rain and the windshield wipers, both beating a steady rhythm as I drove.

I knew that if Rose were still alive, she'd tell me how bullheaded I was being. A stubborn old man, doing something stupid—all because he was addicted to tobacco. But here's the thing about that. When you get to be old, when you're what they call elderly, you lose control of everything. Everything around you isn't yours anymore. Your world, your body, and sometimes even your mind. That makes you stubborn about the things you can still control.

Maybe it sounds cliché, but my heart was in my throat for most of the drive. In the years before the rain, when winter came to visit and the snow piled high, Rose and I didn't go to Renick. For people our age, the winding one-lane road was treacherous even in the best conditions. But after thirty days of rain, it was a nightmare, worse than the harshest West Virginia blizzard.

One side of the mountain road used to be nothing but cornfields and pastures. The other side was a steep drop down a forested mountainside, with only a steel guardrail as a buffer. Now, the rain had flooded the fields and pastures, washing away not only the crops and grass but the topsoil as well. Streams of brown water gushed down the mountain and huge gray rocks jutted up from the mud like uncovered dinosaur bones. Uprooted trees lay scattered across the road, and I had to drive on the sides to get around them. The biggest, an old oak, completely blocked my way.

I spotted the tree as I rounded the corner. I slammed on the brakes, and the truck fishtailed, sliding towards the guardrail. Shouting, I gripped the wheel and did what Rose would have done—chastised myself for being a stubborn, stupid, bullheaded old man. The truck spun. The front bumper slammed into the tree, and the rear crumpled the guardrail. I closed my eyes, holding my breath and waiting for the truck to topple over the side. My heart pounded, and I felt a stab of pain in my chest. This was a stupid way to die, and I expected Rose would be waiting on the other side, shaking her head the way she used to when she thought I was doing something foolish. But I didn't crash through the guardrail and roll down the mountainside. Instead, the truck stalled out on me. I opened my eyes to find myself looking back in the direction I came.

I clutched my chest, trying to get my breathing under control. My pills were back at the house. If I had a heart attack out here, nobody would be around to help me. I imagined I could hear Rose scolding me from on high.

"I know," I said out loud. "You told me so, dear. I'm just being foolish."

Eventually, the pains in my chest disappeared. I got out of the truck to check on the damage, praying I didn't have a flat tire. The damage wasn't bad; just some dents and scraped paint. If I'd been going any faster, it would have been a lot worse. I was pretty sure the truck would start again, and was actually glad it didn't have airbags, since a deployed one would have made it impossible to drive back home. I was a realist. At my age, there was no way I'd be able to walk back up the mountain in the rain. I'd be dead before I made it two miles.

Death. At my age, I was used to the idea. It was imminent. Some mornings, I'd wake up and be surprised I was still here. But when I thought back on my life, I wondered what it was all about. Was it worth it, all the joys and heartaches? What was the point of it all, if it only led to this—an old man drowning alone in a flooded world?

Standing there in the downpour, I heard a flock of geese passing somewhere overhead. I craned my neck skyward, but I couldn't see them. They were lost behind the permanent white haze that covered the earth. The fog bank started just above the treetops and continued into the heavens, blocking out the moon and stars. The disembodied honking sounded eerie and made me feel lonelier than ever. I wondered where they were going, and wished them luck on their journey.

Satisfied that the truck was still operational, I surveyed my surroundings. A few scraggly trees were still standing here and there on the slope, and I looked down on Renick through a break in the tops of them. Or maybe I should say I looked down at where Renick used to be, because the town was gone.

The Greenbrier River had swallowed up the entire valley. There was an ocean in the place where Renick had once been.

Renick had stood at the base of the mountain, nestled in the valley. Beyond it was the state road to

13

Lewisburg (that was a *real* road, with two lanes and a yellow dividing line down the middle). If you traveled from Renick and back the way I'd come, you would have headed up the mountain, passing a few shacks and houses, each one complete with the regulation, rusted-out car propped up on cinder blocks, and a brand new satellite dish on the roof. West Virginia had one of the highest welfare populations in the nation, but everybody had a satellite dish.

You would have then entered Punkin' Center, which consisted of nothing more than seven houses, the combination post office and feed store (run by my good friend Carl Seaton), and then several farms. Keep on going and you'd pass a few hunting cabins, Dave and Nancy Simmons' place, crazy Earl Harper's shanty, the lane that went back to my place, and then miles of West Virginia state forestland. At that point, the road narrowed to a dirt track leading up to Bald Knob. It ended at the lookout tower the rangers used to watch for forest fires in the summer, and their station underneath it.

All of this was deserted and washed out when I made my trek down the mountain. The National Guard had cleared everybody out of Punkin' Center a few weeks before. I stayed behind, though, even when they insisted that I leave. Oh, I guess they could have made me leave if they'd tried hard enough. It isn't too hard to force an old man out of his home. But they didn't. Maybe it was something in my eyes or the tone of my voice, but those young troops backed down quick. This is where I've lived for the last thirty years and I wasn't leaving on account of the weather.

I looked back down on Renick. The town was attainable from our side of the mountain only by means of a steel and concrete bridge that spanned the Greenbrier. On one side of the bridge was the road on which I was stranded. The town lay on the other side. That morning, on Day Thirty, the bridge was gone.

It wasn't just destroyed, mind you. The bridge was *gone*. It had vanished along with the rest of the world, leaving our mountain standing in the midst of a new ocean. That's what it looked like. Either the Greenbrier had gotten very big, or the Atlantic Ocean had gotten very lost and decided to come inland for a spell. Everything was submerged—all the homes and businesses and the school. Everything except for the Presbyterian Church steeple and old Fred Laudermilk's grain silo, jutting up from the water like lone mountaintops.

That was when the full impact of what had happened hit me. There'd be no State Fair down in Lewisburg this year and no cornbread and bean suppers at the American Legion. The rickety yellow school bus wouldn't be making its trip up the mountain to pick up the few kids in Punkin' Center and old Fred Laudermilk wouldn't be bringing in the hay this fall. Ditto for Daniel Ortel's wacky weed crop (we all knew he grew it, but nobody said anything) and Clive Clendenon's corn. My crazy neighbor, Earl Harper, wouldn't have to concern himself anymore about the government conspiracy of the week, and I wouldn't have to worry about poachers on my land this coming deer season.

They always said this would happen because of a hole in the ozone layer. They said that greenhouse gases would melt the polar ice caps, flooding the world. But that's not what happened at all.

One day, a day like any other day, it just started raining and didn't stop. It's as simple as that. We certainly didn't expect it. It was a rainy day, but tomorrow would bring sunshine again. But tomorrow never came. The next day, it was still raining. And the day after that. Every day brought the same forecast; rain, no matter where you lived. Except that there aren't really days anymore—just differing shades of gray and black. I haven't seen the sun or the moon for a long time. They've been reduced to silhouettes, hiding behind the clouds like muted silver dollars.

Everybody had theories. The meteorologists threw around a lot of techno-babble, and the politicians argued, and then the world leaders started pointing fingers at each other.

Here in the United States, the coastal areas went first, along with their cities. Places like San Francisco, Los Angeles, San Diego, Atlantic City, New York City, Miami, and Norfolk. Florida's panhandle and the entire Gulf Coast were instantly wiped out as ten-story waves crashed over them, driven ashore by a massive storm swell and winds of over two hundred miles per hour. Towns like Grand Isle, New Orleans, Apalachicola, and Pensacola were gone in the blink of an eye, submerged along with the two million people living there who never got the chance to evacuate. Interstate Sixty-five, near the coast of Alabama, had been snarled in gridlock when it happened. All of those people died beneath the rushing waters, trapped inside their cars. Tornadoes ripped through the non-coastal areas, leveling trees and buildings, and then those places were flooded, too, relentlessly battered by the rains.

One time, I watched a television program about hurricanes. They said that weather researchers classified hurricanes into different categories, with a category one being just above a tropical storm and a category five being the absolute worst. Well, let me tell you, the super-storm that erupted across the planet was beyond categorization. It would have been a ten. The Federal Emergency Management Agency was unequipped to deal with the disaster, but I reckon no amount of preparation could have saved us even if they had anticipated it.

Within the space of seven days, all of the coastal cities in the United States were obliterated, and the rest of the country started flooding. And that was just the beginning. Then it got worse. The rain kept falling. Some nut in Indiana started building an ark, just like the one Noah had used, and there was a rumor that several governments had done the same, shifting their elite and powerful onto battleships and luxury liners, along with animals and plant life.

The National Guard started evacuating people before the rest of the cities farther inland disappeared beneath the waves, but there was really nowhere to go. The whole damn country was flooding. Then the waters rushed over the rest, as far as Arizona in the West, and up to the Ohio River Valley in the East. It may have gone even farther, but that was when the satellite television stopped working. Last thing I saw on the air was footage of a lake where the Mississippi River used to be. The Potomac flooded over its banks, too, and took out the nation's capitol. The Rockies, the Appalachians, the Smokies, and a few other remote locations were supposedly still above water, just like my own mountain, but I can't imagine life was too pleasant in those places. I wondered if there was another old man like me, trapped on his mountaintop in Colorado, waiting for the waters to rise up and swallow him.

The good old U.S. of A. was a disaster area of biblical proportions, and the rest of the world didn't fare much better. Places like Easter Island, the Philippines, Sri Lanka, Indonesia, and Diego Garcia were gone. Not flooded, but gone. Cuba, Jamaica, and the rest of the Caribbean got wiped out in the same storm surge that destroyed the southern United States. Hawaii had been reduced to a few lonely volcano peaks. I remember watching Nova Scotia get erased live on CNN before the satellite stopped working. Asia, Europe, Africa, Australia—I don't know what the final outcome was, but the television footage hadn't been promising. The Himalayas and Mount Kilimanjaro were probably beachfront property by now.

And now Renick was gone. While I'd seen the damage on television, it took this to finally bring it home for me.

Because this *was* home.

Like everything else, Renick was gone, swallowed up by the Greenbrier River. And the river was gone, lost amid the floodwaters. Down in Lewisburg, Interstate Sixty-four was gone, and with it, the passage to my daughter's home in Pennsylvania.

Pennsylvania was gone. New York City was gone. I'd seen that on TV, too, before the power went out. It was horrible; Manhattan buried under an impenetrable fog and water surging from sewer grates and manhole covers. Hundreds of homeless people drowned in the subway tunnels before the evacuation even started. When it was over, the National Guard and police had to patrol the streets of Manhattan by boat. I remember seeing footage of some jet skiers looting Saks Fifth Avenue, and an NYPD speedboat chasing them off. The water, black with filth and garbage, crept up to the third and fourth floors of just about every building in the city, covering everything under a layer of sludge. Worst of all were the rats. Everything that the camera flashed on swarmed with vermin. The rains had pushed them, streaming and angry, from their underground kingdom. They were hungry, and it wasn't long before they started to eat the dead, bloated bodies floating in the streets. And when they ran out of those, they turned on the living.

The rains had forced the rats to the surface. I wondered what else the rains would force to the surface, and if these things would be hungry, too.

I took one last look at the steeple and the silo jutting up from the churning waters. I just couldn't believe what I was seeing. Rose and I'd had a lot of good times together in that little town, times that would never come to pass again—times that had faded, just like my memories were starting to do. I was suddenly glad Rose hadn't lived to see this. My Rose had loved her Bible, and she would no doubt have had a scripture on hand for this occasion, just as she did for everything.

In the Bible, God sent Noah a dove. I'd done what the Lord had asked me to do for over eighty years, but I didn't get a dove. All I got that day was another nicotine fit.

Dripping wet, I climbed back into the truck. My head hurt, and I shivered while holding my hands in front of the dashboard's heater vent.

I needed a dip.

I put the transmission in drive and returned home, soaked, depressed, with no tobacco and a banged-up truck to show for my efforts. My world—my mountain-top home—was now an island jutting up out of a brand new ocean.

That was Day Thirty. Each day got worse after that. So did the nights. They were the absolute worst. Nights in the country can make a man feel very alone. There are no streetlights or cars, and if the moon isn't out, all you're left with is the chorus of insects. Once the rains started, the insects died, and the moon and stars were swallowed up by storm clouds. Now, nighttime wasn't just lonely—it was downright frightening. With no starlight and no electricity, the darkness was a powerful thing, almost solid. I'd lie in bed craving a dip, unable to see my hand in front of my face, and listen to the rain.

Izaak Walton once said the Lord has two dwellings: one in heaven, and the other in a meek and thankful heart. Well, God must have been in heaven, because the way I felt, He couldn't have lived inside of me.

Each night, I prayed to the Lord and asked Him to let me die. I asked to be reunited with my wife.

And each night, God ignored my prayer.

The sky wept with His tears. I cried, too, but my tears were very small things when compared to those falling from the sky.

CHAPTER TWO

So—let's get back to Day Forty-one. It's hard to believe it was only two days ago. It feels more like two years. Like I said earlier, that's when the earthworms invaded my carport. But something else happened on that day. That was the morning the early worm got the bird.

I reckon that's where we better start. Trust me, I'm fixing to tell you. Everything I've written up to this point was just me trying to avoid talking about what really happened. But that's not going to do us any good. And I'm afraid I might be running out of time. I need to finish this. I'll try to make it as factual as the amount of time and notebook pages allow. As Huck Finn said in the opening chapter of *Huckleberry Finn*, when discussing the previous book, *Tom Sawyer*, "Mr. Twain wrote a little bit about me in that book, and it was mostly true, or some of it was anyhow. The truth may have been stretched a mite, but mostly it was meant to be true."

Keep that in mind while you read this. Because you'll probably think I'm stretching the truth just a bit.

But I'm not. This is what happened, and I swear it's as true as I remember it to be.

You see, the rain was just the beginning.

Day Forty-one. I woke up that morning with a Roy Acuff song stuck in my head, and suffering again from nicotine withdrawal. It wasn't as bad as on Day Thirty, when I tried to make it down to Renick, but I still felt horrible. I opened my eyes, wincing at the pain in the back of my head, right where my spine joined my skull. My jaw ached, and my mouth was dry and tasted like a baby bear cub had used it for a potty. As always, the first thing I heard was the rain drumming against the roof. It was also the last sound I'd heard before falling asleep.

My bedroom was part of that blue world that exists between night and dawn, eerie and quiet—except for the rain. I fumbled for my watch on the nightstand, knocking over a glass of water in the process. I grunted, put on my glasses, found the watch, and focused on the tiny numbers.

Five o'clock, as I'd known it would be.

I'd woken up at five in the morning every day since my retirement. A life spent in the Air Force will do that to you. You get used to a routine, and nothing, not even the end of the world, can vary it. Rose used to complain about it, but there was no curing me.

I reached for the can of tobacco out of habit, and cursed, grinding my gums when I realized it wasn't there. I sat on the edge of the mattress, my feet on the cold floor, breath hitching in my sunken chest. I felt so helpless and alone. I looked back over my shoulder to the spot Rose had occupied next to me and I began to cry.

After a while, I stopped and blew my nose. Then I listened for my buddy outside the window. My special friend stopped by every morning. He would cheer me up, and even though the sun couldn't be seen through the gray skies, it was near dawn, which meant he'd soon start singing.

I pulled back the shades and looked out upon the dreary world. My yard was nothing but muck. White mist obscured my clothesline and tool shed, and hid the trees marking where my yard ended and the miles of sprawling forest began. The only thing not concealed by the fog and drizzle was the big blue spruce outside my window and the robin's nest cradled safe and dry within its broad needles. The robin was the only other living creature I'd seen in the last three weeks, except for a herd of deer I'd spied grazing down near the spring (and by that time, the spring was a small pond). They'd been wet and skinny and half-starved, and I hadn't seen them since. The same went for the horses, cows, sheep, and other livestock some of my neighbors kept. They'd been left behind when the National Guard evacuated Punkin' Center, but I hadn't seen any during my trip down the mountain and I hadn't heard the cows mooing at night. Usually, their sound would have carried over the hills to me. Now there was nothing.

I know now what probably happened to them, but I didn't know then.

The bird was a welcome sight. Each morning, he got me out of bed with his insistent—and very pissed off—song, crying the blues about the weather. The robin hated the rain as much as I did. He left the tree only to catch worms, and then just for a few minutes each morning. It probably sounds funny, but that bird was my only friend and contact since the power went out. Each morning, I looked forward to his visit. Silly, maybe, but then again, I was a silly old man. Rose would have no doubt had something to say about it, but Rose wasn't there.

The bird didn't disappoint me that morning. Like clockwork, I heard the familiar titter as he woke up. His song was hesitant at first, but then it got louder and stronger and angrier. I spied a flurry of wings within the branches of the tree and then he darted out, zipping to the ground as quick as he could, hoping to nab a worm or two and then buzz back to his nest, soaked and miserable.

"Howdy," I croaked, my throat still dry from sleep. "Good to see you this morning. Want some coffee to go with your worms?"

He landed on the wet, spongy ground and began to peck through the mud. He glanced over at the window, and I swear he could hear me. Maybe he looked forward to seeing me as much as I did him. With a final tilt of his head, he got back to business. I smiled, watching in simple contentment as he hopped around, looking for breakfast. Furious chirps punctuated each tiny jump. I laughed out loud. He didn't know how good he had it. At least he didn't have to worry about nicotine withdrawal.

I stared closer at the bird. Something seemed wrong with his feathers. There were splotches of what looked like white fungus growing on his back and wings. I wondered what it was.

The pickings must have been slim that morning, because he strayed farther from the tree, almost halfway to the tool shed, looking for worms. The remaining grass in the yard and the thick, rolling mist almost obscured the robin. I pushed my glasses up on my nose and squinted, trying to track him. Suddenly, he gave a triumphant whistle and leaped at something I couldn't see.

A moment later that chirp of victory turned into a frightened squawk, and the robin shot up into the air, his wings buzzing furiously. Something squirmed through the mud, and then burst upward after him.

I shouted from the window, wanting to warn the robin, even though he'd already seen it. The thing on the ground was hard to see amidst the rain and fog. I caught a glimpse of something long and brownish-white. It was fast. It *stretched* toward the fleeing bird, and then there was empty air where the robin had been a second before.

The thing snapped back to the ground, like one of those Slinky toys my grandkids used to play with when they were little. A second later, it was gone as well, disappearing back down into the mud as if it had never been there at all.

Stunned, I closed the blinds and stood there, my hands and legs shaking in shock and disbelief. After a bit, I put my teeth in and made my way into the living room. Blue darkness had given way to the dim gray haze of dawn.

I stared at the cold and useless fireplace. I'd closed the chimney flue to keep the damp air out. It was built to keep the rain from coming in, but there was so much moisture in the air everything in the house ended up mildewed if I left it open. Above the fireplace was a mantle, made out of a wooden crossbeam taken from my daddy's barn. It was old, like me. Also like me, it had survived numerous tornadoes and storms and hail and lightning and fires and droughts . . . and floods. Many, many floods.

On the mantle, my family stared back at me from their frames. I lost myself in them, trying not to contemplate what I'd just seen. Rose and I on our wedding day, and the portrait we'd gotten taken at the Wal-Mart in Lewisburg for our fiftieth wedding anniversary. She was even prettier in the second picture than in the first, taken a half-century before. Our kids: Tracy and Doug, when they were little. Next to that were snapshots of Tracy on her wedding day, her long, white veil spread out behind her on the grass, and another picture of her with her husband, Scott, taken on their honeymoon. Next to that was a photo of Doug taken in 1967, wearing his green beret, a First Cavalry patch emblazoned proudly upon his arm, just before he'd left for Vietnam.

There were no more pictures of Doug after that. That had been the last one, and I still remember the day Rose took it. I'd told Doug I loved him and that I was proud of him. He'd told me the same.

That was the last time we ever saw him. When he returned home, it was in a mostly empty coffin. The Viet Cong didn't leave us much to bury.

There were more pictures of Tracy and Scott, Rose and myself, my best friend Carl Seaton and me with the sixteen-pound catfish we'd pulled out of the Greenbrier River eleven years ago, and the two of us standing next to the eighteen-point buck that Carl had shot one winter before old age stopped us from deer hunting altogether. Another showed me shaking the hand of our state senator while he gave me an award for being a World War Two veteran who'd lived long enough to tell about it. More numerous than any of these, though, were the pictures of my grandkids: Darla, Timothy, and Boyd.

All of them were probably dead by now, which was something that I'd been trying hard to avoid thinking about. Now it was starting to creep back in, because thinking about their likely deaths was better than thinking about what I'd just seen outside.

I got out a box of wooden matches and lit the kerosene heater. Its soft glow filled the room. I cracked the window just a hair—enough to let out the fumes, but not to let in the rain. Then I put the tin kettle on top of the heater and set the water to boiling, so I could have my instant coffee, which also was running low. My hands were trembling, partly from the arthritis and partly from the craving for some Skoal, but mostly from fear.

Although I didn't want to, I thought about what I'd just witnessed.

The bird. It—

Rose had died of pneumonia three winters ago, quietly fading away in her hospital room in Beckley while I was down in the commissary getting a cup of coffee. Although I'd loved her with all my heart, for some time after she died, I was angry with her. Angered that she hadn't said good-bye. That she went before me, leaving me here to fend for myself without her by my side. Rose had always done the cooking and cleaning and laundry, not because I'm some kind of male chauvinist, but because she'd truly enjoyed it. I was clueless—helpless—after her death. I didn't clean the house for over a month. Tried to fry up some bacon and set off every smoke alarm in the house. The first time I tried to do laundry, I poured in half a bottle of detergent and flooded the basement with bubbles. Then I leaned against the dryer and cried for a good twenty minutes while the bubbles disintegrated all around me.

After that, Tracy and Scott pleaded with me to move up to Pennsylvania and live with them. Their own kids had moved out by then, leaving enough room for an old man like me. Darla was going to Penn State, studying pharmaceuticals. Timothy had moved to Rochester, New York, and was working with computers. And Boyd—well, he had joined the Air Force, just like his grandpa.

Just like me. Boy, that made me proud. He wanted to fly.

The bird. It tried to fly, and then—

The teakettle whistled, startling me. I poured hot water into my mug and spooned in some coffee crystals. I couldn't stop my hands from shaking.

What in the world was that thing? It looked like a—

Instinctively, I knew my family was dead. I can't explain it to you, other than to say that if you've ever felt that too, then you know exactly what I'm talking about. I just knew they were gone—a horrible, gutwrenching feeling. With Boyd, it was more than just intuition, though. Early on, before the storms hit America, I saw the coverage of the tidal waves that took out Japan. He was based there.

Now he was stationed at the bottom of the newly enlarged Pacific Ocean, and there'd be no more Japanese radios or cars or televisions or cartoon programs for a long while.

With the other members of my family, it was just a sense of *knowing*, a knot of tense certainty that settled in my stomach and refused to let go. It was like having a peach pit get stuck in your throat.

It's a terrible thing to outlive your spouse. But it's even more horrible to outlive your children and your grandchildren. A parent should never live longer than their child. The pain is indescribable. As I said earlier, I tried not to think about it. And yet, on the morning of Day Forty-one, I kept it fresh in my mind, picking off the scabs and letting the wounds bleed. I had to.

It was the only way I could stop thinking about what happened to the robin. . . .

And the other thing. The thing that ate the bird. It had looked like a worm, except that no worm could ever grow that big. That was impossible.

Of course, so was the weather we were having. And I was too old not to suspend disbelief, especially when I'd seen it with my own eyes.

Could I trust those eyes? I wondered about that. What if the worm wasn't real, that I'd hallucinated it? Maybe my mind was slipping. That scared me. For someone my age, dementia is much more terrifying than giant worms.

I sat there in the dim light, sipping instant coffee

from a dirty mug and craving a dip. Cool air blew in through the slip of open window. Outside, the rain continued to fall. The fog rolled in and then lifted, then drifted back in again.

I stayed there all morning. Most of my days went like that, actually. There wasn't much else to do. Occasionally, I tried the battery-operated radio, but the empty static always made me uneasy, so I'd snap it off again. Never had good radio reception back here in the mountains. The weather just made it worse, like in the truck on my ill-fated trip to Renick. The AM station in Roanoke had stayed on the air until about the fourth week. Mark Berlitz, the station's resident conspiracy theorist and far-right talk radio host, had kept a lone vigil next to his microphone. I'll admit that I listened in a sort of dreadful fascination as Berlitz's sanity slowly crumbled from cabin fever. His final broadcast ended with a gunshot in the middle of "Big Balls In Cow-Town," an old bluegrass song by the Texas Playboys (a shame, as I'd always enjoyed their music). The song ended two minutes later, then there was silence. As far as I knew, I was the only listener to hear the disc jockey's suicide, except for maybe crazy Earl Harper, who listened to the show on a regular basis and called in to it about every night.

I'd considered suicide as an option myself after that, but soon ruled it out. Not only was it a sin, but I also doubted I'd actually have the courage to go through with it. Certainly, there was no way on earth I could put one of the deer rifles in my mouth and pull the trigger. And I was afraid if I tried to overdose on painkillers, I'd end up paralyzed or something— paralyzed but very much alive. The thought of lying there, unable to move, and just listening to the rain was enough to convince me not to try it. But I thought about it again that morning, before dismissing the idea once more.

The morning went on and the rain continued to fall. I fooled around with one of the crossword puzzle books the kids got me last Christmas. When you get to be my age, your kin are clueless as to what to buy you for Christmas and your birthday. Since I liked crossword puzzles, that's what they decided on. I was fine with that. It sure beat another sweater or a pair of socks.

I gummed the eraser on my pencil for half an hour, then put my teeth back in and gnawed on it, all the while trying to think of a three-letter word for peccadillo. I knew from four across, that it had an "i" as the middle letter, but I was damned if I could figure out what it was.

The coffee was bitter, and I wished for some green tea instead. Then, I sat up so suddenly that the crossword puzzle book fell to the floor.

Tea. Teaberry leaves! I'd known folks who'd quit dipping by chewing on teaberry leaves instead. It grew all over West Virginia, and I'd often picked the red teaberries growing in the woods behind my home, down in the hollow.

Cursing myself for not thinking about it sooner, I got into my rain gear and stepped out onto the back porch. The kitchen had two doors—one that led outside to the carport, and the other, which went out to the back porch. Since the back porch was closer to the edge of the forest, I went out that way.

Maybe if I had chosen the other door, and seen what was on the carport, things might have turned out differently later. Maybe I wouldn't be writing this.

But I doubt it. I'd forgotten all about the robin at that point. The only thing my mind was focused on was the thought of finding some teaberry leaves to chew on.

I slopped through the yard. My breath clouded the air in front of me, and within minutes, my fingers and ears were cold. The fog had decided to stick around for a while. It covered everything. I could see for maybe fifteen or twenty feet, but after that, everything was concealed by white mist.

It was slow going, partly because of the weather, mostly because of my age; but I reached the edge of the forest and stepped into the trees. Under the leafy canopy, the vegetation was in better shape; the trees protected it from the constantly battering downpour. The rain beat at the treetops and dripped down on me. Wet leaves and pine needles stuck to my boots, and I went extra slow so I wouldn't slip. It wouldn't do to lie out here in the woods with a broken hip.

A few of the trees had been uprooted, but most still stood firm, their roots desperately clinging to the spongy ground. I noticed several of them had a strange white fungus growing on their trunks like the stuff I'd seen growing on the robin earlier. It wasn't moss, at least not any kind I had ever seen growing on a tree. It looked more like mold, hairy and fuzzy and somehow unhealthy, sinister even.

Sinister, I thought. *How can a fungus be sinister, Teddy? This nicotine withdrawal is eating away at what's left of your mind. You're losing it, old man. First you imagine that you saw a worm eat a bird, and now you think the moss is an evil life form bent on taking over the planet, like in a science fiction movie.*

There was more of it on the forest floor, clinging to rocks, fallen logs, vines, and even the dead leaves and needles covering the ground. I was careful not to step in any of it.

Despite the havoc the weather was playing with the vegetation, I found plenty of teaberry plants growing up through the leaves on the forest floor. I knelt down to pick some, avoiding any that had that same odd fungus growing on them. As I collected the leaves, a twig snapped. City folks would have noticed that right away, but when you've spent as much time in the woods as I have, you don't pay attention to every little sound the forest makes. You've heard it all before and know how to separate something odd and out of place from the rest of the forest's symphony.

It wasn't until there was a succession of snaps behind me that I turned. And stared.

My breath caught in my throat and the bottom of my stomach fell away.

A deer stood watching me from about twenty feet away; a spike buck, probably two or three years old. Water dripped from his antlers. He showed no fear or hunger, only curiosity. He looked half-starved, and his ribs showed through his wet, slick hide. But that wasn't why I gawked at him.

The buck's legs were covered with the same white fuzz that was on the trees. The stuff was spreading in patches along his belly and up onto his chest. It looked like it had fused with the deer's body, eating through fur and flesh.

Stunned, I rocked slightly backward on the balls of my feet, and like a rifle shot, the deer leaped over a log and sped away, churning up leaves and twigs. As he fled, I noticed that his hind end was covered with the mold as well. Revolted, I hacked up a wad of phlegm and spat it on the ground. Then I made sure that I didn't have any of the fungus on my skin or clothes.

I dropped the teaberry leaves back onto the ground. Whatever the fungus was, if it could spread from plant to animal, then I could probably get it from chewing the leaves in place of tobacco. I couldn't be sure they weren't already infected, so I scrapped the entire idea and slowly started home.

Behind me, from somewhere inside the fog, I heard another twig break. I paid it no mind, figuring it was just the buck again. But then I heard something else that definitely wasn't a deer. A hissing noise, like the wind whistling through a partially open car window. I wheeled around and peered into the swirling mist, but there was nothing there.

Just the wind, I thought. *Just the wind, whistling through the trees.*

Then the wind crashed through the underbrush, sounding like a herd of trampling elephants.

After that, I hurried back to the house. At first the noise hurtled after me, but then it failed again. The memory of what happened to the robin dogged my every step. Occasionally, I stopped and listened, trying to determine if whatever was making the noise was following me. It was hard to hear it above the drumming rainfall. Something stirred beyond my line of site, but I never saw what it was—just a brown flash. At one point, I thought I felt the ground move, but I chalked it up to my imagination.

If I only knew then what I know now . . .

Back inside the house, I took off my wet clothes and collapsed into my easy chair. Just walking down to the woods and back had tired me out. Used to be I walked those valleys and ridges from before dawn until sundown, hunting and fishing and just enjoying the outdoors. But those days were gone, vanished with the sunlight.

Exhausted and lulled by the soft sound of the rain, I closed my eyes and fell asleep in the chair. I dreamed about Rose's blueberry pie.

The rain never slowed. While I slept, the wind had increased, and I woke up to the sound of a strong gust battering the side of the house. It was like the raindrops were being shot from the barrel of a machine gun. Reminded me of the war, in a way. It sounded like a hailstorm outside. I got up, looked out the big picture window, and couldn't see more than a foot away from the house. The rain was coming down so hard now that it was like looking through a granite wall.

The wind blew the rain away from the house for a brief moment. I stared into the downpour; then I jumped back from the window.

Movement.

Something had moved out there. Something big. Bigger than the thing I'd seen earlier. And it had been close to the house. Between the clothesline and the shed.

Cautiously, I peeked outside again. There was nothing there. I chalked it up to old man jitters. *Probably just a deer or even a shadow from a cloud.*

I reminded myself there couldn't be a shadow since there wasn't any sunlight, and then I promptly told myself to shut up. Myself agreed with me. Myself then told myself that I was just a little skittish over what I'd seen happen to the bird earlier, or what I thought I'd seen. Add to that the white fungus growing on the deer and the trees, and the fact that I still didn't have any dip, and I was bound to be a mite jumpy.

I sat back down and returned to the crossword puzzle book.

Three letter word for peccadillo, with an "i" in the middle . . . Three letter word . . . "i" . . .

"Oh, the hell with it!"

Exasperated, I threw the crossword puzzle book down and picked up Rose's Bible instead. It was worn and tattered and held together with yellowed scraps of Scotch tape. It had been her mother's and her grandmother's before that. I read it each day, taking ten minutes for a devotional. Like waking up at five in the morning, it was another one of life's habits I couldn't change, not that I'd have dared. Even with Rose gone, I knew that if I skipped a Bible lesson, I'd feel her watching me reproachfully for the rest of the day. I had no doubt in my mind she checked up on me from her place in Heaven. I opened the Bible. Reading it was like being with her again. Rose's handwriting filled the book, places where she'd marked passages with a highlighter and jotted notes for the Bible study group she'd led every Wednesday night at the church.

A pink construction paper bookmark proclaiming *For Mr. Garnett* in a child's crayon scrawl (a gift from the Renick Presbyterian Sunday School class) marked where I left off the day before, the Book of Job, chapter fourteen, verse eleven.

I read aloud, seeking the comfort of my own voice, but it sounded frail and hollow.

"As the waters fall from the sea, and the flood decays and dries up, so man lies down and rises no more. The waters wear the stones—"

Something crashed outside, and I bolted upright in the chair, yelping in surprise. I waited for it to repeat, but there was only the sound of the rain. Eventually, I stood up, the last words of the section flashing by my eyes as I shut the Bible.

—the things which grow out of the dust of the earth and destroy the hope of man.

When I looked out the kitchen window, all thoughts of the good book vanished from my mind. I yelled, shaking now not with fear, but with rage.

The rain's pace had slackened somewhat and visibility had returned. The woodpile, previously stacked in an orderly fashion next to the shed, had collapsed. Split logs were scattered throughout my swampy backyard. It had taken me a full day to stack it, and I'd nearly worn myself out doing so. Now, kindling spilled out from beneath the blue plastic tarp I used to keep the wood dry. The tarp flapped in the wind, threatening to blow away. The mist swirled.

The firewood was already soaked. That didn't bother me much. I couldn't use the fireplace as long as it was raining anyway. I was more worried about the kerosene. I'd had two fifty-five gallon drums of the stuff also underneath the tarp, sitting on a concrete slab between the shed and the woodpile. I hadn't been able to get them into the shed by myself, and there was nobody to help me move them. The tarp had seemed to be the next best thing. Now, one drum lay on its side in the mud, almost swallowed up by the fog, and the other one leaned at a precarious angle.

From where I stood, I couldn't make out the cause of the destruction. I assumed it was the wind. Even if the worm was real, it couldn't have done this. Could it? It didn't matter. I had to get out there and fix it. Winter was coming, and without the kerosene, I might as well prepare to face my maker or swallow a bullet like the disc jockey.

I opened the hall closet, shrugged into my raincoat, and, with more difficulty than I like to admit, laced up my boots. My fingers were swollen from arthritis that morning, and it was all I could do to wrap them around the doorknob and turn it.

Before I could walk out onto the carport, a sheet of rain blew in through the open door, pelting my face with cold, fat drops. The wind lashed at me. Careful not to slip, I stepped onto the front stoop, my foot hovering above the concrete.

Then the carport *moved*.

THE CONQUEROR WORMS

As my foot froze in a half step, it happened again.

The concrete slab quivered just inches beneath my boot heel.

Then I noticed the stench, an electric mixture of ozone, rotting fish, and mud. That earthy aroma hung thick in the air, congealing underneath the carport's roof. It was the smell of a spring morning after a rain shower. The scent of earthworms on a wet sidewalk.

The carport writhed again and then I understood. It was covered with worms, the concrete hidden beneath a writhing, coiling mass of elongated bodies. Small brown fishing worms and plump, reddish night crawlers. They came in various lengths, the largest as thick as a man's thumb. It gave me a jolt, for sure. I imagined trying to bait a trout or a catfish line with one of those things, and shuddered. I damn near slammed the door.

The worms were everywhere. Literally. The carport was attached to the side of the house, and the concrete slab was big enough for the truck and the Taurus, plus an old red picnic table with chipped paint that had seen better years. The Taurus was out in the yard, covered by a plastic sheet and buried to the bumpers in mud, but the table and my banged up truck looked like islands, lost amidst a churning sea of wriggling bodies. They lay three inches thick in places, twisting and sliding through one another. Groping, glistening, blinded, slithering . . .

Worms.

It was the rain, of course. The rain had driven them topside, just like it always did during a storm. Only this time, every earthworm in a two-mile radius seemed to have discovered that my carport was the only dry spot left in all of Pocahontas County.

My breath fogged the air in front of me and my fingers were already growing cold. I stood there, half in and half out of the house. I couldn't take my eyes off the worms. I probably would have stood there all day, gaping at the night crawlers with one foot hovering in the air, if I hadn't heard the motor in the distance. The tortured sputter of a knocking rod announced Carl Seaton's beat-to-shit, piss-yellow '79 Dodge pickup long before it crested the hill and appeared at the end of the lane, emerging from a cloud of mist.

He careened up the driveway, tires squelching in the sodden ground while the windshield wipers beat a steady rhythm. The truck slid to a stop. Carl's homely, pasty face stared out of the rain-streaked windows.

I stood there in the doorway, and my heart sang. Not only was there somebody else left, it just happened to be my best friend.

The engine didn't so much quit as choke to death. Blue smoke belched from the rusty tailpipe, vanishing into the damp air. Carl rolled down the driver's side window and appraised the situation, staring at my carport in disgust. His nose was a red-veined bulb, and his eyes looked bloodshot.

"Howdy, Teddy," he shouted over the patter of the rain.

"Morning, Carl."

"Boy, am I glad to see you! Figured you'd moved on by now. Gone to dryer parts with them National Guard boys."

"Nope, I'm still here. They wanted me to leave, but I told them I was staying."

"Me, too." He nodded at the worms. "Looks like you're fixing to do some fishing."

"Just tending to my herd. I'm getting too old to raise cattle. Thought maybe I'd give worms a try instead."

"I've never seen anything like that."

"Yeah," I agreed, "it's pretty odd."

He couldn't take his eyes from the wriggling mass between us. "You think it has something to do with the weather?"

"Reckon so. My theory is that the rain's forcing them topside."

Carl had always had a gift for stating the obvious. In mid-July, when the temperature soared to ninety-nine degrees and the fields turned brown, Carl greeted customers to his combination post office and feed store with, "Boy, it sure is hot out there, ain't it?"

Now he said, "Boy, that sure is a lot of worms."

I cleared my throat and changed the subject to something more pressing. "Don't suppose you'd have a dip on you now, would you, Carl? Or maybe some Mail Pouch or a cigarette or cigar?"

His big moon face turned sympathetic. "I sure don't, Teddy. You out of Skoal?"

Like I said, Carl had a knack for summing things up.

"Yep," I answered. "Ran out a few weeks back. Got me a craving for some nicotine. I'd kill for a dip right now."

"I heard that. Wish I could help you out, Teddy. Been hankering for some caffeine myself. I run out of coffee a few days back."

"Well, come on in." I held the screen door open. "I've still got plenty of coffee left. It's the freeze-dried stuff, but you're welcome to have some."

His face lit up at the news of hot coffee. He climbed out of the cab and splashed through the puddles towards the carport. Water dripped from his nose and chin. Then he skidded to a stop, looking at the worms.

"I ain't wading through *that* god-awful mess. Hang on a second."

He ran around to the back of the truck and opened the tailgate. Carl had a camper topper, so the bed itself was dry. He reached inside and pulled out a broom, holding it up like a triumphant deer hunter would hold his rifle.

"I reckon this'll work."

"Carl Seaton, the mighty worm slayer," I quipped. "See that really long one over there, by the picnic table? Maybe you could mount it on your wall, right next to the black bear and twenty-four-point buck."

Ignoring my ribbing, he cleared a path toward the door. The sluggish worms were scooped more than they were swept. The straw bristles speared some and squashed even more. Half worms, severed in the middle but still alive, squirmed and thrashed in his wake. By the time Carl reached my door, he was a bit paler than normal. But his face had a broad grin as he shook my hand. His palms were wet and cold.

"By God, it's good to see you, Teddy." He shook water from his head. "I've been awful lonely. Thought maybe I was the last one left on the mountain."

"I was thinking the same thing." I smiled. "It's good to see you too."

And it was good to see him. Damn good. I'd figured Carl was dead or long gone with the National Guardsmen and the rest of Punkin' Center.

Carl shook a few squished worms off his galoshes. Already, they were closing ranks in his wake, crawling back over the path he'd cleared. He came inside, and I hung up his coat and rain hat, and set his galoshes by the kerosene heater to dry. Then, as I've done more and more in recent years, I slapped my forehead in frustration at my fading memory.

"Damn it, I'd forget my own head if it weren't attached. Carl, make yourself comfortable. I've got to go back outside."

"What's wrong? You'll catch a cold if you stay out there for very long."

"I need to check on something out back. My woodpile and my fuel barrels fell over."

"Shoot." He stood back up and put on his boots. "I'll give you a hand with the barrels. Besides, that ain't nothing. My whole damned place *disappeared into the ground* this morning!"

"What? I saw your house on my way home about a week ago. It looked all right to me then."

"I swear it's true. And by the way, I saw you that day. I was sitting in the house, eating some beef jerky and listening to the rain, when I heard a motor outside. I ran to the window and saw you drive past. That's how I knew you were alive. What were you doing out, anyway?"

"Trying to get to Renick—but it ain't there no more."

"Flooded?"

I nodded. "Yeah, you could say that. The church

steeple and the top of Old Man Laudermilk's silo are still above water, but that's about it."

"Well, I'll be damned. Any survivors?"

"Not that I saw. I reckon the National Guard evacuated everybody before the waters got too high."

Carl shook his head sadly. "I hope so."

"Me too. So why didn't you flag me down that day?"

"I did," Carl said, lacing up his boots. "But you must not have seen me on account of the rain and fog. I hollered as loud as I could. Thought I was going to pop a blood vessel. But I didn't want to leave Macy and her pups alone for too long."

Macy was Carl's beagle, a mangy old rabbit dog that I swear he loved more than any human being on earth.

"That why you hadn't come to see if I was around before now?"

He nodded. "I figured you'd gone with the National Guard until I saw you in the truck. Then after that, I was gonna come check, but I didn't want to leave her alone. Macy and her litter are all I have left. It'd be a shame to just abandon them like that. What if something had happened while I was gone?"

I shrugged. "What could happen?"

Carl's voice dropped to a whisper. "I don't know, Teddy. But sometimes . . . sometimes I heard things at night. Outside, in the rain. Macy heard them as well, and it set her to growling and barking."

For some reason, the Bible verse ran through my head.

The things which grow out of the dust of the earth and destroy the hope of man.

"What kind of things?" I asked.

"I don't rightly know how to describe it. Like a sloshing sound, maybe."

"That's just the rain." I put my hand on the doorknob.

Carl finished with his boots. "No sir, I don't think it was. There was something else—a sort of whistling sound. Gave me the chills when I heard it."

I stared at him. I'd seen Alzheimer's and dementia take some of my closest friends, but Carl didn't seem to be suffering from it. Nor did he seem to have cracked from the strain yet. He seemed like his normal self.

Plus, I'd heard something myself that very morning. Seen it, too.

Something that looked like a dog-sized version of the worms wriggling on my carport.

"All I can say," he continued, "is that it weren't natural."

"Well, I reckon you'd know. Come on and give me a hand, if you're gonna."

We stepped out onto the carport again. As we waded through the worms and slogged through the swamp that had replaced my backyard, Carl told me what happened next.

He hadn't wanted to leave the house because Macy had just given birth and the puppies' eyes weren't even opened yet. He didn't want to leave them alone, not even for the few minutes it would have taken to come find me. Carl had a heart like a big old marshmallow when it came to that mutt.

Carl's house, post office, and feed store were all part of one big, ramshackle building. By the end of the second week, the dirt cellar was flooded, and by Day

Thirty, the foundations had begun to creak and groan. Still, he refused to leave, wanting to be there for his hound and her newborn litter.

He'd woken up this morning at dawn; probably around the same time as what happened to the bird.

"What got you up?" I asked as we walked across the muddy yard.

"Macy was barking and howling enough to wake the dead," Carl said. "Nothing would quiet her. And the puppies were all whining too."

"Well, what had them so stirred up?"

"The house started shaking. I didn't notice it at first, but the dogs did. They said on the Discovery Channel that animals know about earthquakes before they happen. I reckon this was something like that."

"An earthquake?"

"Well, I reckon it must have been. Sure felt like one. Knocked the dishes from the cupboard, and my entertainment center fell over. Busted that big TV I bought down at the Wal-Mart last year."

"Sorry to hear that," I said, and I was. Carl had loved that television almost as much as he'd loved his dog.

He shrugged. "There wasn't anything to watch anyway, what with the power being out and everything. I guess those satellites up yonder are still broadcasting signals and such, but there's nobody left to watch the programs."

"So what did you do?" I prodded, trying to get him back on track. "You said the house sank into the ground?"

Carl's boot sank into the mud and he pulled it free with a squelching sound. "Everything kept shaking and rattling. I ran outside to start the truck. Figured I'd load the dogs and everything else I could carry into it and come find you. Not sure why. I was scared, you know? Wasn't thinking clearly. Don't know what I thought you could do to make things better, but you understand?"

I nodded.

"Anyway, I'd just turned around to go back inside and get the dogs, and then . . ."

His voice cracked.

"Go ahead, Carl."

"Then the whole structure collapsed. It just sank into the ground. My house, the dogs, the store, the barn, the big old oak tree in the backyard that still had the tire swing dangling from it, even the lamppost. It all vanished in seconds, swallowed up by the ground. The dirt was so wet that there wasn't even a cloud of dust or anything. It just all went down into the earth."

"Gone?" I was stunned.

"Gone. The mud just swallowed it up. I reckon it was a sinkhole. Maybe the earthquake opened it up. Must have built my place right over one, and it's been there all these years. Mike Rapp's house down yonder is full of them, and I'm just a little ways up the hollow from him."

I considered the possibility. West Virginia was notorious for sinkholes, especially in the southeast portion, where we were. They dotted every hill and pasture in the county, and the mountains were riddled with limestone caverns, quarries, and old mines.

"I heard Macy," Carl whispered. "She was howling and whimpering down under the ground. The hole had collapsed in on itself. The walls had sealed it up. But I could still hear her, very faint, underneath the dirt. And then she was quiet. I started to dig with my hands, but the mud kept falling in. There wasn't nothing else I could do, and I felt so . . ."

His face crumbled, and he started to cry. Big tears rolled down his weathered, leathery face. His shoulders trembled and his breath hitched in his chest.

"She's dead, and there wasn't anything I could do to help her."

I wanted to comfort him, but I didn't know what to say, so I said nothing. Carl and I weren't the type to hug each other. We weren't in touch with our feminine sides and I dare say we weren't metrosexuals. Men of our generation hadn't been raised that way.

I did the only thing I could. I put my hand on his shoulder.

He dried his eyes.

It was enough.

We walked to the woodpile, and I thought about sinkholes and wondered if my place could be built over one.

But what we found after sloshing to the woodpile was no sinkhole.

It was something much worse.

And it was just the beginning . . .

CHAPTER THREE

"My God," Carl muttered. "That must have been one hell of a big groundhog."

I didn't reply. Grunting, I strained to lift the kerosene drum upright again. Carl came out of his stupor long enough to help me. Getting old is no fun, plain and simple. Fifteen years ago, it would have taken us a minute to lift that drum, but now it took several minutes and lots of puffing and straining between the two of us.

Exhausted, we both stared at the hole.

"You know something?" I panted.

"What's that?"

"I don't think this was a groundhog at all."

"A fox?"

"No. Look at it, Carl. It's too big for a critter."

Something had dug a tunnel beneath the woodpile, as groundhogs and other burrowing animals are apt to do. But if an animal had made this, then it was at least the size of a large sheep.

I knelt down in the rain, my knees sliding in the

mud, and stared at the yawning cavity. There were no piles of dirt, as if something had burrowed up to the surface, and there weren't any claw marks or scratches in the mud to indicate that the hole had been dug from above ground. There was just a dark, round hole, easily five feet in diameter. The walls of the fissure glistened with a pale, almost clear slime.

"What do you figure it is, then? What did this?" Carl asked.

The things which grow out of the dust of the earth and destroy the hope of man.

"I don't know." Still kneeling, I reached out and touched the side of the hole. The odd slime clung to my fingers. Grimacing, I held my hand up and let the rain wash the milky substance off. I raised my fingers to my nose and was reminded of something I hadn't thought of in years.

It smelled like sex. You know, that fishy *almond* odor that is always around in the bedroom afterward? That's what this reminded me of. An otherwise sweet memory, dimmed with age and now twisted with this new significance. It's the same smell you can find drifting in the air on a rainy day after the worms have crawled out to claim the sidewalks. The same thing I'd smelled when I first discovered the worms on my carport.

Carl sniffed. "Something smells funny. Have you been eating sardines today?"

"It's this stuff. Why don't you try some? See what it tastes like."

"No thanks. I think I'll pass. What's it feel like?"

"Snot, like a big old wad of mucous."

Carl's nose wrinkled in disgust. "I don't reckon

you'd better fool with it anymore. Might be some animal's spunk for all we know."

"But what kind of animal?"

Carl shrugged and started stacking the kindling back onto the pile. Then he wandered around the corner of the tool shed, informing me that he needed to take a piss.

Staying crouched over, I looked at the hole and remembered the robin and the thing I thought I saw. Had it eaten the bird or had I imagined it? I kept running over it in my mind. Maybe I was the one getting Alzheimer's. You're probably thinking that I'm obsessed with the disease, seeing as how I wondered if Carl had it too when he told me about what happened at his place. But I'm not obsessed. It didn't run in my family, but when you're my age, it scares you just the same. When your body goes, your memories are the only things that you have left. The only things you can truly call your own. Your memories are your life, and if you lose them—or worse yet, if you can't trust them anymore—then I figure it's time to lie down in a pine box and let them throw the dirt over you.

I thought about it some more and decided that I was pretty sure I saw the whole thing. And that scared me. Scared me even worse than the possibility that it was all a symptom of dementia. Because worms that big just didn't exist. And they sure didn't eat birds.

"We ought to be getting inside now," I said, trying not to show the fear creeping over me.

"What's that?" Carl hollered. He came back around the corner, shaking his limp, shriveled penis, and stuffed it back into his pants. The rain started to come down harder and thunder rolled out of the forest, obscuring what I'd said.

My knees popped as I rose to my feet. My joints were screaming, unused to the exertion I'd just put them through with the barrels. I cupped my hands over my mouth, shouting over the thunder and the drum of the raindrops pounding the leaves.

"I said that I think we should—"

Another blast of thunder boomed over the mountains, closer now. Hidden beneath it, I imagined I heard a muffled thump coming from inside the tool shed.

I hobbled over to Carl and said, "I reckon we should get inside. We're gonna get pneumonia if we stay out here much longer."

"I suppose you're right. I'm soaked clean through to my skivvies."

We slogged back to the house and got out of our wet clothes. I hung them up to dry, lent Carl some clean drawers and a pair of pants and a shirt, then fixed us each a cup of coffee. We sat in the living room, making small talk and letting the hot mugs warm our cold hands. Carl, still the master of stating the obvious, confirmed that it was indeed some weird weather we'd been having. The weather had always been one of his favorite topics, so I figured he was really in his element now.

He rubbed his arthritic knees and winced. "Boy, I hate being old."

"Me too. You ever look at a photo of your younger self and wonder where he went to?"

"Shoot," Carl snorted. "These days, I'm lucky if I can remember him at all."

I rubbed my sore biceps. "Picking those barrels up wore me out. I don't know what I'd have done if you weren't here to help."

Carl nodded. "I'm pretty tuckered out myself."

"The coffee will wake you up. It's strong stuff. You could strip paint with it."

He glanced down at the coffee table, where my crossword puzzle book and a pencil were lying.

"Doing one of your crosswords, are you?"

"Yep. But I'm stuck. I don't suppose you'd know a three-letter word for peccadillo?"

"Peccadillo—isn't that the name of that young fella who wrote those Westerns? The ones with the pregnant gunslinger and the escaped slave and all that?"

"No, I don't think so."

"Oh. Well, then I'm stumped. Never much cared for those books either, to tell you the truth."

He droned on while I wondered why God had seen fit to make Carl and myself the only survivors. I was dying for some good conversation, craving it almost as bad as the nicotine.

"So, have you heard from or seen anybody else?" I asked.

"Nope. No one. Punkin' Center's like a ghost town. I did hear an airplane about a week ago, though. Sounded like one of those little twin-engine jobs. I ran outside to have a look, but I couldn't see anything by then, on account of the cloud cover. And one day, when the fog lifted for a bit, I spotted a helium balloon. I waved my arms and tried to get their attention, but it was a long way off. I don't reckon they saw me."

I blew on my coffee to cool it, and then drained the

mug in one swallow. "Well, at least that means there's still folks alive somewhere."

"There's got to be," he agreed. "I stopped by Lloyd Hanson's place a while back, because his dairy cows were mooing up a storm. He wasn't there."

I thought about the missing livestock I'd noticed. "But the cows were?"

"Not all of them. I reckon a bunch of the herd wandered off somewhere. But the ones inside the barn . . . it was awful, Teddy. Their udders had swollen up and busted since nobody was around to milk them. Most of them were dead, of course, or dying."

I shuddered. "I haven't seen any animals other than some deer and a robin. The pastures have all been empty."

"Maybe they got loose? I'm sure the ground is wet enough in some places that the fence posts probably fell over."

"Could be." But I wasn't sure if I believed that. Images of the robin flashed through my mind. I considered telling Carl, but didn't. I was afraid he'd tell me I really was crazy. Same reason folks don't tell their friends when they see weird lights in the sky.

Carl sat his coffee mug down on a coaster. "There was a hole in the middle of the pasture. Another sinkhole, I imagine. Maybe his herd fell through that."

"One cow, maybe. But the entire herd? They're cows, Carl, not lemmings."

"Those little penguins that jump off cliffs together? I don't think we have those in West Virginia, do we?"

I fixed another cup of coffee and bit my tongue.

"How about you?" Carl asked. "Have you seen or talked to anybody since the evacuation?"

"No one. Like I said earlier, until today, I thought I was alone. Nobody has stopped by. I wonder if there's any other folks left on the mountain?"

"I'll bet crazy old Earl Harper's alive," Carl said. "Ain't no way those National Guard boys got him to leave."

I snickered. "I reckon so. He was liable to put up a fight if they asked him to."

"Think we ought to go check on folks? Drop by some houses and see if anybody's still around?"

I hesitated, remembering my ill-fated trip down the mountainside. It was dangerous for men our age to drive these back roads, especially when the roads were slick with rain, washed out in places, and covered with downed trees and loosened boulders.

"I don't think it's too smart for us to go gallivanting around with conditions the way they are. But I guess maybe we should at least look in on Earl. Make sure he's okay. His shack ain't that far away."

Carl's eyes grew wide. "I don't want to go messing around the Harper place, Teddy. We say howdy to Earl, and that lunatic is likely to shoot us for trespassing."

"He might, but we should still make an attempt. It's the Christian thing to do. What if he's sick and needs help, or what if he's out of food? He could be lying out there with a busted leg or something. If it were us, we'd want somebody to show up and help."

"But he ain't us."

"All the more reason to show him a kindness."

Carl sighed heavily. "I'm telling you, Earl Harper's liable to shoot first and thank us for our kindness later. But I guess you're right. He is the closest after all. Him and the Simmonses."

"Dave and Nancy?" I asked. "Surely they're long gone by now."

Carl nodded. "Yeah, they probably are. Didn't look like no one was home when I drove by."

"Well, let's get this over with." I pushed my chair back and stood up.

Carl's eyes got big. "Now?"

"Yeah. We'll check on Earl, then come back and eat supper."

We finished up our coffee, shrugged back into our rain gear, and slogged back out to Carl's truck. It coughed to life, shot blue smoke from the tail pipe, and rattled and rumbled the whole way out the lane. Carl had a cassette player in the truck, and we listened to Johnny Cash sing about Sunday morning coming down. I always liked that song, but now the lyrics took on a sinister new meaning.

"Damn wiper blades need changing," Carl muttered, squinting through the rain-streaked windshield.

I nodded, lost in thought. Goose bumps ran along my arms and neck, both from the dampness in the air and the sound of the Man in Black's low baritone grumbling out of the speakers. He'd always had that effect on me, especially after his death.

"You're awfully quiet," Carl said. "What you thinking about, Teddy?"

"Death," I told him. "I'm thinking about dying."

"Dying ain't much of a living, boy," Carl said.

After a moment, I realized that he was quoting Clint Eastwood in *The Outlaw Josey Wales*, one of his favorite movies.

"Maybe not, but that's what's on my mind." I wiped condensation off the window with my sleeve.

"Well, that's not very cheerful. Why do you want to be thinking about something like that?"

"Because when you're our age, what else is there to think about? Especially now?"

Carl was quiet for a moment, his brow furrowed in thought. Then he smiled and said, *"The Andy Griffith Show."*

"What?"

"The Andy Griffith Show. You asked what else there was to think about. I like to think about *The Andy Griffith Show* and *Hogan's Heroes*. And *Barney Miller*, too. They always make me laugh."

I agreed that they were among television's greatest comedic achievements, but thought Carl was missing the point.

"There aren't going to be anymore reruns of *Andy Griffith* or *Hogan's Heroes*, Carl."

"They could always do another one of those reunion shows, couldn't they?"

"Who would watch it? Who's left to make the damn thing? It's over. Everything is gone. The world's gone! There's not going to be any more television programs or movies or books or Johnny Cash tapes. Don't you understand? Are you that stupid?"

His face darkened. "Ain't no reason to call me stupid, Teddy."

"I'm sorry. Really, I am."

Carl took the next turn a little too sharply, and our shoulders bumped into each other.

"That's okay," he sighed. "I reckon we're both stressed."

"Maybe, but it still didn't give me the right to call you that."

He grinned. "Hell, we both know I'm dumber than a stump."

I snickered.

Still laughing, Carl turned the defroster off and on, trying to make it work. "So this is the end of the world?"

"Well, something's gone wrong. This rain surely ain't natural."

"But there's got to be other survivors, don't there? People like us?"

I shrugged. "Sure, sitting huddled together high on a mountaintop, watching the waters rise higher and higher all around them. They're just biding their time, same as we are. We're just biding our time until something else happens."

"Like what? Things are pretty bad. I don't see how they could get worse."

"Death. Drowning. Heck, I don't know. Forget about it. I'm sorry. It's just the weather, is all. It's getting me grumpy. Makes my arthritis act up."

"Mine too. I always wanted to live to be old, and now that I'm here, I wonder why I ever wanted such a thing."

I nodded in quiet agreement.

He drove around a big bale of wet hay that had rolled out into the road. "What do you think caused it, Teddy?"

I shrugged. "Global warming? Though I heard some scientists on TV saying the ice caps hadn't melted. Maybe a magnetic shift at the poles? Or a comet . . . or something like that? I don't rightly know. We've been messing with this planet for too many years now. Could be that old Mother Nature has finally decided to fight back."

"Yeah, but the good book says that He promised not to do it again, and God would never go back on His word."

Thunder crashed in the skies overhead and the rain pelted the roof of the cab like thrown stones. The wind hammered into the side of the truck, forcing Carl to swerve.

"Well," I said, "maybe the Lord got tired of us breaking our promises to Him, so He decided to break one of his own."

Carl whistled, a low and mournful sound. "Rose sure wouldn't stand to hear you talk like that. She'd have a fit."

"Rose isn't here, and to be honest, I'm glad she's not. Breaks my heart to say that, but it would break my heart even more to watch her suffer through this—this *mess*."

"Can I ask you something, Teddy?"

"What?"

"Well, you and Rose always knew the Bible better than most, especially when it came to all that prophecy and end-of-the-world stuff. I never understood all that; what with the little horn and the big horn and the lake of fire and the trumpet. But the world wasn't supposed to end in a flood, was it?"

"No." I shook my head. "It wasn't. We were supposed to get a great beast, and I haven't seen one yet."

"Well, maybe the beast will be along before this is all over."

"That's not even funny, Carl."

We continued on down the road, and I saw something out of the corner of my eye—or rather, I didn't see it. I told Carl to stop.

"What is it?" He put the truck in park.

"Steve Porter's hunting cabin."

Carl wiped condensation from the window. "I don't see it."

"That's right."

He tilted his head. "What's right?"

"You don't see it."

"Teddy, are we doing an Abbott and Costello routine here, or what?"

"No." I pointed to the empty, muddy field. "You don't see Steve's cabin because it's not there any longer."

Carl scratched his balding head. "But that's the spot where it used to be. What are you saying, Teddy?"

I fought to keep the impatience out of my voice. "I'm saying it ain't there no more. The cabin is missing."

Carl's jaw dropped. "Well, I'll be . . ."

We both stared at the vacant field, not sure what to make of it. Steve Porter's cabin had sat far in off the road, right next to the tree line. It was hard to tell through all the rain, but it looked like there might be a sinkhole there. There was a depression where the cabin had been.

Carl must have noticed the sinkhole, too, because he

said, "I reckon it must have collapsed into the ground, same as my place."

"Could be." I nodded. "At least we know there was nobody inside. Steve doesn't use that camp except during deer season. This time of year, he works in Norfolk."

"They got flooded out pretty quick," Carl noted. "Guess Steve won't be coming around to use it this year."

"No, I don't reckon he will."

We continued on our way. Carl didn't say much, and I figured he was focused on staying on the road. I stared out at the rain and the mist because there was nothing else to look at.

"Here's what I don't understand," I finally said. "With all this rain, you'd think it would do something to the atmosphere."

"How so?"

"Well, I'm not sure what exactly. But it would seem that a storm this prolonged would affect the oxygen balance or something. Course, I'm not a scientist."

Carl pumped the brakes, bringing us to a slow, sliding halt in front of Dave and Nancy Simmons's place. He stared out the driver's side window.

"Why are we stopping again?" I asked. "Dave and Nancy's house is still standing."

"Yes, it is." Carl squinted through the driver's side window. "But that's not what I'm looking at."

"Well, what are you looking at?"

"I didn't notice it before when I drove past earlier, but their door's open."

"What?"

I looked at the house, and sure enough, the front door was wide open. The screen door hung crooked, swinging back and forth on one hinge and banging into the aluminum siding. Every new gust of wind blew sheets of rain into the living room. Dave's truck and Nancy's Explorer both sat in the driveway, buried up to their bumpers in mud. Dave and Nancy were good folks. Dave worked as a corrections officer down at the prison in Roanoke, and Nancy worked part-time at the telemarketing place in White Sulphur Springs. They were a young couple, early thirties and married for about five years. No children. Both of them had been awfully good to Rose and me over the years, and secretly we'd thought of them as our adoptive kids. Dave had helped to shovel snow in the wintertime and Nancy had come over to socialize with Rose at least once a week before she'd died. She'd come to visit me, too, after Rose was gone. They both had.

Last I'd heard from them was when Dave called to check on me about two days before the National Guard showed up. I didn't realize how much I'd missed them until now.

Carl put the truck in park and left the engine running. The wipers squeaked on the windshield. "You reckon they're still at home?"

"I doubt it. They probably evacuated just like everybody else. More likely that a strong gust of wind just blew the door open."

"Dave would have locked that deadbolt tight before they left. I can't see the wind undoing the lock."

I considered this. "Then maybe it was looters or

someone looking for valuables that got left behind after everybody evacuated."

Carl nodded. "Or maybe it was Earl."

"Well, one thing's for sure." I reached for the door handle.

"What's that?"

"We're not gonna find out by sitting here." I opened the passenger door and stepped out into the rain. Cold drops pelted my face, blinding me for a moment, until I wiped them away.

Carl grabbed his 30.06 from the rifle rack behind the seat, worked the bolt, made sure it was loaded, and then followed along behind me. I wished I'd brought a gun along, too. Even a handgun would have been comforting. A pistol is primarily a weapon that buys you time to get back to the rifle you should have been carrying in the first place, but both of them will make a man dead. And both provided comfort in times like this.

Mud had replaced the grass in Dave and Nancy's front yard. Our boots sunk into the muck, making loud squishing noises. Carl got stuck halfway to the house, and when he tried to pull free, his foot came out of his boot. His sock was dirty and soaked by the time he got his foot back inside.

I crept up the porch, carefully taking the wet steps one at a time so I wouldn't slip and fall. Last thing I needed right then was a broken hip. I also didn't want to give away our presence, just in case there actually *was* somebody still in the house.

Carl clomped along behind me seconds later, shattering the silence I'd worked so hard to maintain. I shot him a dirty look and then peeked inside the home.

My heart stopped. I couldn't breathe, couldn't swallow. Goose bumps prickled my neck and arms and my fingers grew numb. There was an awful, empty feeling in my stomach.

"Good Lord . . ."

Carl pressed against me, craning his neck to see over my shoulder. "What's wrong?"

I walked into the living room and stepped aside. When I did, Carl gasped, and the rifle shook in his hands.

The house, or at least the parts we could see, had been destroyed. The sofa was tipped over, the cushions shredded and leaking their stuffing. The television stand and the bookshelves had collapsed and piles of movies and paperbacks lay in scattered heaps across the floor. All of it was drenched. The coat rack and the antique coffee table were in splinters.

Everything was covered in a thick coat of pale, white slime, and the air stank of that same peculiar fishy smell. Shuddering, I tried breathing through my mouth, but I could still taste it—the stench was that thick. It was like trying to breathe sardines.

"What happened in here?" Carl asked.

I shook my head, then called out for Dave and Nancy. The only answer was the hiss of the rain.

We walked across the living room, broken glass crunching beneath our boots. I entered the dining room. The table had fared even worse than the furniture in the living room, and the hutch had been knocked over, shattering the glassware and dinnerware inside. More slime covered everything. I gagged at the stench.

Carl prodded a pool of the stuff with the barrel of his rifle. It slowly dripped off the blue steel.

"What is this stuff, Teddy?"

"I don't know. It looks and smells like the stuff we found in that hole back at the house. But that don't tell us much."

"Could it be some kind of toxic waste?"

I shrugged. "If so, where would it have come from? No, I reckon this is something else."

He grabbed a dishrag from the sink and wiped the barrel. "You think Dave and Nancy are all right?"

I spotted something splattered across one kitchen wall.

"No." I pointed. "I don't think they are."

A splash of red covered the eggshell-white plaster at waist level. I knew what it was, but my own morbid curiosity got the best of me, and I drew closer to make sure. Blood. My knees popped as I knelt down and examined the floor. Nancy's wedding ring sparkled in the dim light. It too was covered in blood.

"That's Nancy's isn't it?" Carl asked me, and for a moment I wasn't sure if he was asking about the ring or the blood. But I guess they both were.

"Yeah," I whispered, "I think it is."

"What do we do now?"

I stood up. "Let's get out of here. There's really nothing we can do."

"But they might be hurt. Nancy could still be around here somewhere. All that blood . . ."

"It's dried. Been here for a while, by the looks of

things. And see how wet the living room floor is, from all the rain blowing in? Mold is growing on the walls. The house has been wide open for some time."

Carl frowned. "That still don't tell us what happened here."

"I don't know. But it looks like they ignored the evacuation order and stayed behind."

"What makes you so sure?"

"Dave would have never left his truck behind. You know how much he loved that Chevy. So that tells me that they were here after the National Guard evacuated everybody, at least. But something's happened since then. Whatever it was, it doesn't look good."

"Could Earl have done this? Or scavengers? Maybe those no good Perry kids?"

"I reckon anything's possible." But deep down, I didn't believe any of those things had happened. A roving band of looters didn't leave behind a trail of slime. Neither did the Perry kids, or even Earl Harper. The Perry kids did things like blow up mailboxes with M-80s and catch sunfish at the pond and then put them in your swimming pool. This was beyond them. And Earl . . . well, much as I disliked the man, I couldn't see him doing this. The ransacking of the home was pointless and shocking. Not even Earl Harper would have gone that far.

We searched the rest of the house, but it was more of the same. Every room was destroyed and covered with trails of slime, like a herd of giant snails had slithered over it. There was no sign of Dave or Nancy, nor was there any more blood.

I thought about my dwindling supplies back at the house, found a cardboard box in the closet, and loaded it up with canned goods from Nancy's pantry: applesauce, green beans, corn, peas, peaches, tomatoes, pickles, relish, squash, beets, and deer meat (I'd never much cared for the taste of canned venison, but at this point, beggars couldn't be choosers). She'd canned them all herself, as most folks in these parts did. I also took some dried goods that hadn't been opened, a couple boxes of wooden matches, a few dog-eared paperbacks, and a six-pack of bottled spring water. There was plenty of fresh water falling from the sky, but I didn't relish the thought of drinking it just yet.

Carl found the key to Dave's gun cabinet and took a box of 30.06 shells. I searched for some tobacco—cigarettes, cigars, chew—it didn't matter what, or a pack of that gum for people who want to quit smoking, but the house was nicotine free, and I gave up in frustration, cursing a blue streak.

I fished out my wallet and left some crumpled bills on the kitchen counter, along with a note explaining what we'd taken, but I didn't really expect that Dave or Nancy would ever return to find it.

My eyes kept coming back to that stark splash of blood.

We closed the door behind us as we left. Then we plodded back to the truck, climbed in, wiped the water from our faces, and continued on our way.

The dirt lane leading to Earl's shanty was a river of mud. Carl decided not to chance it. Instead, we parked the truck and got out. Barbed wire indicated the property line. An old, weather-beaten fence post had a homemade sign nailed to it that said:

THIS IS PRIVAT PROPTERY
KEEP OUT!! THAT MEANS YOU
TRESSPASSERS WILL BE SHOT ON SITE

Earl was never much for spelling or grammar. Wasn't much for social skills, either. I remember about ten years ago, when he suddenly decided to get himself some religion. Rose used to teach Bible study every Thursday night at the church, and Earl started showing up, sitting in the back and glowering at everyone. Most of us just ignored him, but Rose was delighted. She viewed him as another one of God's lost lambs coming in from the cold and made it her personal mission to tell Earl Harper the good news of Christ's sacrifice.

One night, we were talking about love and how the Bible commands us to love everybody and offer each a chance to worship the Lord. Earl, who hadn't said a word for weeks, stood up and declared, "I'll tell you folks something. There's three types of people in this world that I won't love. The first is the queers. The second is the niggers. And the third is the Jews." Then he sat back down again, having said his piece.

Apparently, he realized that his contribution to the dialogue might have ruffled some feathers, because the next week, he showed up again and clarified his statement. "I reckon I should explain myself a little better. I got to thinking about it this week, and I guess I don't believe that we should forbid folks from coming to church. But maybe we could have a pink row of pews in the back, and the queers could sit there. Then we could have a row in front of that one, painted black, for the niggers. And one painted green for the Jews, since they love money. I reckon that would be okay, and that way, I wouldn't have to sit with them if I didn't want to."

After that, we asked Earl not to come to Bible study anymore. He didn't take that very well. See, while you might be chuckling at his ignorance, or shaking your head, Earl had been serious. He really thought his recommendations would be acceptable.

But now I've gone and started rambling again. I'm wearing this pencil down to a nub (I keep sharpening it with my pocketknife) and we're not even halfway done yet. And the pain is getting worse.

Anyway, Carl and I stood there on Earl's property, staring at that hand-lettered sign. Splotches of the white fungus I'd seen in the hollow grew on the trees along the lane. Carl reached out with his finger.

"Don't touch that stuff," I warned. "You don't want to get it on your skin."

"What is it?"

"I'm not sure, but I saw it growing on a deer this morning. Can't imagine it's too healthy."

Carl shuddered. "No, I don't reckon it is. Hope it's not airborne."

We turned away from the fungus and stared up at Earl's shack.

"I still don't think this is such a good idea," Carl whispered.

I didn't reply. I was thinking about that bloodstain

on Dave and Nancy's wall, and the weird slime that had covered everything.

And about missing houses and buildings swallowed up by the earth.

And about what I'd seen happen to the bird earlier in the morning.

I shivered, and it had nothing to do with the cold or dampness in the air.

We trudged through the mud towards Earl's shack. The clearing was deathly still. Even the rain seemed to fall without sound. We were about halfway there when an explosion split the air. At first, I thought it was thunder. Then Earl Harper shouted, "Stop right there, you two, or I'll blow your goddamn heads off!"

He emerged from the trees, dressed in combat fatigues and a floppy-brimmed rain hat and pointed a twelve-gauge shotgun at us. Smoke still drifted from the barrel. He was soaked, and I wondered how long he'd been outside.

"Howdy, Earl," I tried. "Let's just settle down now. We don't mean you no harm."

He glanced at the rifle in Carl's shaking hands and motioned with the shotgun.

"If you don't mean no harm, Teddy Garnett, then turn right around and head back the way you come."

"We just wanted to see how you're holding up," Carl explained, carefully pointing his rifle away from Earl. "Ain't no call to shoot at us, Earl."

"And there ain't no fucking call to be trespassing on my property, neither, Carl Seaton." Earl's eyes were wide, and his wet face seemed to shine. "You've seen me, and seen that I'm all right. Now get on out of here!"

"Listen now, Earl," I said, fighting to keep my voice calm. "We're fixing to leave in just a second. But I need to ask you something important first."

"What?" He kept the weapon pointed at me, and his expression was suspicious.

I stared down the barrel of his gun, and felt my nuts tighten. "Have you seen or heard from Dave and Nancy Simmons within the past few days?"

"No. I ain't seen them. Not that I'd want to anyway. Why?"

"We just stopped by their place. It looked like there might have been a struggle. I'm worried about them, and just wondered if you might have heard anything."

His eyes narrowed and his grip tightened on the shotgun.

"You accusing me of something, Garnett?"

"Not at all. Just worried about them is all, and you're their closest neighbor."

"I ain't seen nothing of them, but I'll tell you this. Whatever happened to them will happen to you fellas too. You just wait and see."

Carl frowned, and the rifle twitched in his hands. "What are you talking about?"

"There are things in the ground, turning under our feet, crawling through the maze beneath the earth. I hear them at night. They speak to me, and tell me things."

I froze. Carl shot me a wary look.

"I—I think maybe I've seen them too," I said. "What are they, Earl? Do you know?"

"Maybe I do and maybe I don't." He smiled. "But I

ain't interested in discussing it with you, Garnett. Reckon you'll find out soon enough. Now you two get out of here. I mean it!" He jacked the shotgun.

Carl and I kept our eyes on him and slowly backed away. I stepped in a puddle and cold water soaked though my sock.

Earl began to laugh. "You look like a pair of drowned rats!"

"Nice seeing you again, Earl," Carl muttered. "Take care now!"

"You boys think it will rain today?" Earl called.

Carl leaned towards me and whispered, "I told you so. He's crazier than a copperhead in a mulberry bush on a hot day in July."

I nodded. "I already said you were right. Let's go."

But Earl wasn't finished. "Y'all thought I was senile. Crazy! Talking about me, whispering behind my back down at the Ponderosa and your precious church functions. But you'll see. Here's the proof! I warned you about the government's HARP project. Weather control. Heard about it on the radio. Tried telling you, but you just fucking laughed, didn't you? Well, I guess I'm the one laughing now, ain't I?"

"You take care, Earl." I waved. "We'll be heading on home now."

He fired another shot into the air and ejected the shell. It landed in a rain puddle. Wisps of lazy smoke curled from the barrel.

"I see either of you skulking around here again and I'll blow your fucking heads clean off your damn shoulders. Ain't nobody gonna take what's mine, god-damn it!"

Carl pointed his rifle up into the air and held his free hand out, the palm facing Earl. "You don't have to worry about that. Not that there's anything here worth taking anyway."

Earl scowled. "What's that supposed to mean, Seaton?"

"Meditate on it for a bit, why don't you. You're a bright one. I reckon you'll figure it out."

"Carl," I hissed. "Quit antagonizing him. Let's just get out of here."

"Don't you come back, either," Earl warned. He faded into the trees like a ghost, but we could feel his eyes on us, watching as we trudged down the lane.

We made it back to the truck in one piece and climbed inside. The heater warmed us while we got our pounding pulses under control. Then Carl pulled away as fast as he could, spinning the tires and spraying mud and gravel all over Earl's homemade sign.

"Well, the rain certainly hasn't helped his disposition, now has it?" I joked.

Carl shook his head. "No, I don't reckon it has. I told you this was a bad idea."

"I know you did. And you were right. How many times you gonna make me say it?"

"Sorry. But boy, he was fired up. What the hell was that all about, anyway? A maze underneath the earth and such?"

"I'm not sure. Earl was always a crazy son of a bitch, but now . . ."

Carl's knuckles whitened as he gripped the steering wheel harder. "You think he killed Dave and Nancy?"

I hesitated, considering the possibility. "I would, but

you saw the house for yourself. Earl's not as old as us, but he's no spring chicken, either. I don't think he'd have had the strength to do all that damage. Then there's all that slime, and . . ."

Carl turned towards me. "And what?"

"I saw something earlier this morning, before you showed up. Something odd."

"What was it?"

"Well . . . I—I think it was a worm."

"Oh Lord, Teddy, that's nothing. I saw them worms all over your carport too. Sure, that was peculiar, but it ain't worth carrying on about."

"I'm not talking about that. This was earlier, just after dawn. I couldn't see it very well, on account of the rain and fog, but . . ."

"But what?"

"It looked like a worm, but it couldn't have been. It was too big. There's no worm on earth that big."

"I saw a picture once, in an issue of *National Geographic*. One of those native Bushmen fellas was holding up an eight-foot-long night crawler. Gave me the willies something awful. Of course, that was in Africa or some such place, not in West Virginia."

I didn't reply. We drove on in silence, both of us lost in our own thoughts. Carl whipped around a fallen tree limb and turned into my lane. As we drove through the hollow, I looked out on the flooded pasture and froze.

"Carl, stop!"

He slammed the brake pedal and the truck fishtailed, skidding to a halt.

"Take a look at that." I pointed out the window.

In the middle of the pasture, amidst the water puddles and mud, was a hole much bigger than the one in my backyard. A trenchlike track marked where something had slithered out of it and crawled away through the mud. It looked like the marks a snake would make—if the snake were as thick as a cow.

"Something weird is going on, Teddy. That ain't a normal hole."

"Anybody ever tell you that you're the master of understatement?"

"What do you mean?"

"Nothing," I sighed. "Let's just go have a look at that track. Best bring your rifle."

We stepped out into the rain again and walked into the pasture. We hadn't gone five steps before we sank into the mud up past our ankles.

Carl pulled his foot free with a loud sucking sound, and shook the mud off of it.

I chuckled. "At least you didn't lose your shoe again."

"This is no good, Teddy. We're gonna get stuck out here."

Reluctantly, I agreed with him. I took one last look at the hole and noticed the rainwater was running down inside it. Already, the walls of the hole were collapsing. I thought about Steve Porter's missing hunting cabin again and what had happened to Carl's house.

As long as it doesn't get closer to mine, I thought.

"Let's go on home and get dry," I said, slogging back to the truck. "I'll fix us some dinner. And I reckon you'd better sleep here, on account of your house caving in and all."

Carl looked grateful. "That'd be good. To be honest,

I wasn't sure what I was going to do, and I was hoping you'd offer. I sure do appreciate it, Teddy."

I waved my hand. "Don't mention it. That's what friends are for. Can't very well let you sleep outside in the rain. Besides, it'll be good to watch each other's backs."

"You mean from Earl? You think there's gonna be trouble?"

I nodded. I did think Earl Harper was going to be trouble. But I was thinking about other things as well. I was thinking about that white fuzz I'd seen in the woods and what I'd heard crashing around after me. I was thinking about holes and bloodstains and trails of white, glistening slime that smelled like sex.

And worms. I was thinking about worms.

Worms big enough to eat a bird.

I was thinking about the things that grow up out of the dust of the earth and destroy the hope of man.

CHAPTER FOUR

For the second time that day (well, the third for me, and the second for Carl), we shrugged out of our wet clothes and put on some dry ones. Lucky for him we were about the same size and he could pull stuff out of my closet. Our boots were soaked clean through, and I cranked up the kerosene heater and sat them next to it to dry out. Then, while Carl propped his bare feet up and flipped through a four-month-old copy of *American Sportsman*, I fixed us dinner in a pot on top of the heater: a hodge-podge stew of canned deer meat, beans, carrots, tomatoes, and corn. The aroma filled the house, and both our stomachs grumbled in anticipation. My mouth was watering.

I brought the battery-operated tape player into the living room and put on some music, one of those compilation tapes you could buy at the Wal-Mart for a dollar, with bluegrass and country music for old folks like us. When the stew was ready, we ate in silence, listening to Porter Wagoner's "Misery Loves Company," Marty Robbins's "El Paso City" (the version from the

77

70s, rather than his 50s song "El Paso"), Claude King's "Wolverton Mountain," the Texas Playboys's "Rose of San Antoine," and Henson Cargill's "Skip A Rope." Carl joined in with Waylon Jennings for a trip to "Luckenbach, Texas" and wailed about getting back to the basics of love while I suffered and wished for some cotton to put in my ears. He sounded like a cat in a burlap sack that had just been tossed into a pond after being dragged across a hot tin roof. For an encore, Carl sang along with Jack Green on "There Goes My Everything," and I finally told him to be quiet and eat his supper. He did, accompanied by burps and slurping noises.

Despite his terrible singing voice and even worse table manners, it felt good to have him there. I hadn't realized just how lonely I'd been until his arrival. I was surprised that we didn't talk more during that dinner. For the last few weeks, Carl only had his dog to talk to and I'd been conversing with myself. You'd think we would have been a pair of Chatty Sarah dolls, but we weren't. The only sounds we made were the grunts and sighs of contentment when we'd finished. I guess we didn't need to talk. It felt good just to have somebody there with me. To know that there was somebody else still alive.

Carl pushed his empty paper plate away and let out a window-rattling belch.

"Liked it, did you?" I asked.

"My compliments to the chef. So, what do you think happened to all the folks that got evacuated? All of our friends, I mean? Where did they go?"

"I don't know. Maybe they took them to White Sulphur Springs."

White Sulphur Springs had once been the site of the underground Pentagon. I don't know if that's what it really was, but that's what the locals called it. It was a government base carved into the limestone beneath the mountains; an impregnable, indestructible concrete and steel bunker that supposedly would be used to house our elected officials in case of a nuclear war. Vice President Cheney had gone there on September 11th, when the country came under attack. They had bunkers like that all over the country back in the sixties, seventies, and eighties, before Ronald Reagan won the Cold War; back when Iraq was still our friend and George Bush, Sr. was attending cocktail parties with Saddam Hussein. I knew of one near Gettysburg, Pennsylvania, and another in Hellertown, Pennsylvania, and a third in Gardner, Illinois. And then there was the NORAD base in Cheyenne, Wyoming. But the one in White Sulphur Springs was ours, and we had a strange pride about it, even after it was decommissioned and opened up to tourists. Of course, Earl Harper said it wasn't really decommissioned and was now being used as an advance staging area for United Nations security force invaders. But then again, Earl said the same thing about Fred Laudermilk's grain silo down in Renick.

Carl undid the top button of his pants and patted his stomach. He sighed with contentment. "That was a fine meal, Teddy. Best I've had in quite awhile. I'm fit to burst."

"Glad you liked it. If we ever run into Nancy again, we'll have to compliment her on her canning abilities. Most of that was food I took from her cupboard."

"I reckon so."

"We'll have the leftovers for breakfast. And I won't even make you do the dishes."

Carl looked around the kitchen. "What have you been doing with the paper plates, anyway?"

"Throwing them outside."

"But Teddy, that's littering!"

I pointed to the window. "Do you think it really matters at this point?"

"I guess not. Don't suppose Smoky the Bear will be showing up anytime soon."

He was right about one thing, though. It had been a good meal. Damn good. And now I was craving some tobacco again. I think the nicotine desire is at its very worst after you've eaten.

To distract myself, I cleared the paper plates and Styrofoam bowls from the table and put them in the trash. I'd been carrying the garbage bags down to the tree line once a week, and tossing them into the forest. Broke my heart to do so because, like Carl had said, it was littering. But I couldn't just let it pile up inside the house, and burning it outside like I used to do just wasn't possible anymore.

Carl rubbed his arthritic knee. "So, if the National Guard took all those folks to White Sulphur Springs, you reckon we should make our way there too?"

"You still got that old bass boat we used to take down the Greenbrier?"

He shook his head. "No, I sold it to Billy Anderson for fifty bucks and few rolls of hay."

"Sounds like you ripped Billy off."

"He didn't have no complaints."

"Well, without the boat, I don't know how we'd make it. Truthfully, I doubt there's much left in White Sulphur Springs, anyway. Remember, it's in a valley."

"You reckon that it's underwater then?"

"Not one hundred percent sure, mind you, but yeah, I would guess so. I'm pretty sure everything else is flooded, except up here on top of the mountain."

"So it's just us. And the waters are rising." His voice sounded very small and quiet. And afraid. It echoed the same hopelessness I felt deep down in my heart.

"No." I tried to smile. "It's not just us. We've still got Earl to keep us company. Reckon he'll come over and apologize for his rude behavior?"

Carl made a face like he'd just bit into a lemon, while Skeeter Davis sang to us from my little stereo. She was singing about the end of the world.

Time passed. It was a good night—the first good night either of us had enjoyed in a long time. I lent Carl a pair of my pajamas and hauled out the deck of cards. We stayed up late playing poker and blackjack and war and hearts, and switched back and forth between the country music tape and the radio dial, hoping against hope to hear something other than static.

But we didn't. Just the white noise of dead air and the rain coming down outside.

Always the rain.

We talked a lot—about our missing friends and cars and politics and football, and how there probably wouldn't be any of those things anymore. I think that was what really brought it all home to Carl; how he wouldn't be able to watch another West Virginia Mountaineers game next season. We talked about hunting and fishing victories of the past, of our glory days before we got married, of our wives and women we'd known before our wives, and eventually the war.

We both grew pretty maudlin after that, and when Carl farted, it broke the tension like a sledgehammer through glass. I laughed till I thought I'd have a heart attack, and Carl laughed, too, and it felt good. It felt real.

We talked late into the night, bathed in the soft glow of the kerosene lamp. I whooped Carl's butt at cards.

The two things we didn't talk about were what we'd seen earlier at Dave and Nancy's house and the holes that we'd found. The wormholes, as I'd taken to thinking of them, even though God had never made worms that big.

We went to sleep long after midnight. I fixed up the bed in the spare room, and gave Carl an extra flashlight so he could see his way around. Then I went out on the back porch and pissed. The rain had backed up the seepage bed, making the toilet useless, and I didn't feel like making the hike to the outhouse.

It was pitch black outside, and I couldn't even see my hand in front of my face. I thought I heard a wet, squelching sound from somewhere in the darkness. I froze. My breath caught in my throat and my penis shriveled in my hand like a frightened turtle. But when I cocked my head and listened again, all I heard was the rain.

Shivering, I shook myself off and hurried back inside. I made sure the door was locked, and then I double checked it.

On my way down the hall to my bedroom I stopped at Carl's door to make sure he didn't need anything else. I raised my fist to knock, then paused. His voice was muffled, and at first, I thought he was talking to somebody. Then I realized Carl was singing Skeeter Davis's "The End of the World."

"Don't they know it's the end of the world? It ended when you said good-bye."

His crooning still hadn't improved. Carl sounded like a cat with its tail plugged into an electrical socket, but it was the most beautiful and sad thing I'd heard in some time. A lump swelled in my throat. Instead of knocking on the door, I shuffled off to bed. I climbed under the blankets and lay there in the darkness, craving nicotine and missing my wife.

It was a long time before I slept.

When I finally did, Rose came to visit me.

In the dream, I woke up to find that the house had flooded. Everything was underwater and my bed floated on the surface, gently rocking back and forth. The water level grew higher, and my bed rose with it. I had to duck my head to keep from hitting it on the ceiling. The bed swayed. I hollered for Carl, but he didn't answer. I shifted on the mattress, and the sudden movement caused the bed to tilt, spilling me into the water. I plunged downward to the carpet and opened my eyes.

Rose stared back at me, as beautiful and lovely as the first time we'd met. Her nightgown floated around her, the same one she'd been wearing when she died.

She opened her mouth and sang. Each word was crystal clear, even though we were underwater. That's just the way it is in dreams.

"I can't understand, no, I can't understand how life goes on the way it does."

Skeeter Davis. She was singing the same song that Carl had been singing before bed.

"I miss you, Rosie," I said, and bubbles came out of my mouth. But despite that, I wasn't drowning.

"I miss you, too, Teddy. It's been hard to watch what you're going through."

"What? An old man, fooling with crossword puzzles and trying to figure out a three-letter word for peccadillo? Afraid to go out into the rain because he might catch pneumonia? Yeah, I reckon that would be hard to watch. Must be pretty boring."

"That's not what I'm talking about and you know it. Don't you know it's the end of the world?"

"No, it's not," I told her. "It ended when you said good-bye, Rosie. Just like in the song."

"It's going to get worse. The rain is just the beginning. They're coming, Teddy."

"Who is coming? What do you mean? The worms? I thought maybe I was going crazy."

If she heard me, she didn't give any indication. Instead of answering, she swam forward and kissed my forehead. Her lips were cool, soft, and wet. I'd missed them, and I wanted that kiss to last forever.

"They're coming," she repeated, drifting away. "You and Carl need to get ready. It's going to be bad."

"Who's coming, Rosie? Tell me. I don't understand what you're talking about."

"The people from the sky."

"What?"

She suddenly bent over, clutching her stomach.

"Rosie? Rose! What's wrong?"

Convulsions racked her body, and her abdomen

swelled as if she'd suddenly become nine months pregnant. I swam to her, but it was too late. She looked up at me, her eyes wide with panic, and vomited earthworms into the water. They exploded from her mouth, swimming around us. More of them slithered out of her nose and erupted from her ears and the corners of her eyes. Beneath her nightgown, in that magical place that only I had known, the place that had given birth to our children, something squirmed.

"They're coming, Teddy. They're coming soon!"

The earthworms wriggled through the water towards me.

I opened my mouth to scream, and this time, the water rushed in, choking me. With it, the worms slid down my throat.

I woke up clutching the sheets and still trying to scream. My mouth was open wide, but no sound came out. It felt like I was drowning, just like in the dream. My heart thundered in my chest and my lungs exploded with pain. I fumbled on the nightstand for my medicine, popped a pill, and waited for my pulse to stop racing. I was glad for the pills, but they were almost gone, and I wasn't sure how I'd get more.

My pajamas were drenched with sweat, and both the mattress and the sheets were damp. At first I thought I'd wet myself, but it was just perspiration. I shook my head, trying to clear it.

The last few wisps of the nightmare ran through my mind. I wondered what it all meant and decided that it was just my subconscious getting rid of the trash from the day; thoughts of Rose and Carl's rendition of the Skeeter Davis song and the worms from the carport.

But knowing that didn't ease my fears. Even then, I refused to consider the other things I'd seen. My brain just didn't want to accept the weirdness of it. Probably a defense mechanism of some kind.

After a bit, I sat up and lit the kerosene lamp. Rose's picture stared at me from the nightstand. I picked it up and cradled it in my arms, thinking about how we'd met.

In 1943, my sister, Evelyn, and her husband, Darius, owned a five-and-dime store down in Waynesboro, Virginia. Rose and Evelyn were good friends, and she was staying with them and working at the store. Meanwhile, I had been stationed in Panama and Galápagos for ten months, and I came home that April for a seven-day leave. My visit was unannounced. I figured I'd just show up and surprise everybody. I took the train from Norfolk to Waynesboro and got there just after sundown. Darius, Evelyn, and Rose were sitting down for supper when I knocked on the door, looking pretty sharp in my dress uniform, if I do say so myself.

Darius and Evelyn were happy to see me and they made a big fuss. Rose kind of sat there quietly in the background until things settled down, but I saw her right away. The first thing I noticed when we were finally introduced was her smile, and the second thing was her eyes. That was all it took. Just one look into those eyes and I fell in love. Folks these days (what's left of them) may scoff at the notion of love at first sight, but I'm here to tell you that it really happens. It happened to Rose and me.

We communicated with each other that evening through stolen glances, but that was all. There was no real opportunity for us to talk. The next day, Darius and Evelyn gave me a ride to Greenbank, where my parents lived. I told Rose good-bye and that I was glad to have met her. As she shook my hand, I thought that I saw a special look, a message just for me (and later on, I found out that I was right). We piled into Darius's truck. As we drove away, I was surprised to find myself feeling lonesome and sad because I didn't expect to see Rose again. My plans were to catch the train in Greenbank after my leave was up and then head on to Tucson, where I was supposed to be stationed next.

After a short visit with our folks, Darius and Evelyn returned to Waynesboro. I spent the night in my old bedroom, but I couldn't sleep a wink. All I did was lay there in my familiar bed and think of Rose. I couldn't get her out of my head. By dawn, I knew what I needed to do. The next morning, during breakfast, I told my parents all about her and what I'd made up my mind to do. They understood, and I spent the day hitchhiking back to Waynesboro. Once again, I arrived after sundown, and when I knocked on the door and saw Rose, my heart sang. I'd been worried she might not be there.

I asked her out to a movie that night and she said yes. Neither of us had any idea what film we saw. To this day, I couldn't tell you what it was. We sat in the back row and pretty much had the place to ourselves. We never looked at the screen. Instead, we talked the whole time. After the movie was over and the lights came up, we walked home very slowly under the full moon and talked some more. We were awake until one in the morning, but before I said good night I kissed her good-bye.

Holding her picture, I thought about that kiss, and of the next day—the first time I told her that I loved her, and how she'd whispered it back to me, her breath soft and sweet in my face.

I love you. . . .

One week later, I wrote her a letter and asked her to marry me. She said yes. The rest, as they say, is history.

In the darkness, the rain splattered against the roof and windows. Lying back down, I stared at the ceiling, listening to the rain until I finally drifted off again.

I dreamt of Rose again, but this time we were walking down that lane under the same full moon. We stood there and we kissed—one long, lingering moment that lasted until the dawn.

"I love you," she whispered, and the sun was shining bright and there wasn't a single cloud in the sky.

CHAPTER FIVE

The next day—yesterday—was Day Forty-two. That's when the people from Baltimore fell out of the sky.

I woke up the same time as always, still tired and groggy from the dreams about Rose. The bedroom was hot and sticky, and my pajamas clung to me. The weather had sent the humidity climbing. The extremes in temperature were just another weird effect of the constant rain. One moment it was sweltering and the next you needed a sweater to keep warm.

As usual, I reached for my dip out of habit and grumbled when it wasn't there. But I cheered up when I heard Carl moving about in his room. I'd forgotten he was here; his presence was a comfort.

My body creaked and groaned as I climbed out of bed. I rubbed the stiffness from my joints and slipped into my old faded bathrobe. It was ripe enough to stand up on its own, so I reminded myself that I would have to do laundry in the washtub pretty soon. The washtub was an antique; it had belonged to my mother. I'd taken it after she died—sentimentality. But now that the power was out, it came in handy.

Other than the sounds drifting from Carl's room and the endless droning of the rain, the house was quiet. I listened for the bird and then I remembered what had happened the day before. After that, my good mood soured again.

Carl must have heard me moving about. He came out of his room and we greeted each other sleepily. He looked tired, and I wondered if he'd had bad dreams, too. If so, he didn't mention it and I didn't ask. But there were dark circles under Carl's eyes, circles that hadn't been there yesterday, and his face looked drawn and haggard.

I went outside to pee, and while I stood there yawning, I noticed the earthworms were still on my carport—now at least a foot deep. The image of the worms in my dream came to me then and I shivered, forcing it from my mind.

I closed my eyes and listened to the rain. Then I went back inside.

We had leftover stew and instant coffee for breakfast, and when we were done, I fooled with the crossword puzzle book a little more, still trying to think of a three-letter word for peccadillo.

"It has to stop sometime," Carl mused, watching the rain from the living room's big picture window. "I mean, it can't rain all the time, can it? The Lord wouldn't allow something like that."

I gummed my pencil and tried to concentrate.

"Teddy?"

"Hmm?"

"What if it don't stop? You ever think about that? What if the rain just keeps falling?"

"Then it's going to be a mighty rough winter. Can you imagine what will happen once the temperature drops below freezing and all this water turns into snow and ice?"

"No, I hadn't thought of that. As bad as things are right now, I reckon that would be worse."

"Probably best not to think about it."

But now he had me considering the possibility. I tried to imagine all the moisture in the air turning to snow. It would be a blizzard, the type of which hadn't been seen since the Ice Age. The house would be covered within days, and after that . . .

There lay madness. Rather than thinking about it, I returned to the crossword puzzle. Carl picked up an old issue of *Field & Stream* and thumbed through it.

It occurred to me that another Ice Age might occur anyway. Yes, there was still sunlight somewhere above the cloud cover. I knew this because there was a silver disc where the sun would normally be. But would the clouds and fog continue to block the sunlight? What would happen then?

I shivered.

"I'm guessing that the toilet don't work?" Carl asked.

"Yep," I nodded. "If you've got to take a dump, you'll have to use the outhouse. Just don't sit in the spider webs."

Carl frowned. He hated spiders.

"Okay. I'm going to go sit on the throne for a spell."

"Have fun. Don't let anything bite you on the behind."

"That's not funny, Teddy."

Carl put on his raincoat and boots, grabbed an umbrella and slogged outside with the magazine rolled up and tucked under his arm. I got up, wiped condensation from the kitchen window, and watched him make his way across the swampy yard. He was hurrying, so I figured he had to go bad.

But five minutes later, he was moving even faster when he burst through the kitchen door, dripping water onto my linoleum.

"Teddy!" he gasped. "You better come quick. There's something in the outhouse!"

"I told you there were spiders."

He shook his head, and his Adam's apple bobbed up and down.

"Groundhog?" I'd had a problem last summer with them burrowing beneath the outhouse and shed.

Carl swallowed hard. "No, it's not a varmint. I'm not sure what it is, but it sounds big. Just come look, damn it!"

I shrugged into my rain gear and followed him outside in annoyed resignation. The humidity had dropped again. The air was chilly, and the mist seemed to cling to my face. Even still, the fog wasn't as heavy as the previous day, and I could see a little better. I noticed that my apple tree was leaning at a forty-five degree angle, the soil around it too wet for the roots to keep their purchase. Rose and I had planted that tree together when it was just a little sapling, and the sight made me sad.

We reached the outhouse, and Carl suddenly stopped.

"I don't see anything," I said.

"Open the door and have a look inside."

I approached it cautiously, but didn't hear or see anything unusual. I steeled myself and flung the door open. The hinges creaked. I stuck my head inside. There was that faint odor common to all outhouses, and I thought I caught a hint of that strange smell from the day before—the fishy stench. But it was muted. Other than that, everything seemed normal; two holes, three rolls of toilet paper, a bucket of lime to dump down in the hole, a can of aerosol disinfectant, and a lonely spider web hanging in the upper corner.

I stepped back outside. "Yep, that spider sure is scary. Big, hairy sucker. I'm glad you called me out here, Carl. Give me the magazine and I'll kill it for you. Then you can get about your business and I can go dry off."

"There's no need to make fun of me, Teddy. I'm telling you, I heard something inside. It sounded big."

"Well, there's nothing in there now. Take a look for yourself."

He didn't move. "It was down underneath—you know, beneath the outhouse."

"In the pit?"

Carl nodded.

I stepped back inside and stared down into the holes. And then I saw it.

Well, actually, I didn't see it.

If you've never been in an outhouse, I reckon I should explain how they work. When you build an outhouse, you start by digging a pit. You make it as deep as you can—usually at least ten or fifteen feet. Then you construct your outhouse over the hole. The toilet itself goes right over the pit, so that when you do your business, your waste has somewhere to go. You sprinkle a bit of lime down the hole to aid in the waste's eventual breakdown and to cut down on the smell. But every time you look down that hole, you'll see an indicator of your previous visit: a congealed pile of urine and feces and toilet paper.

That's what I wasn't seeing. It wasn't there anymore. The waste pit was gone. There was nothing—just a black, seemingly bottomless hole, certainly deeper than the original pit I'd dug. Something had tunneled up beneath the outhouse, and decades worth of foulness had drained down into the trench and vanished from sight.

"Well, I'll be," I whispered.

"What is it?" Carl asked. "What do you see?"

"I'm not sure. Remember the holes from yesterday? Out by the woodpile and in the field?"

"Yeah."

"We've got another one." I stepped back outside. "Something dug a hole underneath the outhouse and took a really nasty bath."

"Where does the hole go?"

"I don't know, but I'm sure not gonna crawl down inside and see. No thank you, sir."

We stared at each other while the rain soaked through our clothes.

"Teddy, what the hell is going on? What kind of a critter makes a hole like that?"

"I don't—"

A blast of thunder cut me off, and we both jumped.

A second later, another blast followed. There was no lightning in the sky.

That's not thunder, I thought. Somebody was shooting. Heavy caliber, by the sound. Another blast rolled across the hills.

"Did you hear that?" Carl asked me, still a master of asking the obvious.

I put my finger to my lips. "Listen."

There was something else, over the gunshots—a thrumming sound, growing louder and closer.

Carl stiffened. "It sounds like—"

A helicopter exploded through the treetops, seesawing wildly as it roared overhead of us and swooped towards the empty field.

"Maybe it's the National Guard!" Carl shouted above the noise. "They finally came to get us!"

My spirits lifted. It looked like we were saved.

We waved our arms and shouted at the top of our lungs, but the helicopter continued away from us. It looked like it was in trouble. Black smoke billowed from its engine.

Another gunshot rang out, and then a figure emerged from the forest. It was Earl Harper, still dressed in his combat fatigues and looking like a crazy, drowned rat. Just as mean, too.

He hollered something unintelligible, raised the rifle, sighted through the scope, and squeezed the trigger. There was a flash of light and smoke, followed by another blast. Then he lowered the gun and ran towards us.

"Good Lord," Carl grunted. "What's he gone and done now?"

I couldn't answer him. I felt numb, and my feet were rooted in the mud.

Carl picked up a length of dead wood—a thick fallen tree branch—and held it at his side like a club. I just watched the helicopter in stunned disbelief.

It veered to the left and then to the right, as if the pilot were flying drunk. It pitched back toward a grove of pine trees and away from of the field, then shot upward again. The engine whined.

"I hit it," Earl cackled as he ran up to us. "I got the bastards! Didn't I tell you? A black fucking helicopter! It's just like they talked about on the Coast-to-Coast AM show. I warned you all. God damned U.N. invasion troops!"

The helicopter swerved back over the field again. Smoke now poured from the engine in a thick cloud. Earl sighted through the scope again and squeezed off another shot. The gun bucked against his shoulder. Visibility was poor because of the rain and I wondered how he could hit anything, but he did. The fleeing chopper plummeted from the sky like a stone. There was no explosion or big orange fireball like in the movies. Never is. There was just a sickening crunch as metal collapsed and shredded and the whirring blades tore into the earth. The engine sputtered.

Then there was silence, followed seconds later by the sound of people screaming.

Then silence again, except for my harsh breathing, Carl's asthmatic wheezing, and the quiet click of Earl reloading the gun.

And the rain in the background, of course. Always the rain.

None of us moved. We just stared at each other. Earl pulled more ammo from his pocket and slid them into the gun.

Carl gripped his club tightly. "What the hell is going on, Earl?"

"I got them," Earl whispered, a grin splitting his grizzled face wide open. He worked the rifle bolt and trudged toward the twisted, smoking wreckage. So intent was his approach that he didn't see Carl sneak up behind him with the length of wood. Earl didn't suspect a thing until Carl cracked him in the back of the head.

Earl dropped to the ground with a groan, his face sinking into the soggy mud.

Carl looked up at me, his face shocked. "You don't suppose I killed him, do you?"

"Not with that hard head of his. But pull his face out of the mud so he doesn't drown."

While Carl did that and checked Earl's pulse, I grabbed the rifle from where it fell. Then we loped toward the crash site. I clutched the gun so hard that my knuckles turned white. Carl picked up another fallen branch and held it out in front of him like a sword.

"Oh, those poor people," he murmured. "You reckon anybody is alive in there?"

"I don't know. Let's find out."

The stench of scorched metal hung thick in the air.

Carl bent over, coughing. "Good Lord . . ."

"You gonna be okay?" I asked him. "Because I need you here with me right now."

"I'm all right. Just been a while since I saw something like this. Since the war. I'd forgotten how the adrenaline rush can make a man sick. I'm fighting it off."

"Me too," I said, even as the bile rose in my throat.

Black, oily smoke twisted from the crash site, but there was no fire. The weather had taken care of that. It certainly didn't look like a helicopter anymore. Bits of wreckage lay scattered across the field. The cockpit rested at the end of a deep trench gouged into the mud. It was this piece we approached. It had split in half. One section contained something unrecognizable—wet and red, with steam rising off of it. It wasn't until Carl began to retch behind me that I realized what it was.

The pilot. Or what was left of him. I'd seen the worst acts of human butchery during the war; seen living, breathing men reduced to nothing more than piles of shredded, smoking meat, seen the black stuff bubble out from deep inside their bodies—but it had been a long time.

This brought it all back. Carl knelt on the ground, mud squirting through his clenched fists, and threw up his breakfast.

The pilot must have been wearing his seatbelt, and that was what killed him. He was cut into sections, horizontally from his left shoulder and down across his chest to his right hip, and then severed in half again at the waist. His legs and groin remained in a sitting position on the gory seat, along with a steaming loop of gray intestines and splattered feces. His other two pieces had fallen to either side. His innards were spread across everything. As we watched, one length of intestine slithered off the seat like a snake, and plopped into the mud.

It reminded me of a worm.

Carl wiped his mouth with the back of his hand,

leaving a brown smear of mud across his face. He rose unsteadily. His face was stark white.

I found the pilot's head lying in the mud. His lower jaw had been sheared off, and rainwater pooled in his vacant eyes. I bent down and closed them.

"You okay?" I asked Carl.

He spat onto the ground. "Yeah. I'll be fine. Like I said, it's just been a long time since I've seen something this bad. Tell the truth, I'd hoped never to see it again."

"I know what you mean. I thought things like this were behind us now, in our old age."

Carl gagged, and then covered his nose with his hand.

"You sure you're okay?" I asked again.

"I—I'd forgotten what it smells like. Blood and people's insides."

The stench had gotten into my lungs as well and it was making me sick. I fought it off, trying to keep my head. My body ached, reminding me that I was no superhero, just an old man who'd been out in the rain too long.

I turned around to check on Earl. He was still lying in the mud, unconscious.

"We're gonna have to deal with him," Carl said.

I nodded.

There was a groan behind us. We turned and found an old man, probably about our age, lying on the ground and bleeding in a puddle. Carl knelt to examine him and the man moaned, sputtering as the cold rain showered him. His shirt sleeve had ridden up and I caught a glimpse of a black, faded tattoo on his bicep—a pair of anchors and a *U.S.N.* logo. He'd served in the Navy, whoever he was.

"Who—" he began and then broke off, seized by a great, racking cough. He sprayed blood and spittle all over Carl's raincoat.

"You just lay back and rest, mister," Carl assured him. He glanced up at me and then down at the man again. I followed his gaze to the man's leg. Just below the knee, a jagged piece of bone, covered with pink bits, sprouted from his khaki pants. Arterial blood jetted from the wound, turning the rain puddle beneath him a rusty color. The man didn't seem to notice. He lay back as Carl had told him to. Then he began to shake, his eyes rolling and teeth clenching.

"K-Kevin," he hissed. "S-Sarah? G-got t-t-to get . . . it's in . . . in the water. Th-the Kraken!"

"What's he saying?" Carl asked me.

"He's in shock," I said. "Get your belt around his leg, or he's gonna bleed to death right here in the field."

Someone else cried out from the other half of the wreckage. I noticed a petite, bloodstained hand adorned with long, peach-colored fingernails. I stared at them in fascination, marveling that only one nail had broken.

I realized that I was going into shock myself, and I jumped when Carl called out to me.

"Get them out of there, Teddy." Now he was okay and I was the one starting to lose it.

I shoved a piece of steel out of the way and clambered over the frame to where the hand was. I cleared the wreckage and found it was attached to a pretty young woman with long blond hair, sprawled beside a bloodied young man. Both of them were probably in their mid to late twenties, and they seemed unharmed, except for deep cuts in his forehead and shoulder, and the woman's broken nail.

They both blinked at me with big, round, horrified eyes.

"Howdy." I tried to smile.

"We— Are we alive?" the man asked, bewildered.

"You are, indeed," I said. "Must be lucky, I guess. Are you hurt?"

"Th-there was a man," the woman stammered.

"Some son of a bitch was shooting at us," the man said, then noticed Earl's rifle in my hands "You! It was you!"

The woman whimpered, throwing her hands up in front of her face.

"Now hang on there," I said softly. "Just hang on a minute. It wasn't me. The fellow that was shooting at you is my neighbor, Earl Harper. He's a crazy cuss, and I apologize for that. But the important thing now is to get you folks out of this weather and into safety. Are either of you hurt?"

The young man shook his head. "I don't think so."

"My head hurts," the girl complained. "But I'm okay."

I gave them both a cursory check, and looked at her pupils for signs of a concussion, but they both seemed all right. When I turned to check on Carl, I caught a hint of movement out of the corner of my eye. It was just at the edge of the forest, where the field grass met pine trees and the gray light met darkness.

Carl didn't seem to notice.

"What are we going to do about this one, Teddy?" he asked.

The man on the ground grabbed Carl's shoulder. Carl jumped in alarm.

"I c-can't f-feel my l-legs," the older man gasped. "What's ha-happened? I can't f-feel my damn legs."

"Salty," the woman cried out. "Are you okay?"

"S-Sarah," the old man answered. "Is that you, girl?"

I was surprised that he was still conscious. He'd been gushing blood, going into shock, and having a seizure, yet despite this, he remained awake. Hardy stock, I guess. That's why they call us the greatest generation.

The young man and woman climbed out of the wreckage and I helped them hobble over to Carl and their friend.

When the woman, Sarah, saw the bone poking through his torn flesh, she screamed, burying her face in the young man's chest. The one on the ground, Salty, looked at her in puzzlement, and then glanced down at his leg. When he saw what had happened, he began to scream, too.

"My leg! The damn bone's come out!"

I motioned to the younger man. "What's your name, son?"

He eyed the rifle suspiciously and then met my stare.

"Kevin. Kevin Jensen, out of Baltimore."

He sounded tired—and old. Were I to have guessed, I'd say he felt as old as me. I wondered what he'd seen in the past few weeks (other than this helicopter crash) to make him sound that way.

"Nice to meet you, Kevin. Let's start over, okay? My name is Teddy Garnett, and my friend over there is Carl Seaton. We're the Punkin' Center, West Virginia, welcoming committee. We don't mean you any harm. You folks have been shaken up, that's for sure, but we're here to help you."

Salty's screams of pain had turned to whimpers again. He was fading in and out of consciousness.

"Somebody shot at us," Sarah said. Her expression was one of disbelief.

"Like I said, that was my neighbor, Earl Harper. I'm real sorry about that. He figured you folks were the United Nations occupying force or some such nonsense. Earl wasn't wrapped real tight before any of this happened"—I waved my hand at the sky above us— "and I'm sure it hasn't helped his mind at all. In fact, the weather probably made him worse."

Kevin glanced around in a daze. "Where's Cornwell?"

"Who?" I asked.

"Cornwell. Our pilot. Did he survive?"

"I'm afraid not."

I glanced at the wreckage of the cockpit and Kevin started toward it, but Carl pulled him back.

"You don't want to see that, son."

I stared at the ground as Sarah began to sob, her tears indistinguishable from the raindrops on her cheeks.

Carl broke the silence. "Let's get—"

Something cracked in the woods—loud, like another gunshot. I think we all jumped, and Kevin screamed. The noise was followed by the sounds of wood snapping and splintering as a tree crashed to the ground. The echoes rang through the air. I thought about my apple tree and how it was slowly being uprooted. Then I thought about the strange holes we'd found.

"Look." I grabbed Kevin's arm. "We need to make sure Earl can't cause us any more trouble, and then we need to get your friend . . ." I snapped my fingers, trying to remember his name.

"Salty," Sarah said. "His name is Salty."

"Salty," I nodded. "We need to get him inside and check you folks over. You're probably in shock right now. Carl and I are going to go take care of Earl and fix up something to safely move Salty with. Carl's stopped the blood flow, but if we don't sew him up soon he'll be dead for sure. You folks stay here with him until we get back. Make sure that belt around his leg stays tight."

More snapping and popping came from the forest. That's when I really started to get scared.

"What's that in the woods?" Sarah asked.

"Probably just some deer," I assured her, "scared from the crash and all the shooting."

Carl gave me an odd look but said nothing.

I handed Earl's rifle to Kevin. "You know how to use this?"

His face darkened for a moment and he got a strange look in his eyes. "I had a crash course on guns not too long ago."

"Good. Take this one."

I think he saw in my eyes that something was wrong, because he said, "You've seen them, haven't you?"

"Seen what, son?"

"The things from below. You've got them here on dry land too, don't you?"

"I'm not sure what you're talking about, Kevin, but

yeah—I think I heard something out there. We all did. Don't know what it is, but I don't like the sound of it."

He glanced back at the tree line and then, without a word, escorted Sarah over to Salty.

I checked the injured man's makeshift tourniquet, and then Carl and I waded toward the shed.

"Teddy, do you really think we ought to be moving that old fellow? He's hurt pretty bad."

"Actually, I don't." I answered him in short gasps, winded from the last few minutes of exertion. "But I don't see how we've got a choice. If we move him, there's a chance we may hurt him even worse than he is now. I don't reckon there are any doctors around these parts to treat him, and I'm not sure what we can do, other than sew him up with a needle and thread. But if we leave him out here, he's going to die for certain of pneumonia."

"So what do we do? What's the plan?"

"Well, I reckon we'll get some duct tape from the shed and some kindling from the woodpile and make a splint. Then we'll get the wheelbarrow and haul him right up to the house, after we pop that bone back into place."

Carl looked queasy at the prospect of setting the splintered bone. "You know how to do that?"

"Not really."

"But we're gonna try anyway?"

I sighed. "Let's be honest here. No matter what we do, this Salty fellow is probably going to die. He's lost a lot of blood, and even if we do manage to reset the bone and sew his leg up, we don't have anything here to fight the infection. He could get gangrene. But we still have to try."

"We could amputate," Carl suggested. "Cut it off and cauterize the wound, like they do on television."

"Do you honestly think you could do that, Carl?"

"No. I don't reckon I could."

"Me neither."

"What about Earl?" he asked. "He ain't going to be happy when he finally wakes up. I knocked him a good one. Not to mention we helped these folks from the United Nations."

I stopped in my tracks. "Carl, do you really think those poor people back there are U.N. invasion troops? For God's sake, the helicopter wasn't even black."

Carl's wet ears turned red. "No, I guess not."

"Let's just lock Earl up in the shed, till we figure out what to do with him."

"He ain't gonna be happy about that, either. He's liable to be madder than a porcupine in a pickle barrel."

I smiled. "At least he'll be dry."

Earl lay where we'd left him, unmoving. He'd thrown up muddy water all over himself. I checked his pulse and felt it beating beneath his cold, wet, liver-spotted skin. Carl grabbed his legs and I tugged his arms, and we dragged him through the mud to the shed door. As we did so, I noticed the hole next to the wood-pile that we'd discovered the day before had caved in. All that was left was a big depression in the earth.

Carl fumbled with the rusty top latch on the door. It clicked open, and he bent to undo the bottom one. Suddenly, I recalled the muffled noise I'd heard yesterday, from inside the shed, when Carl and I were messing with the drum of kerosene.

"Carl, maybe we'd better—"

The wind ripped the door from Carl's grip before I could finish. The door slammed back and forth on its hinges, allowing us to see inside.

The shed stood empty. Well, not empty, mind you. Just not what I'd imagined might be in there. My riding mower and seeder and wheelbarrow, and my drum full of shelled corn for the deer and squirrel feeders, and my fishing equipment, garden tools, shovels, picks, hoes, and axes, and my workbench . . . but nothing else. Nothing that could dig a tunnel beneath the ground. The oak plank floor was empty of monster worms or giant groundhogs.

We hefted Earl inside.

I noticed that strange smell again; wet, *earthy*—like codfish oil. I wondered if the whole world was beginning to smell like that. Grunting with effort, I let go of Earl's legs and his boots thudded on the floor.

My breathing came in short, winded gasps. I wanted a dip. My body cried out for one. That old television slogan, from the commercial with Charlie Daniels, ran through my mind. *Just a pinch between the cheek and gum . . .*

There was a roll of duct tape on the workbench. I tossed it to Carl, and he began binding Earl's wrists behind his back. I grabbed some bailing twine and went to work on his feet.

"Boy," Carl whispered, "I sure do hope he don't wake up yet."

"He's not going to. You must have really knocked him a good one."

Carl tore off a length of gray duct tape. "I reckon so. Been wanting to for the better part of two decades. He had it coming ever since that time he shot at my dog when she was running rabbits out behind his place. I should have kicked his butt back then and saved us all some trouble."

Earl's chest rose and fell. His breathing was quiet and shallow.

"We'll want to be careful not to jab that piece of bone sticking out of Salty's leg," I said as I unknotted the bundle of bailing twine. "We'll pad the splint with some of those shop rags over there."

Carl nodded and finished binding Earl's wrists.

That was when the floor moved. It wasn't sudden. There was no explosion or jolt. But the wooden planks we were kneeling on slowly began to rise, almost unnoticeably at first. Three inches. Then six. Then back down. Then up again, like the floor was breathing. We froze. There was no sound, save the creaking wood and our own terrified heartbeats, throbbing in our ears.

Carl stared at me with wide eyes, and I stared back at him, probably looking the same.

Then there was a wet sort of rustling; a rubbery sound, like what crinkling paper might sound like under water. I reckon rubbery doesn't go with crinkly, but I don't know how to describe it any better than that. Maybe it shouldn't be described. Maybe it shouldn't be at all. Like I said earlier, I'm not a writer. All I know is I'd never heard a sound like that in my entire life and it was the most unpleasant thing I've ever experienced. Combined with the rolling motion of the floor, which had begun to resemble the deck of a ship at sea, and that same fishy smell that had come creeping back, I suddenly grew nauseous.

It must have shown on my face, because Carl's expression changed from alarm to concern. I opened my mouth to speak, and then I threw up my breakfast all over Earl's chest and stomach. Gagging, Carl turned away.

The floor continued to move. Somewhere in the corner, the planks began to snap. Carl shouted something, but the dizziness had my ears ringing, and I couldn't understand him.

Nausea is never pleasant, and let me tell you, it doesn't get any easier after you pass eighty. I couldn't do anything except lie there, hands clutching the pitching and groaning boards, while my own body betrayed me. That fishy stench was overpowering now, and I think I must have passed out for a brief second.

The next thing I knew, Carl was screaming. I looked up and stared into a nightmare. Then I started screaming, too.

Carl had grabbed my twelve-inch lock-blade hunting knife from the workbench, and he was on the floor, stabbing the knife down again and again between the cracks in the planks. Something jerked beneath the boards as the blade disappeared through the cracks again. I only saw it for a second, but what I saw made me lose control of my bladder.

It looked like a quivering lump of grayish-white jelly, buried beneath the floorboards. The blade sank into the rubbery mass like it was margarine. Brownish ichor spilled from the wound, gushing up from between the cracks in the floor. The boards heaved again, splintering, and then were still.

The thing hadn't made a sound the entire time, not even when Carl stabbed it.

He turned to me. His face was pale and covered with sweat. "Let's get the hell out of here, Teddy!"

"What was that thing?" I stammered, still weak from my dizzy spell.

"I don't know. Oh Lord, I don't know. Let's just go! Please? Let's just lock Earl inside the shed and leave."

I stumbled to my feet and grabbed the rags and the duct tape. Carl kept the knife. We left Earl lying on the floor and dashed back out into the yard. The wind rocked the shed door back and forth, and I fumbled to shut it. Then I realized we'd forgotten the wheelbarrow to haul Salty in.

Carl disappeared around the corner.

"Wait for me," I called out. "Carl!"

Then he screamed again.

Out of breath and panicking, I ran around the side of the building and slid to a halt. The thing that had been underneath the shed was definitely not an oversized groundhog. It had crawled back outside, reopening the tunnel beside the woodpile. Half of it jutted from the hole, thrashing in pain. Stinking fluid sprayed from the knife wounds in its side.

I couldn't believe my eyes.

It was a worm. A giant earthworm, the size of a big dog, like a German shepherd or a Saint Bernard, but much longer. It undulated back and forth in the mud and grass, covering the ground with slime. Watery, brown blood pulsed from the gash in its hide.

More of its length pushed out of the hole and the creature whipped towards me like an out of control fire hose. The worm's tip (what I guess must have been its head, though I couldn't see any eyes) hung in the air in front of me, only an arm's reach away. Then the flesh split, revealing a toothless maw. It convulsed again, and then that horrible, yawning mouth shot towards me. Shrieking, I stumbled backward to the shed door. The worm followed.

Now, as it chased after me, the worm finally made a sound. It wasn't a cry or a scream or a roar or even a grunt. In fact, as far as I could tell, it wasn't composed from vocal chords at all.

A high-pitched blast of air rushed from its gaping mouth, a vibrating noise that sounded like—well, to be honest, it sounded like somebody pretending to fart. You know that sound you make when you put your mouth against your arm and blow? That's the same noise the creature was making. We used to call that a raspberry.

But it wasn't funny. It was the most terrifying thing I've ever heard. And it sounded angry.

The worm heaved its bulk forward and emerged all the way from the hole. I jumped back inside the shed, slipped in the worm's blood, and fell. My teeth clacked together on my tongue, and pain shot up my spine. The worm crawled after me, dripping slime and more of that brown blood in its wake. Outside, I heard Carl shouting for help. I crab-walked backwards, scuttling along the wooden planks. Dozens of splinters punctured my hands and my fingers slipped through a pool of my own warm vomit.

The monster snuffled doglike along the floor, as if smelling me out, but I didn't see any kind of nose or other organs—just that slathering mouth. Maybe it could sense my movements—my vibrations. It occurred to me that while I may have been the smartest man in Punkin' Center, I sure didn't know much about worms other than that birds and fish liked to eat them and that your dog might contract them if you didn't take care of him.

I backed myself into the corner, directly across from Earl, who was still sprawled unconscious on the floor while the world ended around him. More of my vomit was drying on his clothes.

The creature's weight shook the walls, and the rake fell down, hitting me in the head. My vision went blurry for a second. The gray, pallid thing rushed forward, then stopped an arm's length away from me. The tip swayed between Earl's pant leg and me, as if deciding which one of us to eat first.

It wriggled towards Earl. His combat boot vanished into its maw with a sucking sound. The worm's muscles rippled along its length as it swallowed his leg.

Shaking off the panic, I grabbed the pickax from the wall and swung it with all of my remaining strength. The point pierced the monster's pulsating flesh and bit into the hardwood floor beneath it.

The creature coiled and thrashed, twisting its length wildly around the shed. Brown blood gushed around the pickax, and the stench was horrible. The worm knocked a barrel over. Shelled corn spilled out of the barrel, scattering onto the floor. Boxes and tools crashed from the work-bench and the hooks on the wall above it. But the pickax kept the worm pinned to the floor.

I yanked Earl free. His leg and foot slid out of the thing's mouth with a wet, sickening pop. Slime covered his leg from the knee down. Earl groaned and his eyelids fluttered.

"G-Garnett?" he moaned.

"Shit." I limped to the door, looked outside, and then turned back to him. "Why'd you have to wake up now?"

I half wished the thing had eaten him. We wouldn't have been in this mess if not for him.

Earl sniffed the air and looked down at his chest. "Is—is that puke? Who fucking puked on me?"

Kevin and Carl rounded the corner and skidded to a halt on the wet grass, staring at the worm through the open door.

"The fuck is that thing?" Kevin shouted.

"It's a worm," I said, realizing that I'd picked up Carl's gift for stating the obvious.

"Garnett," Earl hollered from behind me. "Get me out of here, goddamn you!"

"You okay, Teddy?" Carl asked.

"I'm all right." Wheezing, I leaned against the door frame. The rain felt cool on my face, and for once, I welcomed it. I wasn't just tired; I was bone weary. My lungs burned, and my chest hurt. It felt like a big fist was squeezing my heart.

I turned back to Earl and the worm. The creature continued thrashing, trying to free itself. Kevin and Carl gaped at it, shaking their heads in either disgust or disbelief, or maybe both. Earl screamed, pushing himself against the wall.

"Shoot it," I told Kevin. "Carl, go get us some pieces of kindling so we can make a splint for Salty."

Carl's eyes never left the worm. "You sure you're okay, Teddy?"

"I'll live. Just got the wind knocked out of me. Now go!"

Carl dashed over to the woodpile, keeping a wide berth around the newly reopened hole.

Kevin set Earl's rifle stock firmly into his shoulder and sighted, going from Earl to the worm. I stepped outside so that he'd have a clear shot.

"That's the guy who shot us down?" Kevin asked.

"Yeah, he's the one."

"I ought to shoot them both."

"Go ahead," I answered calmly, and in that second, I meant it, Christian thing to do or not. There wasn't just one monster inside that shed. There were two of them.

Earl stared out at us, shrinking back against the wall as the worm whipped towards him again.

"Go ahead, you cocksucker! Shoot me!"

Kevin turned the rifle on the worm and squeezed the trigger. There was an empty click, barely audible over the downpour and the creature's crazed throes.

Earl grinned. "It's empty, you dumb fuck."

"Oh, for crying out loud." I slapped my thigh, fear and fatigue giving way to anger and a fresh burst of adrenaline. I marched forward, deftly sidestepping the flailing worm, and grabbed the firewood ax from the wall. Making sure I had a firm grip on the handle, I positioned myself near the creature's midsection and swung the ax down hard.

The ax easily parted the flesh, cutting deep and clean. The worm's gyrations grew frenzied and it began making that hissing squeal again. Wrinkling my nose, I swung the ax again. Pulpy, stinking goo splattered my wet clothes as I chopped it in half. The worm shrieked. Someone else was screaming above the din, and after a moment, I realized that it was me.

The worm was now severed in half. The portion pinned to the floor by the pickax quivered, still leaking fluids. The freed portion flopped around like a fish out of water or a chicken with its head cut off, snaking back and forth across the planks. It tumbled out into the yard. Kevin clubbed it with the rifle, pulping what was left.

Carl returned with the kindling. "I think it's dead now."

Earl sat up and groaned again, struggling with his bound hands.

"Garnett," he snarled through tobacco-stained teeth. "What the hell are you doing, you son of a bitch? Didn't you see the black chopper that came up from the hollow? Why are my hands tied? And who's that fucker with my rifle?"

"He works for the U.N.," I whispered, kneeling to stare into his eyes. "He's here to take over Punkin' Center and Carl and I are helping him."

Earl's eyes grew wide as saucers. "What?"

"It's true. He says that if we help him, he'll give me the deed to your property when we're done, and make Carl the mayor of Renick."

"And then," Carl added, "we're gonna paint the town pink and invite in all the liberals. Maybe even get Clinton reelected for a third term."

I grinned. "Or his wife."

Earl screamed in furious indignation.

"Carl," I said, stepping back into the shed. "Go get us some more kindling. That's not gonna be enough."

"Garnett," Earl snarled, "I'm gonna fucking kill you."

"Not today, you won't."

I tore off another piece of duct tape and placed it over Earl's mouth. He shook with rage and the veins in his forehead and neck stood out. Snot bubbled from his nose. He kicked his heels against the floor. I grabbed his ankles and hauled him outside into the mud, where I left him. Earl shut his eyes against the rain beating at his face.

"Watch him closely," I told Kevin, and ducked back inside the shed for the wheelbarrow. The worm had knocked it over onto its side. I heard Earl grunt, and when I came back outside Kevin was prodding him with his foot.

There was a noise behind us, from inside the shed. We turned to look and both of us took a step back. Even Earl got quiet.

The two severed halves of the worm were now moving independently of each other. One piece slithered slowly across the wooden planks, leaking blood and slime from its wounded end. The other segment wriggled helplessly, the pickax still holding it in place.

Kevin backed away. I slammed the door shut and threw the bolt.

"Will that hold them?" Kevin asked.

I shrugged my shoulders. "I don't know. Doubt it."

As if to prove the point, the entire shed shook as the worm heaved its weight against the door.

Kevin glanced towards the wreckage in the field. "We'd better get back to the others."

"Carl," I shouted, "how are we looking for kindling? Do we have enough?"

"He's not here, Mr. Garnett," Kevin answered.

"Where did he go?"

"I saw him run down to the woods."

Cursing, I dragged the wheelbarrow out into the rain and glanced about. I wasn't sure what was going on, but I assumed that in his confused, panicky state, Carl had ignored the kindling from the woodpile. Instead, he had gone down to the forest to collect sticks and branches to use for the splint instead.

I loved him dearly, but sometimes Carl could be as dumb as a stump. This was one of those times.

"Get Earl up to the house where we can keep an eye on him," I told Kevin. "Tie him to the picnic table or something. Then take the wheelbarrow over to your friends, so we can move Salty in it."

"Where are you going?"

"To find my friend."

"But what about us? What about Sarah?"

"I'm not letting Carl go down into those woods by himself. Not now."

Hefting the ax, I ran after Carl. My breath got shorter and my lungs began to burn again as I pressed onward. I was definitely too old for this type of thing. I wasn't some action movie hero—I was a senior citizen suffering from all the maladies of old age. Several times I skidded, the wet grass giving way beneath me, the sod nothing more than mush after forty-two days of constant battering from the rain.

I passed the little apple tree Rose and I had planted six years ago. It lay uprooted and on its side now, withering and dying as the soil around it turned into quicksand.

I reached the edge of my yard. The woods loomed before me, dark and ominous. A hush fell over the world, and even the rain seemed to fall silently.

"Carl?" My voice echoed through the mist and took on a peculiar quality. Wet branches brushed my face as I took a few hesitant steps into the tree line. I'd walked through those woods a million times, but they looked different now, and I didn't recognize anything. The trees were bent, gnarled shadows. More of that strange white fungus spiraled up the trunks. It hadn't been there the day before, when I was looking for teaberry leaves. That meant it was spreading fast, whatever it was. I wondered how the spores were transported; then I remembered the deer.

Still hovering at the edge of the forest, I glanced back at the crash site. Kevin had managed to get the wheelbarrow over to Sarah and Salty. Rather than dumping Earl at the house, he'd taken him along with him. Earl was now tied to a hunk of twisted metal from the helicopter. From where I stood, it didn't look like Salty was moving. Then the mist thickened and I lost sight of them all.

That's when something exploded from the brush in front of me.

"Oh Lord, Oh Lord Oh Lord Oh Lord . . ."

Carl crashed through the thorns and brambles and sped by me as fast as his old legs would carry him. That now all-too-familiar hissing sound followed in his wake.

"Run, Teddy!" Carl shouted. "Run like hell!"

Four worms emerged from the trees. All of them were bigger than the creature from the shed—about the size of a milk cow, but much longer. Their fat, bulbous bodies undulated, whipping towards us. Rather than crawling, they moved via a series of repeated convulsions, beginning at the back end and rushing through their length like a wave. The motion propelled them forward much quicker than I would have imagined. In the time it took Carl to run past, they were upon me.

I swung at one of the worms with the ax, cleaving its rubbery hide. The fishy reek immediately assaulted my senses and I gagged from the stench. The ground gave way beneath my feet and I struggled for balance in the mud. I let go of the ax handle, leaving the weapon buried in the head of the closest worm.

Carl ran back to help me. As he pulled me to my feet, the ground began to shake. We both lost our footing and fell sprawling in the mud. My knee struck a rock, and agony shot through my leg. The mud sucked at me, trying to drag me down.

The worms had stopped moving as well. They held their heads up high, weaving back and forth like snakes, as if anticipating something. I didn't know what they were waiting for and I didn't care. I tried to free myself, but the mud was like glue.

Somewhere in the woods, another tree crashed to the ground. The worms howled in answer. I sank farther into the slop.

"It's an earthquake!" Carl cried, stumbling to his feet. He was covered in mud from head to toe.

"Help me up," I called. "I'm stu—"

The tremors increased, making speech impossible. Then the yard split open as a huge form rocketed up from below. It surged out of the ground. Mud, water, and saplings tumbled into the hole left in the creature's wake. The worm was easily the size of a school bus, and its hiss was so deep that I felt the vibrations in my chest.

Carl pulled me to my feet and we ran. The worm reared above us, then plummeted downward. Its shadow killed what little light there was, and its pulsating bulk blocked out even the rain. The ground literally *jumped* as the worm crashed into the mud. It began to give chase.

Hysterical, Carl urged me onward. "Run! Run run run!"

The monster squalled behind us.

I caught up with Carl and he tugged at my arm, babbling incoherently. We loped along together, throwing glances over our shoulders. The thing plowed onward, leaving a slime-filled furrow in its wake. The four smaller worms had disappeared back into the forest. Apparently, they were just as terrified as we were. Either that or they didn't want to get in their big brother's way.

Kevin stood still as stone, staring, drop-jawed as we neared the helicopter wreckage. Sarah, on the other hand, kept her wits about her. She pulled a jagged, spearlike shard of metal from the wreckage. She stood ready, like a javelin thrower at the Olympics. Earl struggled against his bonds, straining the duct tape and bailing twine as he rocked backward and forward in an attempt to break free.

"Run!" I gasped. My chest was in agony, and my knee was starting to swell up from my fall.

Carl slammed into Kevin with his shoulder. "Don't just stand there!"

Dazed, the young man looked at him in confusion. "I didn't know there were worms, too. I thought it was just the things in the ocean."

We didn't have time to wonder what he was talking about.

Carl shoved him forward. "Get a move on, boy, unless you want to end up as that thing's supper!"

Sarah stepped past them and flung the makeshift spear. It soared through the air, cleaving through the rain as it arced downward. It sank into the worm's rubbery flesh, jutting from the creature's midsection. Stinking fluids bubbled up from deep inside the creature.

The worm turned.

Frenzied from the wound, it careened through the helicopter wreckage, heedless of the further damage it was doing to itself. Metal shards sliced deep gashes into its pale hide, and that same brownish blood spurted from the wounds.

Earl gnawed at the bailing twine binding him to the wreckage. The duct tape had slipped from his mouth and was dangling from his chin. His eyes were round and frightened. I watched in alarm as the duct tape around his wrists began to rip.

On the ground, Salty finally regained consciousness, took one look at the monster, and screamed. The worm immediately whipped towards him. It emitted another blast of air, and the sound reminded me of Rose's teakettle and the old steam engine railroad up on Cass Mountain.

Shouting, Sarah ran for Salty, but I grabbed her arm and shoved her toward the house instead. Pain shot down my side.

"Garnett," Earl hollered, "you chickenshit son of a bitch! Get back here and untie me, right now!"

Sarah struggled with me. "Salty! We can't leave him behind!"

"It's too late for them. Just run!"

Then it was upon us, and we fled.

I only looked back once. The beast towered over Salty, its slavering mouth open wide, covering him with dripping slime. Then the head stretched forward and swallowed him whole. I made out the faint outline of his body beneath the creature's skin as he slid down its throat.

I turned away and the pain increased. It grew worse with each step I took.

When I looked back again, Earl had succeeded in chewing his way free. He spat the frayed strands of duct tape from his mouth and glared at us as he sliced the bailing twine around his ankles with a sharp piece of metal.

"Ready or not, here I come, you bastards!"

He snatched up another shard of metal and jabbed it into the creature's side. Grunting, he pushed the spear until it sank completely into the hide. The worm's agonized shriek hammered our eardrums. Then Earl ran after us.

THE CONQUEROR WORMS

The fog started to thicken again, as if the clouds were suddenly dropping from the sky.

"Come on," Sarah screamed.

I turned back to the house, took a few more steps, and then doubled over in agony. Pain shot through my kidneys, my stomach, my chest, and my lungs. The giant fist was back, squeezing my entire body.

I collapsed to my knees, which brought a fresh burst of pain.

Sarah knelt beside me. "Mr. Garnett, what's wrong?"

"M-my . . . heart . . ."

"Oh God—are we having a heart attack?"

I tried to answer and found that I couldn't. My lips felt cold. Numb.

"Just hang on," Sarah said. "Stay with me."

"Rose . . . ," I whispered, and blinked the rain out of my eyes.

Cackling, Earl closed the distance between us. The wounded worm slid along behind him, its body shuddering with each undulation.

Sarah helped me to my feet and we pressed on towards the house. We had to wade through the little earthworms on the carport, which was like walking through a foot-deep pile of spaghetti.

Carl and Kevin held the door open for us. Kevin still clutched the empty rifle.

"Hurry," Carl yelled. "They're coming!"

I heard Earl and the worm both bearing down on us. Sarah dragged me through the doorway. We collapsed onto the kitchen floor and Carl slammed the door shut and locked it.

We stared at one another in silence; the only sound was our harsh, ragged breathing.

Stifling a sneeze, Carl glanced out the window.

"Are they coming?" I croaked, as another jolt of pain shot through my chest.

"I can't tell. That fog out there is like pea soup. It's like it came out of nowhere! I don't hear them, though."

"Maybe that thing ate your neighbor," Kevin said, smoothing his wet hair with his hand.

Carl smiled. "If it did, then it's gonna have some really bad indigestion."

I grabbed my chest and closed my eyes.

"You want your pills, Teddy?" Carl asked.

Swallowing, I nodded. "Th-they're on my nightstand."

He hurried off in search of them.

Sarah brought me a bottle of water from the refrigerator (even though there was no power, I still stored them inside the appliance to conserve space). She twisted the cap off and brought the bottle to my lips. I sipped gratefully, choking on the coldness.

Outside, Earl screamed—one long, drawn out wail. Rather than fading, it was cut off abruptly.

Then, everything was still again.

Carl returned with my pills, and the pain in my chest faded after I swallowed a few. I drank some more water, letting it soothe my scratchy throat.

The rain continued falling.

CHAPTER SIX

Twenty minutes later, we were still crouched there on the kitchen floor, sitting in puddles from our wet clothes, huddled together for comfort. We'd have probably been more comfortable in a safer room, but the others didn't want to move me until my chest pains subsided. Kevin peeked outside several times, but there were no signs of the giant worms or of Earl Harper. I bade them both good riddance. The big one had probably caten Earl, and then, having had its fill, burrowed back into the earth.

"Well," I told Carl, "I guess now we know what happened to your house."

He nodded. "And Steve Porter's hunting cabin, too."

Kevin looked puzzled. "What are you guys talking about?"

"Homes have been disappearing down into the ground," I said. "Only thing left behind is a hole—about the same size as that thing out there."

"Shit."

Carl fetched some towels and spare clothes so

everybody could dry off, and we cranked up the kerosene heater to its highest setting. Sarah put on one of Rose's old sweaters and it fit her real nice. It was the first time I'd seen it out of her dresser since she died. Gave me a lump in my throat just looking at it. We didn't say much to each other—just sat there with our teeth chattering and waited to get warm.

When the pills kicked in and I felt better, I went to the spare bedroom and unlocked the gun cabinet. Kevin still had Earl's rifle, and I found some ammunition for it. I gave Carl the Winchester 30-30, and I took the Remington 4.10, loaded with punkinballs. Then I pulled out Rose's old Ruger .22 semi-automatic pistol (I'd bought it for her one birthday long ago, and Rose had become an excellent shot—even better than me). I handed it to Sarah. I considered asking her if she knew how to use it, but something told me she did.

She eyed it skeptically. "That's all? Don't you have anything bigger?"

"Afraid not. But that there pistol will surely kill a man if you aim right."

"It's not a *man* I'm worried about. I was just thinking about stopping power. And as for killing, I don't need a gun to do that."

Carl and I both shuffled our feet, not sure how to respond. After a moment, we realized that she was smiling.

"You're a regular spitfire," Carl said, chuckling.

Kevin positioned himself at the kitchen door and continued staring out the window. "There's no sign of them. Those things, I mean. We might be okay. Maybe they won't come back."

"Even still," I replied, "I reckon one of us ought to stand guard at all times."

"What were those things?" Carl asked.

I shrugged. "Worms."

"Teddy Garnett," he scolded, "don't you ever make fun of me for stating the obvious again!"

Sarah and Kevin were silent.

"Have either of you seen anything like them before?" I asked.

Sarah shook her head, but she seemed hesitant.

Kevin was quiet for a moment and then said, "No, not like them. But we have seen some weird things. Not worms, but similar creatures, in a way."

"Like what?"

"I'd rather not talk about it right now, if that's okay?"

"Sure." I put my hand on his shoulder. "Let's rest up first. You can fill us in later. I imagine we all have a tale to tell."

I looked at Sarah standing there in Rose's sweater, and I suddenly missed my wife real bad. My eyes welled up. I excused myself, rushed down the hall, and locked myself in the bathroom.

I put the commode lid down and sat on it, and that's when it hit me. All of it. The horror I'd just experienced and the despair of the last two months and the sheer loss. It crashed down on me like a lead balloon. I sat there for twenty minutes, and I shook and I cried. But I did it quietly, without uttering a sound. I didn't want the others to hear me. And to be honest, I was afraid I'd start screaming and not be able to stop.

When I came out, they were all sitting around the kitchen table, drinking instant coffee while Carl told them about Old One-Eye, the legendary catfish that was supposed to inhabit a part of the Greenbrier River we locals called the Cat-Hole.

"So then Hap Logan took his little bass boat out one night, about two weeks after Ernie Whitt's dog vanished while swimming across the Cat-Hole. It was a quiet night, and Hap had just about nodded off, when all of a sudden his boat started rocking. He sat up and looked around, but he didn't see anything. But the boat started swaying more, like it was bumping against a rock or something. So he grabbed his flashlight and pointed it at the river's surface, and guess what he saw?"

"What?" Kevin asked.

"Old One-Eye. He'd come up under Hap's boat. There was one good eye on the left side of the boat, and a blind, milky eye on the other. Scared him something awful, he said. A lot of folks thought he was making it up, but I'll tell you one thing—Hap Logan never went fishing in the Cat-Hole again."

Sarah grinned. "Sounds like those worms aren't the only big things around here."

As implausible as it sounded, the thought of sitting in a boat on the river at night and seeing one unblinking fish eye staring at you from one side, and a white, sightless orb from the other, had always made me shudder.

I heated up what was left of the stew and served everyone a bowl, along with some crackers from the pantry. But nobody seemed to have much of an appetite.

"The bathroom's available if anybody wants it," I announced. "You can't use the toilet, but I've got a wash basin in there and a five-gallon bucket of spring water to clean up with."

"Ugh." Sarah wrinkled her nose. "I've had enough of water for right now, but thanks anyway. Maybe later."

Kevin asked, "So where are we supposed to go to the bathroom?"

"Good question," I said. "To be honest—and my apologies to Sarah—but I've just been going out on the back porch when I had to go number one, and down to the outhouse for number two."

Carl shivered. "You ain't getting me back in that outhouse again."

"No," I agreed, "I don't think any of us will be venturing back out there anytime soon. I reckon we'll use a bucket, and then dump it outside when we're done."

Kevin sighed. "Boy, there's nothing like roughing it. This reminds me of summer camp back when I was a kid."

Carl crossed his arms and leaned back against the wall, eyeing them. "So are you two . . . together?"

"Us?" Sarah threw her head back and laughed.

Kevin joined her a second later.

Carl's ears turned red. "I reckon that's a 'no.'"

"Sorry," Sarah giggled. "You just have to know us. I'm gay, and Kevin, well . . ."

A shadow passed over Kevin's face and Sarah trailed off, her grin fading. I could tell they didn't want to talk about whatever it was, so I tried to change the subject.

"By any chance, would either of you happen to have some cigarettes?"

"Sorry," Sarah apologized. "I don't smoke."

"And I was getting ready to ask you and Carl the same thing," Kevin said.

"You a smoker?" I asked, hoping he'd say yes. Then at least I'd have someone to commiserate with. My misery needed some company.

"I wasn't," Kevin replied. "But after what we've been through today, I'm tempted to start."

Chuckling, I dumped the uneaten stew back into the pot and put the crackers in the pantry. Then I poured myself some hot water and instant coffee into a mug, and pulled up a seat at the kitchen table.

Sarah gestured to the pictures in the living room. "Those pictures—are they your family?"

"They were. I don't reckon my daughter or my grandkids . . . Well, they lived closer to the ocean. And Rose, that's my wife, she passed away of pneumonia three years ago. I figure I'll see them all sooner rather than later."

Carl nodded and sipped his coffee. Kevin didn't reply. Sarah stared out the window, then turned and looked at the hutch, where Darla, my granddaughter, stared back at us from a silver frame.

"She's beautiful."

"Thanks," I said. "You remind me of her, actually. You've got her strength."

Sarah smiled, and yes, she *did* remind me of Darla at that moment.

Carl sat his mug down on the table. "So what did you folks do before—all of this?"

Kevin brightened for a moment. "I worked in a video store."

"I worked for McCormick," Sarah added. "The spice manufacturer."

"Sure." I nodded. "So you're both from Baltimore?"

"We are," Kevin said. "Or were. What's left of it, at least."

He let his gaze roam around the kitchen. It lingered on my three houseplants, and I wondered if he was some sort of amateur gardener. When he spotted my framed picture of Johnny Cash hanging on the wall, he turned to me.

"You're a fan of the Man in Black, huh? I saw him in concert when I was younger. Great show."

"You like country music?" Carl asked.

"Some—but not all of it," Kevin replied. "I guess I'm pretty eclectic. Mostly rock, metal, and hip-hop. But I liked Johnny Cash. And Shania Twain and the Dixie Chicks are pretty cool. Or were. I bet you guys like them, right?"

"No sir," Carl said. "Don't care much for that new country at all. We like the classics. Folks like Conway Twitty, Loretta Lynn, Porter Wagoner, and Patsy Cline."

"And Jerry Reed," I added. "Can't forget about some of those seventies trucking songs."

With a grin, Carl started humming the theme song from *Smokey and the Bandit*.

"East bound and down," I chuckled.

"We're gonna do what they say can't be done," he answered.

Kevin looked stunned. "No Dixie Chicks or Shania?"

"The Dixie Chicks make me break out in hives," Carl said. "And Shania Twain is about as country as that rock and roll band, Metalli-something."

Kevin grinned. "Metallica."

We all laughed then, except for Sarah, who stood up and moved to the kitchen window. She looked out the rain-streaked pane, but her eyes weren't fixed on anything. I could tell her thoughts were far away.

"What is it?" Kevin asked her softly.

"There are no more Dixie Chicks," she said. "There's no more Shania Twain or Metallica, and no more radio and Baltimore and—and I saw Cornwell after the crash, and he'd been sliced into three—" She stopped, unable to continue, and shut her eyes. "And poor, poor Salty."

"Baltimore's flooded?" I asked, even though I already knew the answer.

"Are you kidding?" Kevin snorted. "Baltimore's fucking gone, man. Just like everything else."

"What happened out there," Carl whispered, more to himself than to anybody. "What the hell happened?"

"God broke His promise," Sarah said from the window. "Decided He was tired of us messing up this nice planet He gave us and flooded it again."

"Can't say as I blame Him," Carl muttered.

"I'm serious," Sarah continued. "How else do you explain it? One morning, kiddie porn is a multibillion dollar industry, the President is pardoning drug dealers in exchange for campaign contributions and declaring war on any country he feels like, teens are shooting each other in school, and terrorists are blowing up places of worship. The next day, we wake up, and Pennsylvania's Amish country is beachfront property and the survivors are making a pilgrimage to the Rocky fucking Mountains in Colorado!"

"And Leviathan and Behemoth are loosed upon the earth," I added.

Kevin and Sarah both jumped, and Kevin's coffee mug crashed to the floor.

Carl rose to his feet. "You okay? What's wrong? Did you see something outside?"

The two young people shot wary glances at each other.

"Sorry," I said. "Didn't mean to startle you. My Rose taught Sunday School for thirty-some years. Behemoth and Leviathan were both biblical creatures. The book of Job, if I remember correctly."

"Rose always did know her Bible," Carl said.

Suddenly, bursting into tears, Sarah ran out of the kitchen and down the hallway. We heard the spare bedroom door slam shut.

"What is it?" I asked Kevin. "Did I say something wrong? I'm sorry if I offended her."

He shook his head. "No, you didn't. The word Leviathan . . ."

He grabbed a towel and mopped up his coffee. Then he sat back down, folded his hands, and looked at Carl and me. His face was grave.

"Maybe I'd better tell you guys our story. Then you'll understand. You see, those worms aren't the only things out there."

"There's other things?" Carl asked. "Worse than the worms?"

"Oh, yes." Kevin's voice was barely a whisper.

I refilled Kevin's mug. He stirred the crystals, watching them dissolve in the hot water. None of us said anything. Carl got up and stood at the window, keeping watch.

After a bit, Kevin took a deep breath. His hands were shaking.

This is what he told us. . . .

PART II

UPON US ALL A LITTLE RAIN MUST FALL

Water, water, every where,
Nor any drop to drink.

The very deep did rot: O Christ!
That ever this should be!
Yea, slimy things did crawl with legs
Upon the slimy sea.

About, about, in reel and rout
The death-fires danced at night;
The water, like a witch's oils,
Burnt green, and blue and white.

—Samuel Taylor Coleridge
The Rime of the Ancient Mariner

CHAPTER SEVEN

The Satanists were surfing down Pratt Street when I found Jimmy's head floating outside the fifteenth floor of the Chesapeake Apartments.

Earlier that day, a jellyfish almost stung me while I was paddling off the roof of the Globe Capital building. It was a good place for scavenging since the top floors were still above water. I went in from the roof, looking for guns, food, cigarettes, disposable lighters—anything that might be useful. While untying the raft from the roof, I was busy wishing the National Guard Armory wasn't at the bottom of the ocean, and didn't notice the jellyfish until it was almost too late.

All in all, between the rain, the Satanists, and the jellyfish, it was a bad day to be outside.

I'd always hated rainy days. They brought me down. I hadn't been happy in a long, long while.

Finding Jimmy's head did nothing to improve my mood. I barely managed to keep from screaming. I bit through my lip, tasting blood and stifling a yell, while the Satanists whooped and shouted to each other in the distance. Their surfboards were painted black.

I turned back to Jimmy.

There he was. My best friend. The guy I'd grown up with, reduced now to a severed head floating on the crests of the misplaced Atlantic Ocean.

"Shit, Jimmy. What the fuck did they do to you?"

I grabbed him by the hair before the tide could take him.

His pallid skin felt like cottage cheese and his mouth was frozen in an expression of surprise, as if he'd died saying, "Oh!" But it was his eyes that *really* got to me. I shut mine, but I could still see that death stare, floating in the darkness.

I opened my eyes and closed his.

Blood and water dripped from his neck, pooling around my rubber boots. It didn't matter. I was wet anyway. I hadn't been dry in so long that I'd forgotten what being dry actually *felt* like. Most of us had developed rashes, and we'd lost about two-dozen people to pneumonia and colds. My uncle used to talk about jungle rot, something they got in Vietnam from having damp feet. We had a new type of fungus, a version that covered your entire body in white fuzz. In fact, that's what we called it: the White Fuzz. It ate at you until there was nothing left—a horrible way to die.

Choking off my emotions and trying to be clinical about things, I turned over Jimmy's head in my hands. It didn't appear severed. Rather, the windpipe and neck were pinched and flattened like the end of a toothpaste tube. It looked like his attacker had *squeezed* the head off his body. I couldn't be sure, of course. I'm not a medical examiner or crime scene investigator or anything like that. I'm just a guy who worked at a video store—until the rain started.

The thing on his cheek was the worst, a reddish-purplish sore, open and leaking. It looked like Jimmy's killer had given him a hickey and gnawed through his face at the same time.

I knew who'd done it. The Satanists. Who else?

My mind flashed back to fourth grade. Spending the night at Jimmy's house, reading comic books until his parents went to sleep, and then sneaking a peek at his father's porno magazines, staring at the pictures of naked women and reading the letters, and trying to figure out what it meant when a woman said "eat me." Summers spent inner-tubing down the Codorus Creek, and buying more comic books at the flea market, and camping out in my backyard, and riding bikes all over town.

We got our driver's licenses at sixteen, and our bikes were replaced with muscle cars. About the same time, the girls from the magazines were replaced by flesh and blood, and we learned *exactly* what a woman meant when she said "eat me."

We'd planned on joining the Marines together, but then Jimmy got his DUI after a car wreck just over the border in York, Pennsylvania, and I got Becky pregnant. For our nineteenth birthdays, Jimmy went to jail for manslaughter (his girlfriend hadn't survived the crash) and I got a job at Crown Video & DVD in Cockeysville, just outside of Baltimore. I've often thought that life is like a Bruce Springsteen song, and looking back on those days always reinforces that in my mind.

Jimmy did three years at Cresson State up in Pennsylvania. Thanks to overcrowding, they let him out on parole. While he was gone, Becky and the baby ran off with some Lexus-driving yo-boy she met at a club. Secretly, I was relieved. But it still hurts sometimes, knowing there's a kid out there somewhere who looks like me.

Well—probably not anymore.

We had a welcome-home party, and Jimmy readjusted to civilian life. He landed a job at the casket factory. Things were good. We chilled, marveling over the fact that our five-year high school reunion was coming up.

Then the rain started, washing it all away.

I wouldn't cry. I *wanted* to, but I couldn't. There were many times since the rain started that I'd wanted to cry, especially now. I felt like screaming, ranting at the gray haze that had replaced the once blue sky. I wanted to collapse, cradling my best friend's head, and just stay there, not moving or thinking ever again.

I couldn't cry because I'm incapable of it. Sure, when I was a little kid, I cried when I skinned my knee or didn't get my way. But I've never been able to do it over death. I used to think there was something wrong with me. When I was twelve, my grandmother died. At the funeral, I couldn't cry, and I felt like a complete dick. My parents were crying, my sister, my aunts and uncles—but not me. I just stood there with a stupid look on my face. Sure, I was *sad*. I grieved. I loved my grandma. But when the time came, the tears were absent and I couldn't summon them, no matter how hard I tried.

I looked up at the sky, letting the rain beat against my face and pretended the drops of water were tears. They were phony tears, but it was the best that I could do.

Voices carried over the roaring waves. Ducking down so the Satanists wouldn't see me, I quickly took stock. The Globe Capital building had been a complete bust (except for the jellyfish), but the Chesapeake Apartments had yielded a dozen bottles of spring water. It seemed obscene that with so much water falling from the sky, fresh water was like gold. But the rain had a high salt content, at least in our area. I'm not sure why. Don't know if it was some freak ecological occurrence or what. We'd heard from passersby that it was better in other places. I'd also found some canned goods, a flashlight that still worked, a fifth of Jim Beam, a half empty bottle of vodka, two dry cartons of smokes (almost as valuable as the bottled water), a few paperbacks and magazines that hadn't begun to mold yet, a box of crayons, and most importantly, a houseplant, a bag of potting soil, and three little envelopes of seeds—carrots, marigolds, and sunflowers.

And Jimmy's head.

Sighing, I placed the loot inside one of the nylon backpacks I carried with me, so that it would all stay dry during the trip back home. Then I dropped the backpack into a garbage bag for extra insulation. Finally, I wrapped Jimmy's head in a plastic bag and stuffed it inside the backpack as well. The pockets of my raincoat bulged with smaller items: cigarette lighters, waterproof matches, vitamins, silverware, toothpaste, aspirin and other medicines, pens, batteries, candles—anything I thought our group could use.

The only thing I left behind was cash. That was good for starting fires, and then only if the bills were dry.

After I finished, I waited for the Satanists to leave. Starting the boat motor would have been like shouting, "Hey guys, here I am!" Paddling off the rooftop without the motor running would be futile because of the waves. They'd push me right back onto it.

I waited about an hour and eventually they moved on. I guess the surfing was better in another part of the city. When I was sure it was safe, I untied the boat from the flagpole and started home.

The blue-green ocean seemed huge and endless and lonely, and it was pretty quiet, except for the waves, the seagulls, and the rain hitting the water. I kept glancing around for signs of pursuit, but I was alone.

"Raindrops keep falling on my head," I sang. "But that doesn't mean my eyes will soon be turning red. Crying's not for me, cause I'm never gonna stop the rain by complaining, because—"

My voice bounced back to me off the remains of a skyscraper, and I stopped singing. The echoes gave me goose bumps.

Debris floated by: wooden crates, aluminum lawn furniture, bodies and pieces of bodies. I tried to snag a few of the crates so that I could examine the contents, but the tide carried them out of my reach. We didn't need the lawn furniture, and I already had Jimmy's head, so I left the other body parts alone.

Water dripped from the oars, oily and slimy. I shuddered to think what was in it, all of the chemicals and pollution from the flooded buildings and industrial sites, and the bodies of the dead, of course.

To pass the time, I wondered about what the rest of the world was like now, if it was raining and flooded there, too. Occasionally, people sailed through Baltimore and stopped at our building, wanting to trade with us, or just looking for a dry place to dock and rest. When this happened, we'd hear news. Most of it concerned pockets of survivors like us, scattered across the country; but some of the things we heard were just plain weird.

The crew of a Coast Guard cutter reported that the population of Estes Park, Colorado, had resorted to cannibalism and human sacrifice. Some yuppie investment banker who had sailed all the way from Philadelphia swore he'd seen mermaids and that his friend made love to one and was never seen again. We traded him two cases of bottled water and some batteries for fishing tackle and a handgun with extra ammunition, and then quickly sent him on his way. Dude was obviously crazy.

Two folks named Ralph and Holly arrived in a traffic chopper, and stayed with us for a week, while we treated Holly for an infected dog bite on her leg. They said that giant carnivorous earthworms were rampaging through most of the Appalachians. Supposedly, the creatures killed some friends of theirs in North Carolina. At the time, I didn't believe them. But the kids believed them, and after they left, we went through a week of little Danielle waking up every night screaming about giant worms coming to eat her. Old Salty believed them, too, but Salty believed in everything.

I'd seen Salty around before the rains came. I don't know what he did before he was homeless, but at one time in his life he'd been a sailor. When I first encountered him, he was a regular fixture at Baltimore's Inner Harbor, telling sea stories for pocket change and watching the boats sail in and out. We used to give him money on Friday nights while barhopping in Fell's Point.

Salty was a walking encyclopedia of nautical myths and superstitions and he never missed a chance to warn you of them. Bananas onboard a boat guaranteed you'd catch no fish. If you overturned a basin of water at home, disaster would follow at sea. It was unlucky for fishermen to count the contents of the first net hauled up for the day. When you stepped onboard a ship, you should always go with your right foot first. If the ship's captain tripped while coming down a ladder, it was some bad mojo. Stuff like that. When one of the other girls offered to trim Sarah's hair for her, Salty begged them not to. According to him, cutting your hair while the sea was calm would raise a storm. We pointed out that the sea hadn't been calm for months and that it didn't look like the storm would stop anytime soon.

So we had Salty, Sarah, and little Danielle (who we found clinging to the roof of a car, her family dead and bloated inside, gnawed on by the fish). There were two other kids—ten-year-old James and eight-year-old Malik. There was also Lee, a paunchy, balding schoolteacher from Texas. He'd been in Baltimore for his mother's funeral and got stranded when the government halted all airline and rail service. The same thing happened to Mike, a middle-aged nuclear engineer from Idaho visiting Baltimore for a convention. Anna was a widow in her late-sixties, plump and matronly. Louis was sort of a beatnik. Always wore a beret. He'd owned a music store down in Fells Point, and his life partner, Christian, ran some kind of investment Web site. Nate was an architect, pompous and arrogant. Thought he was better than the rest of us. Juan was a Baltimore city cop. Hard as nails, but a nice enough guy. And smart. Then we had Taz, Ducky, and Lashawn. Taz had been a drug dealer and so was Ducky (I often wondered if those were their real names or just their street names, but I never found out). Taz was a big, hulking guy, built like a linebacker. Ducky was the exact opposite, thin and scrawny. Lashawn was Taz's girlfriend, and while I don't think he knew that she was also sleeping with Ducky, the rest of us did. We had two other women. Mindy had worked for an office supply company. She was smart and funny. Lori was about my age, and had gone to Johns Hopkins University. I'd had a crush on her and Mindy both—and Sarah, too, until I found out that she only dug other women. Finally, there'd been Jimmy and myself, the two amigos, reduced now to just one.

That was our group—all eighteen of us. There'd been more at one time. Some people left, sailing off in search of dryer pastures, and we never heard from them again. Cholera and typhoid were bad in the early days, before the dead were all washed out to sea. Two people died of heart attacks, and another from what we think was probably diabetes. One guy named Hector died from an impacted wisdom tooth infection. Amazing how something so minor can have such dire consequences without access to even basic medicine. A simple wisdom tooth cost Hector his life. The others who died succumbed to pneumonia, the White Fuzz, or else they drowned or simply vanished. We suspected that a few of these last ones probably fell victim to the Satanists.

Our neighbors weren't *real* Satanists, of course. Real Satanists didn't kill people or have orgies and black masses. I once dated a girl who was into Satanism, and I knew that real Satanism was a philosophy that was atheistic in nature. Satanists believed they were their own gods and that they controlled their own destiny. They didn't actually believe in the Devil, but used Satan symbolically, to represent the opposite of Christ. Cool concept, but it wasn't for me. I'd had a strict Methodist upbringing, and though I considered myself an agnostic, there were still enough of the old-school teachings ingrained in me. I dumped both the girl and her philosophy after two weeks.

Anyway, our neighbors weren't real Satanists, but that's what Juan started calling them. Then Taz and Ducky started using it. After a while, the name stuck.

Like I said, real Satanists didn't kill people, or have orgies and black masses—but these fuckers did just about every night. In the beginning, Juan and a few of the others suggested we take them out—do unto them before they could do unto us. But they had the numbers and an attack would have been suicide. They were bad news, so we just tried to avoid them as much as possible.

We had set up shop in the ruins of the big Marriott Hotel in what used to be the Inner Harbor district. Many upper floors of the city's skyscrapers were still above water, but most of the buildings were flooded inside. Miraculously, ours wasn't one of them. Somehow, the hotel had escaped any broken windows or cracks in the walls. The bottom floors were underwater, but from fifteen to twenty, everything was relatively dry. We lived on the top two floors.

The Satanists lived downtown in what was left of the Baltimore Trade Center. I'm guessing that, like our building, it had escaped major damage. I don't know how many of them there were, but while our numbers were shrinking, theirs seemed to be growing. They had enough people that they could afford to sacrifice someone every evening, at least.

We'd watched them from the rooftop a few times, through a telescope that Lee found in one of the hotel rooms, but none of us had the stomach to keep spying for long.

Not after what we saw.

The fire was the first indication that something wasn't right with our neighbors. With no streetlights or electricity, the Trade Center was barely noticeable at night. Until they lit the bonfire, that is.

The rain *never* stops. Sure, it changes. It has patterns. Mist to downpour, gentle breeze to gale force winds. But it never stops. Still, every night, despite the rain and the winds, the Satanists lit a huge bonfire on their roof, right in the middle of the helicopter pad. You could see it with the naked eye, a small, orange pinprick in the dark. But when we looked through the telescope . . .

It was bad. Water-soaked wood that shouldn't have been able to burn did so anyway. The rain didn't put the fire out. Once it was going, they tied people to posts and roasted them alive. Others had their throats cut or were weighted down with cement blocks and then tossed over the side—sacrifices to whatever deep-sea denizens the Satanists worshipped.

One night, Juan, Christian, Jimmy, and I took a boat out to investigate. It was against my better judgment and in hindsight a really stupid thing to do, but we had to know more. We got close enough to hear them chanting. The words weren't English. Hell, I'm not even sure they were in a language. It was like something out of a cheesy horror movie and it freaked us out pretty bad, so we left.

The Satanists weren't our only neighbors. There were other survivors scattered throughout the city, but they were loners or madmen and kept mostly to themselves. I'm sure some of them ended up captured and sacrificed in the rituals.

Early on, the Satanists tried to raid our building twice, but we'd repelled both attacks, and they took some heavy casualties. Since then, they'd left us alone, but we still kept a guard posted on the roof twenty-four hours a day. We weren't stupid enough to believe they wouldn't eventually return.

I kept a wary eye out for them while I paddled over the submerged highrises and office buildings, but the Satanists had vanished. The only living creatures I saw were a school of dolphins frolicking over the space where Camden Yards used to be, and flocks of seabirds soaring far overhead.

When I returned to the hotel, Jimmy's head still securely tucked away in the backpack, it was Lee and

Mike's turn on watch. I saw them through the downpour, water dripping from their plastic-covered rifle barrels. I tossed them the rope and Lee tied me off.

"Jimmy's not back yet," he said, sounding scared. "And it's getting late."

I took a deep breath.

"What's wrong, Kevin?" Mike asked.

I exhaled. "He's not coming back."

"What do you mean? What the hell happened out there?"

"Get everybody together and I'll tell you. I don't want to rehash it over and over. It . . . it hurts too bad."

Like a Viking returning home, I grabbed the plunder and walked inside.

Mike and Lee called after me, but I couldn't hear what they said. Their words were lost in the rain.

I still wanted to cry. I still couldn't.

So I let the sky do it for me instead.

Each floor of the hotel had a small lobby located next to the elevator doors. We'd turned the lobby on nineteen into a common area. While I hung up my wet clothing and toweled off, Mike and Lee gathered the others together. When I came out, they were all waiting for me, lounging on the couches and chairs.

"Bring us back anything good?" Mindy asked.

I nodded. "Always do, don't I?"

I gave the paperbacks to Lee, Christian, Mindy, Sarah, and Lori, since they were the readers in the group. Louis, Taz, Ducky, Lashawn, Juan, and Salty divided up the cigarettes. Nate got the flashlight since he didn't have one in his room and had been relying on candles. The Jim Beam and vodka were passed around and practically everybody took a swig except for the kids and Mike. He said that he'd managed to stay sober and on the wagon for ten years, and would be damned if the weather was going to make him start again. Sarah and Anna did most of our cooking, so the food went to them for safekeeping. Finally, I gave the crayons to the kids, and the grins on their faces cheered me up momentarily—until I felt the bulge of Jimmy's head, still inside the bag.

"I wish you could find some jazz or blues discs, Kevin," Louis said. "All we've got around here is hip-hop and classic rock."

"That reminds me," Lee chimed in, "we need more D batteries, too, if you find any. The boom box runs on them."

"I could use some more vitamins," Christian said.

"Fuck that, playa." Ducky grinned. "What we *need* is some chronic."

"Chronic?" Nate looked puzzled. "What's that?"

"It's street slang for weed," Juan said, "and under the circumstances, it wouldn't be a bad thing. Can't believe I'm saying that." He shook his head wistfully.

"All of you can fill out a shopping list," I muttered, and sat down. "I'll pick it up on my next trip outside."

Lori handed me a warm can of soda and I sipped it gratefully. The carbonation soothed my upset stomach.

"So where's Jimmy?" Mike asked.

I glanced at the kids.

Anna took the hint and herded them out of the lobby. "Come on, children. Let's go color some pictures for everybody with those new crayons!" Anna had lost her family, including two grandchildren, and Danielle, James, and Malik had adopted her as their grandmother.

After they were gone, I cleared my throat. Everyone looked at me, waiting patiently. I guess they already suspected what I was going to say.

"Jimmy's dead. I found him while I was on the supply run."

They were silent, and then Juan spoke, saying aloud what they were all thinking. "The fucking Satanists."

"I guess so. Who else could it be?"

"Where is he now?"

"In my bag. There's not much left. He was . . . decapitated."

They stirred.

"Show us." Again, he wasn't asking.

"I don't want to see that," Sarah protested. "Isn't it bad enough—"

"Show us, Kevin."

I paused, choosing my words carefully. I felt tired, and all I wanted to do was sleep. "Juan, where's the sense in doing that? I mean, what, you don't fucking believe me?"

Juan held out his hands. "Calm down, man. Of course I believe you."

"Then why do you need to see his head?"

"Because I want to remember it for every one of those cultist motherfuckers that I put a bullet through. I want the image burned into all of our brains."

"Word," Taz seconded, and then turned to me. "You don't seem that upset, dawg. I thought you two was homeboys and shit."

"We are—were. For fuck's sake, man, he was my best friend! I knew him since we were little kids! I just . . . fuck it."

I unwrapped Jimmy's head and hoisted it by the hair, holding him up in the glow of the lanterns. Several of them gasped, and a few turned away—but not as many as I would have expected.

There was silence for a few seconds while they all got a good look.

"Doesn't look like it was cut off." Juan stroked his goatee. "It looks *squeezed* or something."

"Yeah," I muttered. "I noticed that, too."

"What would do that?" Nate asked. "What kind of weapon could squeeze his head off? And what's that weird bruise on his cheek?"

"A jellyfish sting, maybe?" Mike offered.

"Maybe it wasn't the Satanists," Taz said, cracking his knuckles. "Could have been a shark or some shit. Bit his head off and swallowed the rest."

He started humming the *Jaws* theme, and Ducky and Lashawn broke into wild laughter. For a second, I seriously considered killing all three of them. Juan and Sarah both shot them a dirty look and they shut up.

"Weren't no shark."

Salty hovered in the rear, his back to the elevator doors. He lit a cigarette.

"Weren't no shark," he repeated. " 'Twas a Kraken."

Ducky giggled. "A crackhead?"

"A Kraken," Salty corrected him, and then grew quiet again.

Mindy looked at Lori and Sarah and rolled her eyes.

A few of the others were grinning. But for a moment, Salty reminded me of Quint, from *Jaws*. I half-expected him to start showing us his scars.

Juan stared at him. "What the fuck is a Kraken?"

"A mythological beast," Lee spoke up. "It's like a giant squid or octopus, except bigger. Much bigger. They show up pretty frequently in the old sea stories. I once had my ninth-graders do a paper on them and other Old World myths."

"Ain't no myth, either." Salty inhaled cigarette smoke, coughed, and then focused on us with his bloodshot eyes. "You're a smart man, teacher. I'm sure you know all about grammar and famous people and splitting the atom, but you don't know shit about the sea. There's been whales that have sucker scars on them the size of truck tires."

Lee shifted uncomfortably in his seat. "Well yes, marine researchers have reported that from time to time, but a Kraken? Those were just a legend, based on mariner sightings of the giant squid. There's nothing in the ocean big enough to pull an entire ship down!"

"Tell that to the crew of the *Alecton*," the old man snorted. "Eighteen sixty-one it was, when the *Alecton* sailed from France to the island of Madeira. Crew saw something round and flat and full of arms. Looked like a tree pulled up by the roots. They decided to catch it. Harpooned the thing and slipped a rope around its tail. Tried hauling it back to port, but it began to rot and they had to let it go. Nobody believed them. Said they were crazy."

He lit a cigarette, hacked up a wad of phlegm, swallowed it back down, and continued.

"Another washed up on the beach in Dingle-Cosh, Ireland, back in sixteen seventy-three. Had a long body, two huge eyes, and ten tentacles. They say it measured over forty feet long. Carnival owner by the name of James Steward came to see the monster. He cut off two eight-foot sections of tentacle and put 'em on display in his carnival. The rest of the carcass washed out to sea. Nobody believed him, either—said he made it up."

Everybody sat still, transfixed by the story. Even Taz and Ducky, who could usually be counted on to make a mockery of anything, were quiet.

"During the winter, I used to sit in the library on cold days. I'd read a lot. Wasn't much else to do. Nobody ever believed them folks, but today, the giant squid is recognized as an animal. Scientists say they live way deep down in the ocean. Biggest one accepted by science was found on November second, eighteen seventy-eight. A fisherman named Sperring and two of his buddies were fishing off the coast of Newfoundland. Spotted something big in the water, bigger than a whale. Thinking it was part of a wrecked ship, they rowed toward it. But when they got closer, they found out the damned thing was alive."

I drained my can of warm soda, listening.

"It got stranded in the shallows," Salty continued, "and it was beating at the water with its tail and arms, trying to get back out. Must have been an awful sight. Sperring was spooked by its eyes. He said the eyes looked human, but they were more than a foot and a half across.

"They watched it for a while and saw that it was

wounded and weak. Then, just like the crew of the *Alecton,* they slipped a rope around its tail, and when the tide went out, that thing was high and dry. They cut it up for dog food, but not before a scientist come along and took some measurements. It was at least fifty-seven feet long, from the tip of its tail to the tentacles."

"That's a lot of fucking dog food," Taz snickered.

Salty glowered at him.

Lee cleared his throat. "Those are indeed some fascinating stories, Salty. But that's all ancient history."

"Wrong. There were reports of one coming up out of the Chagos Trench in nineteen eighty-five. People stationed at the Navy base in Diego Garcia saw it. Over twenty-five witnesses, and the government had pictures, too. And another one washed up on the beach in St. Augustine in nineteen twenty-seven, and there're samples of its flesh preserved at the Smithsonian and Yale. I'm sure you'd believe *them*, teacher."

Lee shrugged. "I'm familiar with those, but they were simply giant squid. That's all. As I said, the Kraken myth was based on ancient sightings of those creatures."

"No, it wasn't. And they weren't just giant squid. Those things were the Kraken's *babies*."

"If you guys don't mind," I interrupted, "I'd like to go bury my friend now. You can all stay here and play Jacques Cousteau if you want."

I stalked out of the lobby with Jimmy's head cradled under my arm. Behind me, Lee and Salty continued to debate nautical myths. I heard some of the others get up, starting to drift away as well.

Lori ran after me. "Kevin?"

"Yeah?" I stopped and turned.

"Are you all right?" She touched my shoulder, and her fingers felt warm. The moment was brief, fleeting, but I relished the sensation. There's so little warmth these days.

"Sure, I'll be okay." I tried a weak smile, and almost managed it.

"I'm here if you need me."

"I know. I appreciate that. Thanks."

I left her standing there. Any other time, I would have welcomed her presence. But not then. Not at that moment. I pushed the stairwell door open and walked up one flight to the twentieth floor, listening to my footsteps echo in the shadows. Even in there, the air was damp. Water stains were starting to appear on the ceiling, and black mold grew in patches along the walls. We were going to be in trouble if that continued. But I was too exhausted to worry anymore about it just then.

I exited the stairwell and went to the room at the end of the hall. *My* room.

My *garden*.

Originally, it had been a king-sized business suite; the conference room type, with a television built into the wall and lots of space for meetings and parties. The TV didn't work anymore, and neither did the minifridge behind the bar. But that was okay since I didn't plan on throwing a party anytime soon.

The room's best feature was the large skylight in the center of the ceiling. It measured ten feet across, facing out into the gray sky. At night, I'd lie in bed and listen to the rain beat against it. The sound of the rain was always there, day and night, no matter where you went. Eventually, you got used to it and it became nothing but background noise. At night, though, it got pervasive again.

I wasn't a gardener, but I'd started a garden anyway, directly beneath the skylight. It didn't matter that there was no sunshine peeking through the clouds. I still wanted to try it. Maybe it was hopeless or perhaps I just wanted to break the monotony. Maybe I thought some ultraviolet rays would creep through and photosynthesis would magically happen. I was also just fucking tired of eating fish, seabirds, and kelp, along with the occasional scavenged bag of potato chips or a can of corn from an abandoned building.

Jimmy and a few of the others had helped me bring some pool tables up from the sixteenth floor. They were the heavy, slate-bottom type, and it had been a full day's work. We'd placed them beneath the skylight, and then used plywood to shore up their sides. I filled them with what little dirt we could find at the time and added to it when I found more. Now there was a foot of soil layered evenly on top of the tables. We used fish bones, bird feathers, and other organic waste from our catches for fertilizer. The smell was bad, but I'd grown used to it. At one point, Lee suggested we use our own excrement for fertilizer, but I'd balked. I still had to sleep there and wasn't thrilled at the idea of smelling and tilling through my fellow castaways' shit.

So far, nothing was growing, except for some potatoes and a few baby pine trees and spider plants that Jimmy and I had scavenged from other buildings.

Anna and Sarah used the potatoes sparingly, careful not to deplete them all until we were sure they'd continue growing. On the rare occasions when they did cook with them, they made a wonderful addition to our seafood diet. Desperate for some greens, we'd even debated eating the pine trees and spider plants, but decided we couldn't. Not yet, at least.

I pulled out the houseplant, the bag of potting soil, and the seed packets that I'd found earlier that day, and then I unwrapped Jimmy's head. For a moment, I saw him standing there, not so long ago.

He had stooped over a baby pine tree, inhaling the fresh scent.

"Damn, that smells good, dude! I forgot how pine trees smelled."

"Yeah." I sipped instant coffee, brewed with saltwater to avoid depleting the fresh water supplies. It tasted like shit, but it was still better than eating the instant coffee with a spoon. "I'd give my left nut to be standing in a pine forest right now, feeling the needle carpet beneath my feet and breathing that in."

"Hell," Jimmy had laughed, "while we're at it, I'd give both nuts to be in bed with Hillary Duff and Britney Spears, and have a nice, rare sirloin steak to go with them. One that's cold and red in the middle. And maybe a baked potato, too, with butter and sour cream, and an ice-cold beer. God damn, that would hit the spot, wouldn't it?"

"Fucking aye, brother," I'd agreed.

"Fucking aye."

How long ago had that been? It was hard to tell

these days. Calendars and holidays seem to have been washed away with the rest of civilization. No one even looks at their watches anymore. At least, I don't. What does it matter what time it is?

I held up Jimmy's head and looked him in the eyes.

"Well bro," I said, "I couldn't get you the girls or the steak or the beer, but you liked the pine tree, so I guess this will have to do. Sorry, man."

I dug a hole near one of the baby pine trees and then placed Jimmy's head in it, covering him up with the potting soil. When I was done, I planted the seeds and moved the houseplant from its tiny pot into the garden. I placed it directly over his head, so that it could feed as it grew.

While I did this, I thought about when we were kids.

I tried really hard to cry, but it didn't happen.

Across the room, Jimmy's bed sat empty, the sheets still rumpled from the night before. His things sat nearby, odds and ends he'd gathered during various scavenger trips: automobile and nudie magazines, cigarettes, a boombox and a half-dozen compact discs, toiletries, a half bottle of Jim Beam, and a Rolex that had taken a licking but was no longer ticking.

The room seemed quiet without him. I made sure there were batteries in the boom box and then put in a disc by Pantera. I played "Cemetery Gates," which had always been Jimmy's favorite song.

I said good-bye to my friend.

When it was over, I took out Pantera and played some Lewis and Walker. The acoustic guitar melodies washed over me and I closed my eyes, thinking about life before the rains came. It seemed like it had all happened a long time ago, and to someone else, as if I'd seen it in a movie or read it in a book.

I couldn't remember being dry. Or warm. Or safe.

Later in the night, Lori slipped into my room. I heard the door creak open, and when I rolled over in bed, she stood beside me, wearing a flimsy nylon nightgown. She smiled, and I smiled back. I opened my mouth to speak, but she put a finger to my lips, looking at me with those sad brown eyes in the soft glow of the lantern. She held out her arms and we melted together. Silently, we undressed each other and then, without a word, we made love. Even our orgasms were quiet, despite their intensity. When it was over, I trembled in her arms, but still, I did not cry.

After the tremors subsided, I snuffed out the lantern and we lay there in the dark, in a room smelling faintly of rotting fish and pine trees, until the rain lulled us both to sleep.

For the first time since the rains started, I didn't have any nightmares.

My dreams were as dry as my eyes.

CHAPTER EIGHT

Lori was still sleeping beside me when I woke up. Her honey-brown hair spilled across her face, and I don't remember ever seeing anything quite so beautiful in my life. She looked so peaceful—but troubled at the same time. Her brow was furrowed, and her eyes darted beneath the lids. I wondered what she was dreaming about. The whole thing seemed unreal. I'd forgotten how good it felt to be with someone. Not just the sex, but to actually have someone there *with* you, to hear them breathe, feel them move, watch them sleep. I snuggled close to her, shut my eyes, and sniffed her scent. Our musk from the previous night still clung to the bed and I savored it.

So this was love. Or the start of it, at least.

I liked it.

She felt warm—and dry. Dryness had never been erotic before the rains came, but now I couldn't think of anything more pleasurable.

I wasn't sure what would happen with us next. I'd been lonely. Sarah was off limits, Mindy had hooked up with Mike, and Anna was out of my age range. I'd been interested in Lori all this time, but so had Jimmy. Because of that, I'd never made a move. Now, Jimmy wasn't even twenty-four hours in the ground and here was Lori, sleeping next to me.

She stirred, then opened an eye and stretched like a cat.

"Morning." She smiled, flashing white teeth. Looking back on it now, that was the exact moment I fell in love with her. God, she had a beautiful smile.

Yep. This *was* love.

And I liked it more and more with each passing moment.

"Morning yourself," I smiled back. "How'd you sleep?"

"Better than I have in a long time," she yawned. "You?"

"Amazingly. Especially after—well, you know." It wasn't in my nature to play coy, but Lori had a weird effect on me. I glanced at the garden and then back to her. My ears felt hot.

Smiling, Lori nodded in understanding.

We both blushed. Neither of us spoke for a minute.

"You know what's weird?" she asked, breaking the silence.

"Hmm?"

"Every morning, I still wake up and look at the alarm clock. But, of course, it doesn't work. I should just throw it out."

I laughed. "I do that too, sometimes. A few days ago, I was dreaming about life before the rain. When I woke up, I thought I was late for work. Jumped out of bed, threw on some clothes and shoes, and then it hit me. There is no more work. The video store is gone. It really bummed me out. Never thought I'd say this, but I actually *miss* work."

"I don't. College maybe, but not work. I miss television—and music, too."

"Yeah," I said. "There's a lot of good movies they were in the process of making that we'll never get to see. The third *Star Wars*, and the remake of *High Plains Drifter*. It's just so weird that they'll never be seen by anyone."

"I know what you mean." She snuggled closer. Her breasts brushed against my forearm. Her nipples were erect and I felt myself harden in response.

We grew quiet again, lost in our own thoughts. She felt so warm beside me. I could have happily stayed there all day.

"You know what else I miss?" She said it so quietly that I almost didn't hear her.

"What's that?"

"The sun. I miss waking up and feeling it on my face when it comes through the window, and hearing birds singing outside. The only birds I ever hear now are those damn seagulls."

"Yeah. Sometimes I can't remember what the sun felt like. You know what I mean?"

"Mm-hmm." She stretched again, and as she yawned, the sheet slid down an inch, revealing the dark triangle between her legs. I stiffened even more.

"Lori, about last night . . ." My voice was thick.

She pressed a finger against my lips. "Don't say it, Kevin. Don't say anything. You needed someone. I wanted to be that someone. Neither of us has to explain it or make excuses for it. What happened is what happened."

I grinned. "Does that mean it can't happen again?"

Giggling, we disappeared beneath the covers.

Later, I figured we'd go to breakfast together, but Lori went back to her room instead, saying that she wanted to fix herself up. I accepted with a smile and a kiss, but after she left, I wondered if she didn't want the others to see us together.

Even in a post-apocalyptic world, women were still women, and I still didn't fucking understand them. Some things don't change, despite the weather.

The hotel's restaurant and kitchen on the lower floors were both underwater, so we'd converted one room on the twentieth floor into a galley. When I walked in, Anna and Sarah were hard at work making breakfast, and Juan, Nate, Lee, Mike, and Mindy were already eating. I pulled up a chair and joined them.

"Morning, sleepyhead," Anna said. "Late night?"

"Yeah, I guess so."

Juan, Nate, and Lee chuckled. Lee elbowed Juan in the ribs and shoved some bacon into his mouth.

I wondered where the bacon had come from, but before I could ask, Mike interrupted.

"I *know* so." He grinned. "Mindy and I heard you guys all night. Hard to sleep with all that racket."

"Mike! Stop it." Mindy elbowed him in the ribs, making him wince. She turned to me and said, "My apologies, Kevin. Mike's being an asshole this morning."

I felt my ears turning red.

"Sorry," Mike chuckled, glancing warily at her elbow, poised for another jab. "It's cool, Kevin. We're happy for you guys. About time, too. Nice to see that Louis and Christian and the two of us aren't the only couples."

Lee sipped his coffee. "Don't forget the Taz-Ducky-Lashawn triangle."

"That whole thing's messed up," Mindy snorted. "One of these days, Taz is going to figure it out, and Ducky and Lashawn are going to have some serious explaining to do."

Sarah stirred a pot on the stove. "It's like a post-apocalyptic soap opera."

"I hope not," Lee groaned. "It takes a year to resolve the plotlines on those things."

"If you hadn't made a play for Lori," Nate told me, "I would have. Was getting ready to, in fact. You beat me to it."

"Shit," Juan muttered. He sipped weak green tea from a recycled and reused tea bag. "I think you're a little older than what Lori's looking for, Nate."

"I'm sorry about Jimmy." Sarah sat a bowl down in front of me, along with a chipped ceramic mug of instant coffee. "He was a good guy. We're all going to miss him. He made me laugh."

"Thanks," I said simply. I didn't know what else to say. The lump was back in my throat again. It felt strange not having Jimmy sitting there with us. By now, he'd have been razzing Nate and flirting with Sarah.

I stared at my breakfast—fish stew with a few sparse chunks of potato, one strip of bacon, and some of the canned corn that I'd brought back the day before.

"Where did the bacon come from?" I asked.

Sarah sat down at the table. "Louis hooked a Styrofoam cooler yesterday while he was fishing. Inside was some bacon packed in dry ice and a few cans of soda. The bacon was still good, so enjoy it."

Lee smirked. "If it really *is* bacon."

"Well what else would it be?" Anna asked.

"Maybe you and Sarah are feeding us long pig."

Anna frowned. "Long pig?"

"That's what the cannibals used to call the white settlers that they ate."

Anna made a disgusted face. "That's sick."

The others laughed.

I glanced around. "Where are Christian and Louis?"

"I sent them out for salvage duty," Juan said, mopping up his broth with a cracker. "I figured you might want to take a break today. I hate to ask, but I don't guess you saw Jimmy's boat yesterday, did you?"

"Nope, just his—well, you know. His head."

He chewed his lip. "That's what I was afraid of. Now we're down to one boat. We'll have to see what we can put together."

Lee stood up. "Well, I've got to get started with the kids. You ready, Mindy?"

"Yep!" She stood up and gave Mike a quick peck on the cheek. Then she and Lee left in search of Danielle, James, and Malik. Poor kids. I felt sorry for them. End of the world, and they still had to go to school every day. Lee had set up a classroom in one of the hotel suites and Mindy helped him out. When Anna wasn't cooking, she'd join them as well.

Nate pushed his bowl away and turned to Juan. "Where do you want me today?"

"I want you on watch duty, actually."

"Watch? Come on, man. We've got Taz, Ducky, Lashawn, and Salty on the roof already, hunting and fishing. Do we really need someone else up there on guard duty?"

Juan took his time finishing his coffee before he answered. He sat the mug back down and gazed into it. "After what happened to Jimmy? Yes, I think we do."

Nate stared at him for a moment. Then, without a word, he left the room and headed for the roof.

"Prick," Juan muttered.

I cleared my throat. "What would you like me to do, since Louis and Christian went salvaging?"

"Take the day off. Relax. Don't do anything at all. Shit, Kevin, your best friend was killed yesterday and you're the one who found him. I think everybody will understand if you need some time off for a few days."

"No offense, Juan, but that's the last thing I want to do. I need something to keep my mind off of it."

He shrugged. "Okay, if you're sure. Why don't you give them a hand up top for now? Mike and I are going to inspect the building for any recent leaks or damage we might not know about. When we're done, you can help us look below for material to make a new boat or raft. Cool?"

It was. I told them about the water damage I'd noticed in the stairwell the night before, thanked Sarah and Anna for breakfast, and then grabbed my raincoat and went up to the roof.

I don't remember how or when Juan became the leader of the group. It just sort of happened. Maybe it was because he'd been a Baltimore city cop, or just the way he carried himself, his calm air of self-assuredness.

But he was smart, fair, and we rarely argued with him. Occasionally, Taz, Ducky, and Lashawn gave him a hard time, or Nate would get a little haughty, but that was it. I'd always gotten the impression there might be a history between Juan, Taz, Ducky, and Lashawn predating the rain, but I'd never had the nerve to ask. Maybe Juan had busted them at one time for drug dealing or something. Jimmy had suggested that one time and Louis had given him shit about thinking all black people were drug dealers simply because of the color of their skin, but that was bullshit. Taz and Ducky proudly bragged about their street cred all the time. They were proud of dealing drugs.

Anyway, they had new jobs now. We all did. Lee and Mindy taught the kids in the makeshift school. Anna helped them out and gave Sarah a hand preparing our meals. Jimmy and I usually had salvage duty, switching off with Mike and Nate when the need arose. Salty was in charge of fishing, helped by Louis and Christian. Taz, Ducky, Lashawn, and Lori did odd chores where needed. And of course, we all took turns on guard duty.

I walked out onto the roof, blinking as a gust of cold rain blew into my face. Salty and Nate stood at opposite sides of the roof, holding deep sea rods and carefully watching their lines for a bite.

Taz and Ducky were feeding the birds.

The Alka-Seltzer had been Salty's idea, one he'd suggested when Juan stressed that we needed to save ammunition to defend ourselves from the Satanists and couldn't use it all up shooting seagulls. Our initial skepticism at Salty's solution vanished when we saw the results.

Taz and Ducky stood in the middle of the roof, the rain beating down on their heads, while a large flock of seagulls circled above. Their slim white and gray bodies glided gracefully out over the water and then back to where the two men stood.

The guys threw a mixture of fish guts and other food scraps into the air, and the shrieking gulls darted forward, snatching the morsels before they came back down. Once they had the birds' attention, they tossed up a handful of Alka-Seltzer tablets. The birds lunged for these, too, gobbling them up as quickly as Taz and Ducky could throw them.

Then they let nature take its course.

"Rats wit' fucking wings, yo!" Ducky said to me as I walked toward them. "What's up, playa?"

"Figured I'd give you guys a hand," I said. "How's it going?"

Ducky threw another handful of tablets into the air.

"Here comes the boom." Taz leered, watching intently. "Ka-blam!"

According to Salty, a bird's digestive system was different than a human being's. Since it couldn't burp or fart, the Alka-Seltzer sat in its stomach, fizzing away, until the gas and foam built up to the point where it had nowhere to go. The bird's stomach would then expand beyond its limits and pop.

There was no explosion of blood and feathers, nothing so gruesome. The seagulls faltered, becoming so bloated that they could no longer fly, and then plummeted to the roof, foaming at the beak and making a horrible sound. At this point, Taz and Ducky stomped on their heads with their boots, ending the creatures' struggles.

It was quick and easy, and it was much easier to find Alka-Seltzer in the ruins than it was bullets (one of the buildings still above water had a pharmacy inside) and simpler to kill the birds by feeding them the stuff than trying to get a bead on a moving target. We'd tried Salty's method on the occasional duck and goose as well, when we saw them passing through, and it worked just the same.

When it was over, nine carcasses lay on the wet roof.

"Nice shooting," I said. "Look's like we got enough for a couple days."

"Yeah," Taz pulled out his pocketknife and began gutting the kills. "Gonna get these things cleaned up, then take 'em down to Anna and Sarah. Now if you could find some motherfucking barbecue sauce or some hot sauce while you're out scavenging shit, we could have ourselves a *real* dinner!"

The rest of the gulls had flown away, screeching their displeasure. I knew from experience that they'd be back within minutes.

Hands shoved into his pockets, Ducky moved towards the door.

"Yo, Ducky," Taz called. "Where you going, playa?"

The smaller man jumped, his shoulders jerking. He turned and smiled, but his eyes were nervous.

"Just figured I'd go see what Lashawn and Lori are up to. See if they need some help."

"Man, fuck that. They're okay. You need to help me clean these seagulls, dog."

"I'm getting wet, Taz!"

"You ain't been dry since this shit started. Go on, with your punk ass self. Kevin can help me instead."

Ducky vanished down the stairwell. The wind slammed the door shut behind him. I wondered how many minutes it would be before he and Lashawn were engaged in a quickie, frantically screwing before Taz finished his task and came to look for them. For a moment, I considered going to find Lori and engaging in a quickie ourselves, but I decided against it. The last thing I wanted to do was scare her off.

Instead, I helped Taz field dress the birds, slicing them open and pulling out their insides. Steam billowed from the wounds. We dropped the guts into a slop bucket, already half full with rainwater in the brief time we'd been outside. They would be recycled, either as fish bait or fertilizer for my garden. Later on, Sarah and Ann would remove the feathers and finish the preparations. Salty was an expert at fly-tying, so the feathers would then be recycled into fishing lures.

"Nasty job," I commented, wiping the sticky blood from my hands. Steam rose from the gutted carcass at my feet.

Taz shrugged and slid his knife through a bird's belly. "I don't mind. The blood keeps my hands warm."

"I never thought of it that way," I admitted. "But it makes sense."

"I hate the cold. Never did like it. Winter always sucked ass. But you notice something?"

"What?"

"It's like, August and shit, at least according to my calendar. But it's fucking cold. Colder than it should be in the summer, you know? Why you think that is?"

I shrugged. "I guess the clouds are blocking out the sun."

"Gonna be a rough fucking winter, if that's the case, yo. We need to start thinking about ways to keep warm. Course, now that you and Lori are knocking boots, you shouldn't have any problems."

"Jesus Christ! You know about that too?"

He laughed. "Shit, dude, the whole damn building knows about it. Ya'll made enough noise last night. Sounded like a porno movie."

I sighed and shook my head. My ears burned.

Still chuckling, Taz took the gutbucket and the cleaned birds inside. After he was gone, I crossed over to Salty's side of the roof. The end of his fishing rod drooped sullenly over the railing, droplets of water rolling off it. I noticed he wasn't watching the line. Instead, he stared out to sea. His eyes had a lost, faraway look, and he was standing in a puddle. Water seeped over the tops of his boots, but he didn't seem to care.

"Any bites?" I asked.

He shrugged. "A few nibbles. Got one sea bass, but it had the White Fuzz growing on it, so I had to cut the line. Later in the day, it'll be better. Fish aren't hungry right now."

"That's no good."

"At least we haven't hooked another dead baby."

I nodded. Early on, after we'd just set up shop inside the hotel, Jimmy had accidentally hooked a dead infant with his fishing rod. It must have been in the ocean for quite some time, because it fell apart as he reeled it up onto the roof. I can still see it in my mind—one tiny arm hanging by a thin shred of muscle or tendon, fish bites pocking the white, bloated flesh. That had left all of us shaken, even the hard cases like Taz, Ducky, and Juan.

The old man sniffed the salty breeze. "Listen, Kevin, I'm sorry about your mate. He was a good lad, Jimmy was."

"Yeah, he was. Thanks, Salty."

"It's a real shame what happened to him."

I was quiet for a moment, considering my words carefully. "Salty, I like you. And more importantly, I respect you. But do you really believe that was what got him? A fucking Kraken?"

"Of course I do, boy. Saw the proof with my own eyes, same as you did."

"Granted, it looked weird, but I still don't see how a tentacle could have done that."

"Hurricane Agnes, nineteen seventy-two."

"Huh?"

"Hurricane Agnes," he repeated, and then spit over the side. "It come roaring up the East Coast, raising hell in the Carolinas, Virginia, Maryland—even as far inland as central Pennsylvania. I was still in the Navy then. At the time, I was assigned to an LPD, the *U.S.S. Miller,* out of Pier Six in Norfolk. I was too smart to be a bosun's mate, and too dumb to be a radioman, so they put me on the signal bridge."

He gazed out over the waves as he talked. I followed his glance in time to see a school of dolphins frolicking over what had once been an on-ramp to Interstate 83. I'd driven over that ramp many times, before the rains.

"The hurricane, she come out of nowhere and headed up the coast like a banshee. They put all of us that wasn't in dry dock out to sea, double-time. I'd drawn the unlucky watch, while my mates stayed below. I was huddled up in the signal bridge, cold and wet and miserable and thinking about home.

"We were off the coast, somewhere near Little Creek, trying to outrace the storm. I was out of cigarettes, but a friend of mine, Danny Ward, who worked down in CIC, dipped Copenhagen, and the CIC center was on the deck below me. Figured I'd nip below, bum a pinch from Danny and be back up topside before anybody was the wiser. I stepped out, struggled in the wind, and the ship rolled on me. Thank God there was a rail or I'd have gone over the side, into the drink. Instead of falling into the ocean, I slid into the rail and held on for dear life while the ship rolled with the wave. That was when I saw it."

Something silver flashed in the water in front of the dolphins. A school of fish. I tore my eyes away and focused on Salty.

"I didn't see all of it—don't think I could have. It was *that* big. I was clutching that rail, waiting for the deck to hold still, when I spied a huge form—gray and pale and slick. It wasn't a whale, which is what I thought at first. The thing rocketed up out of the water and I stumbled back. It just kept going up and up—a tentacle the size of an oak tree. It waved in the air, and then darted towards where I was standing. I crawled back as far as I could go, and it crashed into the rail a second later. The rail *bent* under its weight. The thing wriggled around, feeling the deck, searching for me like a big old rubbery worm. I screamed, but nobody heard me. It crawled closer. Then the ship rolled again, and it was gone, disappearing back into the spray. I'd never been more scared in my life.

"I learned later, from another mate of mine, Greg Blumenthal, that they'd picked up a large object coming toward the ship. But nothing else ever came of it. Nobody mentioned it again and I never told anyone, either. Not even Greg or Danny. Never breathed a word, until now."

I was quiet, not knowing what to say or how to respond. Salty slicked his wet, thinning hair back across his scalp and smiled at me. The rain ran down his face in rivulets.

"You understand why I'm telling you this, Kevin?"

"I'm not sure, but I have a good idea."

"Guess you think I'm senile, huh?"

"No." I shook my head. "To be honest, Salty, I don't know what to think. But I don't think you're crazy, if that helps."

"Well," he shrugged, and turned away. "There it is. That's my tale. Do with it what you want. I've got to get some more tackle and bait."

Another bird landed on the roof, just a few feet away from us, begging for fish guts. I stomped my boot to scare it away, but Salty stopped me.

"Don't. It's an albatross."

"So?"

"You need to respect it, lad. Bad luck if you harm it, or scare it away."

I smiled. "Why is that, Salty?"

"The poem. The one by that Coleridge fella. An albatross is good to have when you're at sea."

"True." Then I surprised him with my own knowledge of nautical legend. "But did you know that the assistant navigator on the *Titanic* was named Albert Ross?"

Salty grunted. "Is that a fact?"

"It is indeed. Guess he wasn't so lucky to have around."

"I don't get it." He frowned.

"Albert Ross," I repeated, slowly. "Albatross. Get it now?"

Salty laughed, loud and boisterously. Then he walked away, splashing through the puddles and was almost across the roof when he turned and called to me again.

"One other thing, Kevin. That tentacle I told you about . . ."

"Yeah?"

"The suckers had teeth in 'em. Sharp little teeth. They weren't suckers at all."

"What were they?"

"Mouths. The suckers were little mouths."

He disappeared through the door.

Nate sidled up beside me. He'd been quiet until now, keeping his distance and eavesdropping on us.

"You believe that shit?" he asked. "The old man has clearly lost his mind. Don't tell me you buy into that fish story?"

I shrugged. I didn't care much for Nate. He was pompous and arrogant, and even after all this time, still carried himself as if he were better than most of us. Somehow, the fact that his fully tricked-out Audi, brand new condo, and enormous expense account were gone hadn't fully settled on him yet.

"I don't know," I said. "Probably not, but then again, I never believed the story of Noah, either, and now look around us."

His laughter was sharp and brittle.

"I'm guessing you don't believe him?" I asked.

"Of course not," he said. "For Christ's sake, Kevin! A giant tentacle with mouths for suckers? The rain is one thing, but that? It's crazy." He shook his head.

"Stranger things have happened, man. And you heard what Lee said yesterday. There *are* such things as giant squid. This could be some sort of genetic mutation or something."

"Maybe. But it's more likely that old man is just nuts. Alzheimer's, I'm guessing. And if he is, then what's to stop him from hurting himself—or one of us? Are you willing to take that chance? What if he snaps and goes after one of the kids?"

"Oh, come on!" Anger welled up inside of me. "Senility doesn't make somebody fucking homicidal."

"He's talking crazy, Kevin!" He snorted, clearing his sinuses, and then spit out over the roof. We watched the falling wad of phlegm as it dropped toward the water below.

"So," he said, changing the subject, "let's get back to you and Lori. Tell me this—is she any good in the sack?"

"What the fuck? Does everybody need to know every minute detail between the two of us? Are you people that starved for gossip?"

"Chill out. I was just wondering, man."

"It's none of your fucking business, dude."

"She's a cute one," he continued, as if he hadn't heard me. "Like I said, I was going to make a play for her myself, but—"

Suddenly, Nate cocked his head sideways and jumped as if startled. He dropped the fishing rod and picked up the rifle. "Did you see that?"

He stared out at the water, craning his head back and forth. The tide tugged on his fishing line.

"What was it?" I asked.

"Nothing." He sounded embarrassed.

"Dude, what the hell did you see?"

"It's nothing! I thought for a second that I saw a woman out there. It—it sounded like she was singing."

It actually wasn't that farfetched. There could have been somebody out there. Another castaway, stranded when her vessel overturned or her dry patch got flooded out. I scanned the ocean but saw nothing. Even the dolphins and the seagulls had mysteriously disappeared.

"A singing woman? You sure she wasn't shouting for help instead?"

"No," His eyes seemed troubled, his voice barely a whisper. "She was singing, man. I'm sure of it. It was—beautiful. Very soft . . ."

"Well, she's not there now."

He didn't seem to hear me. "She was naked. She had long blond hair, like Sarah's, and a huge pair of . . ." He held his cupped hands out in front of his chest, then stopped.

"A naked, singing blonde with big tits." I giggled, unable to help myself. "Was it midnight on the water? Did you see the ocean's daughter?"

He stared at me, uncomprehending.

"ELO, man! Electric Light Orchestra? Didn't you ever hear that oldie, 'Can't Get It Out of My Head'? Midnight on the water. I saw the ocean's daughter?" I sang a few more lines, but he turned back to the ocean.

"Fuck you, Kevin." He put down the rifle and picked

up his fishing rod, reeled in the line, and walked farther along the rooftop.

"Hey," I called after him. "Now you're the one that's talking crazy!"

"I know what I saw," he said over his shoulder. "So knock your shit off."

He stalked to the other side and cast the line out again. His shoulders were tense, his jaw clenched.

I stared back out at the water again, but all I saw were the raindrops coming down and the waves rising up to greet them.

I went back inside and looked for Lori, but she was busy doing laundry with Lashawn and Sarah, and I didn't want to intrude on them. Even now, I still wasn't sure how to act around her—especially since it appeared that everybody knew about us. I wondered if Sarah and Lashawn were giving her a hard time, the way the guys had given me.

Later in the day, Mike, Juan, and I went down to the lower levels, searching for materials to build another boat. The lower levels always gave me the creeps. If you stood still, you could feel the ocean pressing against the sides of the building. It was eerily quiet. The only good thing about the stillness was that since we were below the surface, the constant sound of the rain was noticeably absent.

We'd found a round, wooden coffee table that looked promising, and Mike and I were lifting it when he suddenly stopped.

"Too heavy?" I asked.

He didn't reply.

"Mike?"

He sat his end of the table down. "Did you guys hear something?"

Juan shrugged. "Not me. Why, what did you hear?"

"Voices," Mike whispered. "Or a voice."

"Down here?" I asked, sitting my end down as well. "I'm not sure."

All three of us listened, but heard nothing.

We picked the table back up, struggling to move it. Damn thing was heavy. Mike started humming "Riders On The Storm" by The Doors.

Juan opened his mouth to speak and then froze.

Somebody else was singing, too.

The voice was beautiful. Melodious and faint and definitely female, that much was certain. I couldn't understand the words, but I *felt* them. As I listened, my grief for Jimmy disappeared, along with everything else. I forgot about Lori and the rain and our predicament. The voice made me feel good. Alive. It had a calming, hypnotic effect. I wanted to get closer, so I could understand what was being said. Mesmerized, I shuffled forward.

"What the fuck is that?" Juan whispered.

"One of the girls," Mike guessed, "playing a joke on us? Sarah, maybe?"

I shook my head. "That's not Sarah. Whatever it is, it's coming from the other side of that wall."

"What's on the other side?" Mike asked.

Juan and I looked at each other.

"The ocean," I said.

"Bullshit." Mike shook his head.

"He's right," Juan insisted. "Think about it. We're at least fifteen feet below the surface right now."

The singing grew louder.

"So then what the fuck *is* that?"

"Somebody's in the water!" Mike shouted. "It's a chick's voice. There's a woman out there."

"A castaway?" Juan asked. "How's she singing underwater?"

Mike stepped around the table. "I don't fucking know, man! But you heard her, too."

"Maybe we'd better go see," I suggested.

"Good idea," Juan agreed.

I remembered what Nate thought he'd seen—a naked blond woman, singing in the water. I started to tell Juan, but he was already running for the stairs. Mike and I dashed after him.

The others came out when they heard us thundering up the stairwell and we told them what was going on. They all followed us up to the roof. We ran through the door and into the rain. We startled Salty and he almost dropped his fishing rod.

Nate whirled around, his rifle at the ready. "What's going on? What's wrong?"

"Have you seen anything?" Juan asked.

"It's been raining," Salty chuckled. "Oh, and some birds flew overhead, looking for Alka-Seltzer. But other than that, no."

"What's going on?" Nate asked again.

Juan and Mike ran to the edge of the roof and looked out over the water.

Salty frowned. "What are you lads doing?"

"We were down below," Juan said, "and we heard a woman. Sounded like she was outside, in the water." He turned back to the group. "Were any of you down on the lower levels?"

They shook their heads.

"I knew it!" Nate stomped his feet. "I *told* you I saw something out there, Kevin!"

Juan glanced at me. "What the hell's he talking about?"

"Earlier today," Nate told him, "when Kevin was out here, I thought I saw a woman in the water. She was singing. And she was nude."

"Oh, for Christ's sake," Lee scoffed. "First Salty with his mother of all squids and now this?"

Nate's ears turned red. "Listen asshole, I know what I saw!"

Lee refused to back down. "Be rational, man. Even if there were somebody out there, how long would she last? Do you have any idea how cold that water is or how rough those seas are?"

"You calling me a liar?" Nate stepped towards him, his fists clenched.

"Back off, man," Lee warned him.

"Or what?"

"Keep it up and you'll find out."

Juan stepped between them. "That's enough, both of you. I don't know what's going on, but I want the watch doubled. Taz and Ducky, you guys relieve Salty and Nate. Sarah, I want you and Lashawn out here with them."

Little Malik stepped forward, clutching Anna's hand. "It's the fish lady."

"What?" Juan asked.

"The fish lady," the boy repeated. "I see her sometimes at night when I sleep. She sings to me."

"Me too," James echoed. "She makes me miss my mommy. She used to sing to me at night, too."

Juan took a deep breath. "Okay. Taz, Ducky, Lashawn, and Sarah, you guys are on watch. Everybody else, head down to the common area. We need to talk about this in detail."

"Yo," Taz called, "what do we do if we see this naked bitch?"

"I know what I'm gonna do." Ducky grinned, rubbing his crotch. "I'm gonna get me some pussy."

"Great," Sarah muttered under her breath. "Juan, why did you stick me with these assholes?"

"Hey!" Taz protested.

"Because Christian and Louis aren't back yet," Juan told her. "If they don't get back soon, I'll send Kevin or Mike up."

Dripping, we followed him downstairs, shrugged out of our rain gear, and took our seats.

"Okay," Juan said, shaking the water from his hair, "anybody else hear or see this mysterious woman?"

Nobody spoke.

"All right. Nate, give me a rehash. Tell us exactly what you saw."

"Kevin and I were out on the roof, talking about what Salty said last night, and I heard somebody singing. When I glanced out at the ocean, just for a second, I saw a woman."

He paused, lost in thought, and then continued.

"She was beautiful. She had long, blond hair, and

even though she was far away, I could see her eyes very clearly. It was weird. Felt like her eyes were looking right through me."

"And she was singing?" Juan asked.

"She was singing. Then she vanished beneath the waves."

"And that's all?"

"That's it." Nate glanced at Lee, but Lee didn't challenge him this time.

"Kevin," Juan said, turning to me, "did you see this woman, too?"

I shook my head. "I didn't see anything. To be honest, I thought Nate was full of shit. Now, I'm not so sure."

"Apology accepted," Nate grumbled.

Juan knelt down and looked at the kids.

"James. Malik. What did you guys mean up on the roof, when you said you'd heard a lady singing to you?"

They stared at the floor and shuffled their feet nervously.

"Go on, boys," Anna urged, "it's okay. Tell us."

"The fish lady," Malik began, not looking up. "I dream about her every night. She sings outside my window, and tells me to jump in the water. I . . . I tried, but I'm not strong enough to get the window open. I'm too little."

The regret in his voice was almost heartbreaking. The windows weren't designed to open, so that Baltimore's elite wouldn't take a swan dive after a bad day on the stock market. But a kid like Malik wouldn't have known that.

"Malik," Juan prodded gently, "why does she want you to jump in the water?"

"She said that she would teach me how to swim. And when she talks, I can't help it. I have to do what she says."

A shadow crossed his face. When he spoke again, his voice was choked. "She's a nice lady—but scary, too."

Juan turned to James. "You've seen her as well?"

He nodded. "Yes sir. At night. I heard Malik talking to her through the window. That's when I first saw her. She said if we came down, she'd give me a big hug like my mom used to."

"We tried to—" Malik began, but the older boy shot him a warning glance.

"Tried to what?"

Malik was silent.

"Boys," Juan sighed, "you're not in trouble, okay? But I need you to tell us the truth. What did you try to do? Open the window?"

Malik shook his head. "No. When we couldn't get the window open, we tried to sneak out onto the roof one night. She said she'd be waiting for us, down in the water. We didn't want to go, but we couldn't help it. So we snuck out of our room while everybody was sleeping. But when we got up to the roof, Taz and Ducky were standing guard and they told us to go back to bed."

"And those idiots never thought to mention it to the rest of us," Juan muttered. "Boys, when did you first start seeing this lady?"

"Just a few nights ago," James whispered. "Malik's seen her four times, and me only two."

"Danielle," Sarah interrupted, "have you seen this lady too?"

"No," Danielle picked up her doll and began combing its hair. "Girls can't hear the fish lady. Just boys."

"How do you know that?"

"Because that's what she told Malik and James. They told me, and I thought they were making it up to play a trick on me. So they asked her and the fish lady told them I couldn't see her."

Lori spoke up. "So why do you guys call her the fish lady?"

Malik said, "Because she doesn't have any legs. Just a tail like a fish."

None of us knew what to make of their story. It was impossible to tell where the truth ended and childhood imagination began. But Juan, Mike, and I had all heard something, and Nate had seen a figure in the water.

After dinner, Lori and I went back to my room. I checked the garden while she lounged on the bed, reading an out of date issue of *Cosmopolitan*.

"So what do you think, Kevin?" she asked.

"I think this houseplant is going to do fine," I said, gently fingering the leaves, checking for brown patches. "I just wish I knew what it actually is. I'd love to find a book that identifies plants. We'll have to wait a few more days to see what happens with the seeds I planted."

She rolled up the magazine and swatted at me. I grabbed her arm, pulled her off the bed and we collapsed to the floor, wrestling with one another. Our laughter turned into a kiss—long, soft, and lingering.

"I'm not talking about the garden," she said with a smile, lying on top of me. "I'm talking about this 'fish-lady.' What do you think?"

"Well, if it was just Nate, I'd say he's cracking under the strain, and if it were just the kids, I'd say they were having bad dreams. But all of them together, plus what happened with . . ." I glanced at the mound of dirt covering Jimmy's head. "With what happened yesterday—I don't know anymore. It's like reality and fantasy are blending, you know? I can accept the rain, and I can accept the Satanists. I can even consider the possibility of Salty's giant sea monster. But mermaids? That's pretty fucking hard to swallow."

"Yeah," she whispered, her breath tickling my ear. "It does seem a little far-fetched. But these days, I'm willing to believe just about anything."

She pointed to the skylight. The rain drummed against it, obscuring the sky.

"A year ago, I wouldn't have believed that it would just start raining one day and never stop."

I looked into her eyes. "A year ago, I wouldn't have believed I could be with a girl as beautiful as you."

She sat up on top of me, her pelvis cradling mine. She grinned, gave me a playful squeeze, and then got to her feet. "So you really think stuff's going to grow in here without direct sunlight?"

"Sure." I shrugged. "It's worked pretty good so far."

"Yeah, I've got to admit, it has."

She flopped back down on the bed and opened up the magazine. I turned back to the plants.

"When were you born, Kevin?"

"September twenty-second. Why?"

"I'm reading the horoscopes." She scanned a few pages and then smiled. "Hey, you're a water sign. That's pretty appropriate, isn't it?"

"I guess so. A little fucking dark though, don't you think?"

She giggled.

I tilled the surface soil with my fingers, carefully avoiding Jimmy's resting place.

Lori was quiet for a moment, and then she made a small sound in her throat.

I turned. She was frowning.

"What is it?"

"Nothing." She snapped the magazine shut.

"Come on, Lori. What is it?"

"The magazine. It—it said that we're destined for a doomed relationship."

"Really? It says that?"

She nodded, chewing her lip.

"Who the fuck writes those things? Jesus—I thought they were just supposed to tell you good stuff."

She gave me a weak half-smile, and I pressed on.

"Come on. Who cares what a year-old magazine says anyway? I don't think we're doomed. Do you?"

She hesitated before she answered. "No."

Brushing the dirt from my hands, I lay down next to her, stroking her hair and gazing into her troubled eyes.

"Lori, when this started, I wondered what the sense was in staying alive. I can't tell you how many times I thought about just ending it all. I mean, what's the point? The fucking world is flooding and it doesn't look like it's going to stop. I felt that way again yesterday, when I found Jimmy. He was my best friend, my last link to my old life. With him gone, there just didn't seem to be a point to life anymore."

She started to speak, but I pressed a finger to her lips.

"But you make me want to stay alive, Lori. *You* are the point. You're my reason now."

I kissed her again.

"Kevin," she breathed. Her body was trembling, her eyes filled with emotion. "You haven't said much about what happened with Jimmy. If you want to talk, I'm here for you. Or if you want to cry."

"Thanks. I appreciate that. Right now, it still hurts too much to talk about it. As for crying, well, I don't cry. You might as well know that now."

"I'm serious." She frowned. "You don't need to impress me, so stop with the macho stuff already. If you need to cry, it's okay. I'm here."

"Lori, I'm serious, too. I don't cry. I've never been able to." I told her about my grandma's funeral and everything, and she said that was sad, but that she understood.

But despite the emotional pain, I did open up and talk about Jimmy. I told her about the first time Jimmy and I met (playing with Hot Wheels together in the dirt lot between our houses), and what it was like growing up together, fights we had with our parents, the crazy shit we did in high school, those sort of things. Then she told me about her best friend and her parents and her brothers and sisters, and the guy she'd been dating when the rain started.

When we were finished, we made love again. It was better this time, perfect in fact. It was everything I'd ever seen in movies and read about in books— lovemaking on an epic scale. Maybe that sounds corny to you, but that's what it was. I'd never felt this way with anyone else. Our relationship was less than twenty-four hours old, but we were already learning our way around each other's bodies. We both lasted a long time, and when it was over, we lay there, holding each other and listening to the rain beat against the skylight.

I almost fell out of bed when the pounding started. Somebody was at the door.

"Kevin? Lori? Open up."

Juan. The door shook in its frame as he hammered at it again.

"Kevin! Wake up, man. We've got trouble! Are you in there?"

"Yeah! Hang on a second!" I struggled into my boxer shorts and jeans, and Lori pulled the sheets up around her, concealing her nakedness.

I opened the door. Juan stood there, his eyes wide and frantic. He grabbed my shoulder and the strength and urgency in his grip made me cringe.

"What's up? What's going on?" I asked.

He took a deep breath. "It's Louis and Christian."

"Yeah? Are they finally back?"

"No."

I frowned.

Juan's face had grown pale. "The Satanists have them."

CHAPTER NINE

Anna kept the kids inside, despite their protests and insistence that they should be allowed to go outside and see what was going on. The rest of us ran out onto the roof. I think that most of us didn't *want* to see, but at the same time, we were unable to help ourselves. Christian and Louis were our friends, and in some strange, fucked up way, we owed it to them. We were obligated to bear witness.

The group crowded around the edge and took turns with the telescope. Lee accepted it from Mike, put his eye to it, and the color instantly drained from his face. Without uttering a word, he handed it to me.

I looked and felt my stomach fall out from under me. A dozen Satanists milled around on the Trade Center's roof, waiting for darkness to fall. Some of them carried wet kindling in preparation for the bonfire to come. Others were securing the evening's sacrifices.

The evening's sacrifices being Louis and Christian.

I recognized them even from a distance, through the blurry, raindrop-distorted image in the telescope. Their hands and legs were bound with heavy chains, the ends of which were secured to cinder blocks. In addition to Louis and Christian, there was a young woman with a baby, not more than a few weeks old. I watched as the baby began to cry, squirming helplessly in its captor's grasp, and then I could watch no more. The look of terror etched on both the baby and the mother's faces made me sick to my stomach. I closed my eyes and handed the telescope off to Sarah.

She pursed her lips. "Oh my God . . ."

"Those motherfuckers," Taz growled. "Those dirty, evil motherfuckers!"

"What are we going to do?" Mindy whimpered.

As usual, we all turned to Juan for guidance. He was trying to light a cigarette, but the rain kept putting it out. Giving up, he flung the soggy butt into the wind. A seagull darted for it. He watched the shrieking bird snatch the cigarette and wheel away, and then he met our eyes.

"Do? We're going to go get them back."

"Word!" Ducky pounded his fist into his palm. "That's what I'm talking about. Put a hurtin' on their ass."

"Some Rambo-style shit," Taz agreed. "Bust in, break some off, and bring them home."

"I'm up for it," Sarah said.

Mike stepped forward. "Count me in, too."

"Are you crazy?" Mindy shouted. "That's suicide! How many of them are over there?"

Mike took her hand in his. "It doesn't matter, honey. Juan's right. We've got to try. This is Louis and Christian we're talking about."

"You'll be slaughtered! Then what will I—the rest of us—do?"

"Goddamn it, Mindy." Mike's face turned red. "Those are our *friends* over there! What do you want me to do? Stand here and watch while they get butchered? I'm going along to help!"

"No, you're not," Juan told him. "And neither are you, Sarah. But me, Kevin, Taz, and Ducky are going to."

I jumped when I heard my name. "Me?"

"Why not?" Mike asked. "You can't just expect me to stand here while Christian and Louis are their captives."

"I can and I do," Juan said. "You've got a woman here that loves you, Mike. And more importantly, I trust you. Let's be honest here. Chances are I'm not going to make it back, and if that happens, I need you to take over here. Somebody needs to lead and my choice is you."

"Well then why the hell do Taz and Ducky have to go?" Lashawn angrily jabbed a finger at Lee. "Send Mr. Science here instead."

"Hey," Lee shouted back, "don't call me Mr. Science, bitch!"

Taz took a step towards him. "Don't call her bitch, motherfucker."

Lee refused to back down. "Or what, you two-bit thug? Tell me! What are you going to do about it?"

"You best get the fuck out of my mug," Taz warned him. "Unless you want to get your fucking face split. You ain't messing with Nate now."

Juan sighed. "Both of you knock it off."

Sarah frowned at him. "I still don't see why I can't go. I'm just as capable as the rest of you. Is this because of some bullshit macho creed or something? Because if that's what it is, Juan, then—"

I could see the anger building in Juan seconds before he snapped.

"All of you shut the hell up, right fucking now!"

Shocked into silence, they waited for him to speak. He stood there on the roof, his chest heaving, rain dripping from his face, fists balled in rage. Slowly, he unclenched them and his voice returned to a normal tone.

"Now that I have your attention, here's how we are going to play it. Despite what you might think, this is *not* a democracy and it is *not* open for debate. Those things died with the rest of our civilization. Welcome to Juan's world."

Sarah opened her mouth, but he cut her off again.

"You've all trusted me up to this point and you'll have to trust me now. Sarah, Mike, and Lee have talents that are irreplaceable to the group. I need them here in case something happens to us. Taz and Ducky are used to guns and violence. I need them with me, for what we are about to do. We're not going over there to sell Girl Scout cookies, people."

"But why does Kevin have to go?" Lori whispered, so softly that we almost didn't hear her above the rain.

Juan grinned. "Because I like him. And because I think he might like to pay those sick fuckers back for what happened to Jimmy."

I tried to smile back, but my mouth didn't want to work. I felt sick inside. My stomach was a ball of lead.

Salty, who'd been hiding in the back of the crowd and standing under some ductwork to block the rain, stepped forward. "Wasn't the Satanists that did that to Jimmy."

"Not now, Salty," Anna whispered.

"You're forgetting something," Sarah pointed out to Juan. "Louis and Christian took the last boat, and now the Satanists have that, too. So how will you get over to the Trade Center?"

Juan's shoulders sank.

"Shit!" Mike threw his hands up in frustration. "God damn it, she's right, Juan! What the hell do we do now? You can't swim over there."

"Why don't you use those washtubs?" Salty suggested.

"What?" Juan blinked at him.

"Those plastic washtubs downstairs," Salty said. "They float. Just strap 'em together with rope."

Juan glanced at Mike. "Would they hold us?"

"I think so. We haven't exactly been eating well." He sized up Juan, Taz, Ducky, and me. "None of you are small guys, but you've all lost weight. I think it would work."

"No," Lee said, "I don't think that's a good idea. What happens if you guys start sinking halfway there? All it would take is one big wave to flood those things. Then you'd be stranded in the water—or worse."

"Then what do you suggest?" Juan asked.

"We build a raft, and quickly. It doesn't have to be anything permanent. Just enough to get you guys there and back again."

"Do we have time to build something like that?"

Lee glanced at the sky. "I think so. It's hard to tell exactly when sunrise and sunset occur, but I've noticed that they don't start their ceremonies until well after dark. We've got at least an hour. Maybe even an hour and a half."

"All right," Juan barked. "Taz, Ducky, Kevin—you guys come with me. The rest of you help Lee out and give him a hand putting the raft together. Lee, you're in charge. Nate, you stay up here and keep an eye on the Trade Center. Holler quick if it looks like they're starting without us."

Nate didn't reply.

"Nate?" Juan stepped towards him. "You hear me?"

Distracted, Nate stared out over the water.

Juan put a hand on his shoulder. "Nate? You okay?"

"Yeah," Nate shook his head as if trying to clear it. "Just tired is all."

Juan studied him a second longer, then took me by the arm and led Taz, Ducky, and me back inside. Taz and Ducky ran off to their room to fetch their guns. I followed Juan to his suite. It looked like a tornado had hit it. Dirty clothing and bed linens lay tossed about and food wrappers, empty beer bottles, and other debris littered the floor. There was an overflowing trash can in the corner.

"Sorry about the mess," he said, embarrassed. "Housekeeping hasn't been by lately."

"I think you should complain to the front desk." I grinned, but he must have seen the fear in my eyes.

"Kevin, look—you'll be okay. The truth is, I need you along on this. I don't trust Taz and Ducky one hundred percent, and I need somebody to watch my back in case they try to smoke some pork along with the bad guys. I know how it is now, but I also know that back in the day, I was a cop and they were gangbangers. Old loyalties die hard and I'm still not sure where they stand. You understand what I'm saying?"

"Yeah." I felt like puking, and the blood drained from my face.

Juan noticed it. "Seriously, man. It's going to be okay. I've got your back, and you've got mine."

He pulled open the closet door and brought out a very mean-looking rifle.

"What's that?" I asked.

"This is an M-16 assault rifle. I actually prefer the M-1 Garand. It's a lot more reliable, especially in rapid-fire situations. But this is all I brought with me, and beggars can't be choosers. I've kept it cleaned and serviced, so hopefully it won't jam on me. These are my extra magazines. They hold the bullets."

"I knew that. I've seen movies."

"Okay then," he chuckled and pulled out another piece of equipment. "Know what this is?"

"An elephant gun?"

He laughed. "Not quite. This beauty is an M-203 grenade-launcher. I can install it on the M-16. And these little babies here are antipersonnel ammunition for it."

"Antipersonnel ammunition?"

"Grenades."

"Christ, Juan. We should change your name to Rambo."

He winked at me and then fished around in the dresser drawers.

"Do I get one, too?"

"No. But you do get this."

He handed me a pistol. I'd held pistols before, during guard duty and when Jimmy and I found them while scavenging, but it felt different this time. It was heavy. Cold. I admired the weapon, curled my fingers around it. It felt good in my hand.

"That's a Sig P245," Juan told me. "It's a .45 caliber, holds six rounds in the magazine and one in the pipe. As with all Sigs, there is no manual safety. It's a double-action pistol, single after the first shot, with a de-cocker."

"I don't understand," I admitted.

"I don't have time to give you the schematics or read you the sales brochure. What you need to know is this— the trigger is here. We've only got the one clip for it, so try to make your shots count. You've got seven. When you run out of bullets, that's all we have. Hopefully, by then I'll have done some damage to the Satanists and we'll have rescued our friends and be on our way home."

"Juan, I've never fired a gun before in my life."

"It's easy, Kevin. Just point and shoot. That's all you have to do. Point. Shoot. Repeat as necessary."

Before I could reply, there was a knock at the door. Juan opened it and Taz and Ducky bustled in, acting like excited little kids around the tree on Christmas morning. This was the happiest I'd seen them since they'd joined our group.

"Yo, check it out." Ducky nudged Taz. "Kevin's got a Sig."

"Nice one," Taz said in appreciation. "You know how to use it?"

"I'm a fast learner."

Taz laughed. "You go, playa."

Ducky flashed a smile. "I got me an MP-5."

Juan whistled in obvious admiration. "Heckler Koch, right?"

"You know what time it is. The mini-uzi is dead, but this motherfucker here," he lifted the gun with pride, "is alive and well. There's no kick at all. It shoots exactly where you point it. You got to be retarded to miss with this thing."

"Keep that in mind when we're over at the Trade Center," Juan said.

"See this?" Taz showed me his machine gun. "This is an AK-47—when you absolutely, positively want to eradicate every motherfucker in the fucking room. Accept no substitutes."

"It's big," I said.

"Big dick, big gun."

They both giggled uncontrollably and I caught a hint of weed wafting off of them.

"Are you guys stoned?" Juan asked.

They shrugged.

"We can still do our job if that's what you're thinking," Ducky said, leaning against the dresser.

"Why?" Taz sat down on the bed, the mattress springs creaking under his weight. "You gonna arrest us, Officer?"

Juan shook his head. "No. Actually, I was going to ask if you had any more. I could use a hit right about now, and I bet Kevin could, too."

I nodded. A nice buzz would have taken the edge off of me right about then.

Taz's expression was one of surprise, and then regret.

"Shit, I wish we did have more. This was the last of the stash. We been saving it for a special occasion, but we figured this might be the last chance, you know?"

"Yeah, I know," Juan said. "I've got something that I've been saving for a special occasion, too."

He pulled open another drawer and held them up. All three of us gasped.

"Are those—more grenades?" I stuttered. They looked huge.

"White phosphorous grenades, a kind that was only used by the Special Forces and Black-Ops units. But I managed to get some from a friend of mine, right before everything collapsed. There's one for each of us, so use them only as a last resort, okay?"

Taz and Ducky started laughing again. I took mine warily. It was heavier than I would have thought, even heavier than the gun. Holding it in my hand scared me, but I felt a little better after they explained how to use it.

"So what's the plan?" Ducky asked.

"I don't know," Juan admitted. "I'm making this shit up as I go along. We don't know enough about them, where they post guards, if there are any entrances at water level, what kind of weaponry they have. All we know is what we've seen from the roof. When we get there, we're going to have to think quickly and play it by ear. Taz, you and I have the heavy shit. I figure we'll open up, and keep those fuckers busy, while Ducky and Kevin try to free Louis and Christian."

"What about the girl and the baby?" I reminded him.

"Sure, them too. And any other prisoners we find. We'll keep the cultists pinned down while you rescue the captives."

Taz stood up and scratched his groin. "Be straight with us. You really think we can pull this shit off?"

"I don't know." Juan shrugged. "Worst case scenario, we take as many with us as we can, so that the rest of our group doesn't have to worry about them. It just pisses me off. We should have done this a long time ago, but we didn't. And now Christian and Louis might pay the price."

We fell silent then, each lost in our own thoughts. Finally, Juan stirred. His joints popped as he stood up, and they sounded loud in the silence.

"Okay, you guys get your shit together. I'll meet you on the roof in five minutes. Hopefully, Lee and the others have got that raft ready."

I sought out Lori and found her hurrying up the stairs with an armload of rope. I called her name and she turned. She started to speak, but I quieted her with my mouth, pressing my lips to hers as I pulled her tight against me. Her hair and clothes were wet, but her body was warm. Then I pushed away and looked into her eyes.

"I love you. I need you to know that before I leave. Maybe it's too soon to say it out loud. It's only been a few days—what we have—but I'm in love with you."

A tear ran down her face. I watched it, mesmerized.

"I love you too," she whispered. "Be careful."

Swallowing, I assured her that I would and wiped her tears away with my finger.

"I wish I could cry," I told her. "I wish I could show you how much—"

Lori silenced me with another kiss, then let go and turned away.

"I'll be here when you get back."

She disappeared up the stairs.

After a moment, I followed her out into the rain. On

the roof, the rest of the group was clustered around the raft. Tabletops and plywood had been lashed to seven big metal drums. The raft was rectangular and pointed at one end. It looked ready to fall apart.

Ducky pointed at the makeshift craft. "We're gonna go over there in *that?*"

"Trust me," Lee said, "it will work. A raft floating on two ten-gallon drums will support approximately one hundred and eighty pounds of weight. Like we said before, none of us have been eating well, so we're all safely under that. According to my calculations, this should support the four of you, plus Louis, Christian, and the other captives. We added some buckets and Salty's tubs for extra buoyancy."

"But why is it pointy?" I asked. "Rafts are supposed to be square, aren't they?"

"Pointed rafts are easier to propel, especially if they're rectangular, rather than square. We fashioned you some crude oars using push brooms and mops from the janitor's closet. Hopefully, they'll work."

"They'll have to," Ducky said.

"You did good." Juan shook Lee's hand. "Thanks, man."

Taz pointed at a rusty, multipronged piece of metal with a length of rope attached to it, lying in the raft. "What's that shift?"

"A grappling hook," Lee said. "Improvised at the last minute, of course, but it should suffice. It always seemed to work for the pirates."

Juan and Lee laughed, and seconds later the rest of us joined in. It felt good—good but surreal, as if the laughter could take away the gravity of what we were about to do.

Ducky picked up the grappling hook and squinted at the rest of us. "Ahoy bitches! I'm the dread pirate Ducky."

It was stupid and silly, but we laughed harder. I got a stitch in my side, and tears ran down Juan's face.

That was when the singing started.

We all heard it this time. Well, at least the men heard it; a beautiful, clear melody that carried over the roar of the waves and the sound of the rain. We stopped and cocked our heads, entranced. The women stared at us like we'd lost our minds. We turned just as Nate jumped off the roof and plunged into the water.

"Shit!" Sarah shouted.

The spell was broken. We raced to the edge, staring in disbelief. Nate was entwined in the arms of the most beautiful woman I have ever seen. Long blond hair, glistening with droplets of water, cascaded over her milky skin and breasts. Their mouths met hungrily, their tongues seeking each other. Nate went limp, surrendering himself to her embrace, locked in her arms. The woman in the water wrapped herself tighter around him, twisting her body. Her lower half crested a wave.

From our vantage point on the ledge, Sarah, Mindy, and I gasped in unison. We couldn't believe what we were seeing. Instead of legs, the woman in the water had a fishlike tail, grayish-silver and covered with scales. She flicked it back and forth, as if she was waving at us with it, and then both she and Nate vanished below the surface.

"Nate!" Sarah shrieked.

Mike stepped out of his shoes and balanced on the ledge, preparing to jump.

Mindy grabbed him, "What are you doing?"

"We've got to get Nate! She's drowning him!"

The water churned and then the mermaid's head broke the surface again. Nate was no longer with her. The mermaid stared at us and I lost myself in her eyes. Then she opened her mouth and began to sing.

"Listen," Lee breathed. "It's beautiful." As if asleep, he shuffled toward the edge of the roof.

Mike nodded his head in agreement. "It sure is. It's the most beautiful thing I've ever heard. I've got to get closer."

"I don't hear nothing," Lashawn said.

Lori shook her head. "Me either."

"Women can't hear it," Anna gasped. "Remember? That's what the kids said."

I tore my gaze away from the mermaid, but her voice filled my head.

Mike struggled with Mindy as she fought to pull him back. Anna jumped in front of Lee and shook him. He stared at her blankly; then she pinched him.

Taz and Ducky headed for the edge, too. I noticed that both of them had an obvious hard-on jutting from their wet pants. My own penis was stirring as well. Still, I tried to fight. Then my feet betrayed me and I joined the procession, stepping up onto the ledge. My erection strained against my zipper, throbbing.

Lori grabbed my arm. "Kevin, what are you doing?"

"Stop me, Lori," I whimpered. "It's too strong. I can't fight it."

"You have to!"

Salty stuffed his fingers in his ears and the veins stuck out in his neck as he tried to fight the siren's call. "Shoot her, Juan! It's a sea-witch! A harpie! Shoot her!"

Juan ignored him, slack-jawed and mesmerized by the song. Sarah slapped him and he shook his head, glaring at her.

"Don't listen to her!" Sarah snapped.

"Get away from me." Juan shoved her backward.

Sarah stepped toward him again and Juan slapped her hard across the mouth. Reeling, she brought her hand to her lips. Her fingers came away bloody. Juan pushed past her, toward the edge of the roof.

"Fuck this," Sarah growled. She reared back and then lunged for him. One hand darted between his legs, grabbed his balls, and squeezed. Howling, Juan collapsed to his knees, dropping the rifle. Sarah picked it up.

"Everybody get back," she yelled. She stepped to the edge and swung the rifle downward. The thing in the water directed her song towards Sarah, and her aim wavered. Then, slowly, she started to swivel the weapon back around towards us.

"What's wrong with Sarah?" Anna moaned. "It's not supposed to work on women. That's what you guys said!"

"Don't listen to it, Kevin," Lori urged me.

Hands over my ears, I stepped off the ledge and back onto the roof and ran towards Sarah. *She's gay,* I thought. *She prefers other women. Maybe that's why it's working on her.*

The M-16 continued its turn towards us. Sarah's eyes were vacant.

I grabbed her wrist. "Block it out, Sarah, and shoot the bitch!"

Gritting her teeth, Sarah shook her head, focused, and then squeezed the trigger. She missed—on purpose or not I'll never know.

"Somebody stop me," she pleaded.

Her face grew clouded again and she turned back towards us. Before she could aim, Lashawn and Lori jumped on her, wrestling Sarah to the ground. Lee, Mike, Juan, Taz, Ducky, and Salty all moved towards the edge, and Malik and James were following close behind.

The mermaid's voice crept into my head again and I could feel her picking through my brain—invisible fingers that poked and prodded, trying to control me. Mentally shrugging her off, I pulled my pistol, aimed as best I could, and fired. The first two bullets missed. The third, fourth and fifth didn't, immediately silencing her song and obliterating one bobbing breast and most of her head. She sank beneath the waves in a crimson froth.

Nate never resurfaced.

"You killed her," Lee rasped, holding his head.

I nodded, unable to speak.

Lashawn and Lori let Sarah up. Panting, she rose to her feet, slammed a fresh clip into place and stepped away from the edge.

"Can I have my gun back?" Juan asked her.

She handed it to him without a word, blood trickling from her split lip.

"Sorry about that," he apologized.

"Don't sweat it," Sarah said. "She was in my head, too."

Juan pointed at the still smoking Sig in my hand. "How many shots did you fire?"

I shrugged. "Five, I think."

"That means you've got two left. Keep that in mind when we go next door."

"Okay." I wasn't sure what I'd do once the gun was empty. Throw it at the Satanists, maybe, and hope I knocked one out?

Wincing, Taz pressed his fingertips into his forehead. "Damn, yo. My fucking head hurts."

"Mine too," I sympathized. "It's like she was inside my brain."

"Poor Nate." Anna shook her head sadly.

"Shouldn't we look for him?" Lori asked.

Nobody answered her.

Juan tilted his head from side to side, cracking the joints, and then turned to me. "All right, let's go. The darkness is coming quick."

Using the telescope, Lee checked on the Satanists and reported that they were still making preparations. He, Mike, Sarah, and Salty dropped the raft into the water, and we all held our breath. It started to sink, and then bobbed back up again, floating aloft on the waves. Mike untied the rope, securing it to the roof.

We said our good-byes. I noticed that while Lashawn hugged Taz, she was simultaneously staring at Ducky over his shoulder. Moving away from the others, Lori and I embraced, and she started to cry again.

"I'll come back," I whispered to her, and didn't believe a word of it.

"You better," she whispered back, and I could tell that she didn't believe it, either.

We clambered out onto the raft. It rocked under our weight, but stayed afloat. Ducky and I each grabbed an oar and began paddling, while Juan and Taz positioned themselves at opposite ends, their weapons at the ready. We pushed off from the building and struggled against the current. For one harrowing moment, I was convinced the waves would smash us against the side, but then we were free and it became almost easy.

The sun's gray silhouette vanished in the sky and the water turned black.

Ducky shifted his weight and the raft rolled. "So, what the hell was that thing back there?"

"You saw what it was," Juan said.

"A bitch with a fish tail. A mermaid."

"Yep."

"That's fucked up, dawg. That's really fucked up."

"Lori and I were talking about that earlier," I said. "It's like fantasy and reality are blending now. The rain, I could accept. But a mermaid?"

"Yeah," Ducky repeated, "that's fucked up. Some goddamn Walt Disney shit."

Thunder rolled across the sky and the rain fell harder.

"Ya know what's fucked up?" Taz said. "Back in the day, when I was dealing, at the same time, I was part of the neighborhood watch. Even got a commendation for it. How fucked up is that?"

"That's pretty fucked up," Juan admitted. "What are you now?"

Taz grinned in the darkness, raindrops running down his face. "Shit, dawg. I'm *still* the neighborhood watch. We all are."

Juan laughed. He looked out at the choppy ocean and said, "This is our hood now."

Cloaked by the rain and the darkness, we drifted towards the Trade Center and the confrontation that awaited us there. My breath hitched in my throat and the others heard it.

"It'll be cool, Kevin," Taz assured me. "You ain't gonna cry or nothing, are you?"

"I can't cry," I said. "I don't know how."

"That's pretty fucked up, too."

The rain beat against the raft and we drifted on in silence. It took us about twenty minutes to reach the Trade Center, each second seeming like an hour. A heavy fog rose from the water, obscuring everything, and we fretted that we'd miss the building completely or worse, drift past it and out into the open sea. Just as we were about to admit defeat, the bonfire erupted to our left. It was close. Closer than we'd realized. We still couldn't see the building, but the bright orange flames were hard to miss, impossibly shooting sparks up into the heavy downpour.

"I'd still like to know how the fuck they get that shit to burn in the rain," Taz commented.

We drifted closer.

"Okay, let's do this," Juan hissed. "Everybody knows the plan, right? Taz and I lay down a distraction while you guys rescue the others."

Taz and Ducky nodded. I smiled, trying to look self-assured but feeling scared and foolish and very small.

My sphincter muscles contracted and my balls shriveled up to the size of raisins. I flipped the wet hair out of my eyes, took a deep breath, and tightened my fingers around the pistol.

Then, suddenly, directly in front of us, the building emerged from the fog like some island cliff face. Upraised voices drifted through the mist, echoing around us. Chanting words that I'm sure weren't part of any language spoken on Earth. I shivered; wet and cold and miserable.

Juan leaned forward, peering through the rain. "Anybody see Louis and Christian's boat?"

Silently, we shook our heads.

"Maybe the Satanists took it inside," Ducky suggested. "Put it with their surfboards and shit?"

"Could be," Juan agreed. "Keep an eye out for it. We might need it to get everybody back home, if there's a lot of prisoners."

We pulled alongside the building, next to an office window. Ducky and I struggled to hold the raft in place while Juan stood up, peered through the window, and investigated.

"I don't think there's anybody inside the room," he said.

"Want to go in that way?" Taz asked.

Juan nodded. "It beats the hell out of using that grappling hook."

"Word," Taz agreed. "I'm not up for that *Pirates of the Caribbean* shit, anyway."

Juan tried opening the window.

"It's locked," he whispered, "but I've got a key."

He smashed in the glass with the butt of his rifle. I

held my breath, waiting for sounds of discovery or alarm, but the chanting continued. I noticed that Ducky was holding his breath as well.

Juan looked back at us. "Let's do it."

He gripped the sides and climbed through the hole. Taz and I followed after him. Ducky tossed us the rope, and I tied the end to a desk leg, securing the raft against the tide. Then he clambered through as well.

It was dark inside the office. What little light there was came from two fluorescent green glow sticks hanging from a nail in the wall. The damp, rotting carpet felt like a sponge under our boots. The musty air clogged our lungs; the furnishings were covered with mildew.

Juan clicked on his flashlight.

Somebody had spray-painted graffiti on the wall and the cubicle partitions. I recognized some of it—the obligatory pentagram and 666, snakes, demonic faces, and symbols from albums by Iron Maiden and Blue Oyster Cult—all standard high-school amateur devil worship crap. But there were other things, too, figures that I'd never seen before, figures that made me shiver just looking at them. There was writing:

KANDARA RULZ! IA DE MEEBLE UNT PUR-TURABO! THERE IS NO GOD BUT OB! KAT SHTARI! LEVIATHAN DESTRATO UR BEHEMOTH!

"Yo, what the hell is that shit?" Taz whispered. "Who the fuck is Kandara and Ob?"

"I don't know," I answered. "Could it be a gang thing?"

Taz shrugged. "I never knew a brother named Ob. And there ain't no crews in Baltimore named Kandara. Must be from out of town. Probably New York or something."

Another drawing showed a circular maze spiraling in on itself. In the center of the spiral, there was a squiggly blob with half-moon–shaped eyes and tentacles. It was cartoonish and crude, like something from a kid's doodle pad—but unsettling, too. The eyes seemed to be staring at us. Below the image was scrawled,

HE WAITS AT THE HEART OF THE LABYRINTH!

"The fuck does that mean?" Ducky asked. "What's a labyrinth?"

"It's another word for a maze," I explained.

"Maybe they was into Pac-Man and shit," Taz joked, but his smile flickered, and there was no laughter in his voice.

Juan hesitated, then reached out and touched the graffiti. His fingertips came away red. He sniffed them.

"It's blood," he hissed. "Fresh fucking blood!" With a look of disgust, he wiped his fingers on his pants.

"This is bad," Ducky whispered. "This is really fucking bad. Maybe we should just go, ya'll?"

"Man, screw that!" Taz punched his shoulder. "You fucking scared, man?"

"Hell yes, I'm scared! You are too, motherfucker!"

"I ain't scared, bitch! I ain't scared of nothing. I'm ready to smoke these fuckers."

"Both of you shut up," I said. "You're going to give us away."

Taz scowled at me, but kept quiet. Ducky skulked away.

I picked up a wet book. The cover had some kind of Arabic writing. I opened it up, but the pages were like wads of cottage cheese. I dropped it. My fingers felt greasy.

Ducky noticed my discomfort. "That book didn't have that White Fuzz shit on it, did it?"

"No," I said. "Just felt *nasty*. Oily."

Juan crept toward the open door. We tiptoed along behind him. The hallway was empty and lit with more hanging glow sticks. The air reeked, so I breathed through my mouth. Rotten food and other refuse littered the floor. A pile of feces with flies crawling over it. Empty beer cans and wine bottles. A moldy porno magazine. A withered head of lettuce covered with maggots. Several used condoms. A severed human hand, also swarming with maggots. An eyeball with a strand of gristle or muscle still attached to it. Ducky and I both recoiled in disgust when we saw it.

Taz kicked a round object with the toe of his boot. The object skittered across the floor towards me.

It was a human heart. Worms crawled through the meat.

I turned away, gagging. Bile crept up my throat.

"You okay?" Juan asked.

I nodded, unable to speak.

We came to the end of the hallway, and Juan pointed to a closed door marked EXIT. As we approached it, my breath caught in my throat. I imagined a dozen black-robed Satanists on the other side, their daggers held high, just waiting to jump us.

Taz nudged the door open with the barrel of his gun, and the hinges squeaked. Flakes of rust and chipped paint showered us from above. The stairwell was pitch black and quiet. After a moment, we slowly started up toward the roof, with Taz now in the lead. The darkness seemed almost palpable, like a living thing, pressing against me. My faltering hand found the cold handrail, and I felt like screaming. I gripped my pistol tighter.

Carefully, we continued upward, one floor, then two. We could hear the chanting clearly now, along with the crackle of the flames and the frightened cries of the captives.

"This is the top floor," Juan breathed in my ear. "The roof is on the other side of the door. Be ready and be quick. Don't freak out on us, Kevin."

I felt him leave my side, and I started to hyperventilate. I tried to swallow and found that I couldn't. There was a slight scuffling sound as Juan and Taz moved towards the door. Standing next to me, Ducky mouthed a Hail Mary.

I had time to wonder if there really was a heaven, and if so, would I be welcome there.

Then Taz kicked the door open and all hell broke loose.

"Neighborhood watch!" He opened fire. "You motherfuckers are bringing the property values down! Consider yourselves evicted!"

Everything happened very quickly after that. I wasn't sure what to expect. I guess I thought that everything would happen in slow motion, like in a movie. But it didn't. Juan followed Taz through the doorway and began shooting as well. I heard gunshots and an explosion, unintelligible shouts and then more gunfire. My ears were ringing and the gunshots reverberated in my chest.

Juan and Taz were both screaming, and I was surprised to find myself screaming, too, as I burst out the door behind them. The rain lashed at my face. The bonfire had turned night into day, and the flickering flames cast weird shadows around us.

About three dozen Satanists were gathered on the roof. None of them had weapons, except for the ones guarding the prisoners and a guy who must have been the leader or high priest. He clutched a long, curved dagger and held an old, leather-bound book in his other hand. The only part I could make out was the title, illuminated in the flashes of light from Juan's M-16. It was in Latin or something—*Daemonolateria*. The leader recited from it, shouting over the roar of the machine guns, seemingly oblivious to the hail of lead around him.

"Ia verminus Leviathan! Ia destrato Leviathan! Leviathan!"

Christian and Louis were lying at the far edge of the roof, still chained to the cinder blocks. The woman and her baby cowered next to them. The two cultists standing guard over them ducked behind an air-conditioning vent for cover and returned fire. Juan unleashed a barrage in their direction. As Ducky opened fire next to me, I watched in horror as one of the men darted forward, picked up the baby and flung it into the water without hesitation. There was a splash and the mother shrieked.

"Oh my God—" My mouth went dry.

"God does not live here," a voice hissed into my ear. Something heavy slammed into my back and I fell to the roof. Rolling, I managed to get a knee up just as the attacker leapt for me. My knee sank into his abdomen, and the air whooshed out of his lungs. His sour breath reeked, and I turned my head to cough. He punched me in the face and my teeth rattled. Blood filled my mouth, warm and salty. My stomach churned, and I felt nauseous. His weight crushed me.

"You have interrupted the ceremony," he growled. "Leviathan will not be pleased. He's waiting to meet you, under the sea. I will take you to him, after I wring your scrawny neck!"

His meaty hands closed around my throat. I swung the pistol, knocking him in the temple with the butt, and he rolled off of me, groaning as the blood began to flow from his scalp. Several more Satanists closed in on my position. A second later, something that sounded like a swarm of angry bees ripped through the air, dropping them where they stood. Gunfire.

"Go," Juan shouted at me. "Get them untied, and hurry!"

Ducky was already halfway across the roof. The Satanist who had thrown the baby into the water picked up the cinder block attached to the screaming mother and tossed it over the side as well. She had time to let out one terrified shriek as the chain trailed along behind it and then she was gone, jerked over the side.

"Motherfucker!" Ducky aimed, fired, and the man's kneecap disintegrated. He fired again, and kept firing, finally severing both of the man's legs. Then Ducky rushed forward, pointing the smoking gun at the other guard. The second man scurried away in fear, then grabbed Louis and used him as a human shield.

"Don't come any closer! Shoot me and you shoot him too!"

"Shit . . ." Ducky froze.

Louis met our eyes and then suddenly rammed his head backward, smashing into his captor's nose. Blood gushed down the Satanist's face and chest. Louis wrenched away and fell forward onto his stomach.

He looked up at Ducky. "Shoot him!"

Ducky did. His gun sang out and the Satanist toppled over the side of the building, his hands clawing at the edge for purchase. His fingers closed around Louis's ankle, and Louis began to slide with him. I ran forward, but both men went into the water before I could reach them. I saw Louis's head disappear beneath the waves.

"Get Christian untied," I yelled to Ducky, and then I tossed my gun aside and jumped in after them.

The surface of the ocean was hard and sharp. It felt like I'd dived into a sheet of ice. My skin stung as the cold water closed over me. It was dark at first, but then I noticed a strange, green glow coming from the depths below me. It was bright enough that I could make out Louis, sinking like a stone. There was no sign of the woman or her baby. Kicking with all of my strength, I swam after Louis. His terrified eyes pleaded with me. It sounds impossible. There's no way I could have seen it underwater, and yet, I did. The green light illuminated everything. Louis opened his mouth to scream and black water rushed in. I reached out my hand— and that was when it happened.

Something long and thick uncoiled from the center of the green light, spiraled towards us, and wrapped itself around Louis's feet. A tentacle. It flexed and then he was gone, pulled into the light.

He vanished inside the glow, and the last thing I saw were his eyes, wide and terrified and still very much alive. I think that image will stay with me till the day I die.

Another tentacle rose toward me and dozens more followed in its wake. Frantic, I kicked for the surface. One of the tendrils brushed against my foot and I opened my mouth to scream, forgetting that I was underwater. Frigid salt water rushed into my lungs. The tentacle caressed my ankle. I lashed out with my foot, knocking it away.

My head broke the surface. Gagging, I clutched a drainpipe and hauled myself upward. The metal surface was slick, and I started to slide back down toward the water. Something splashed below me and I struggled back up again, afraid to look behind. Finally, I rolled onto the roof and coughed up water. I shrank away from the edge, watching for more of the tentacles, and retrieved my Sig, remembering that I still only had two shots left in it.

It took me a few seconds to realize that the shooting was over. Black robed bodies littered the roof, their blood already being washed away by the rain. Ducky had untied Christian and was checking him for injuries, while Taz kept guard at the stairway door. Juan stood over the cult leader's supine form. The dagger and the leather spell book lay next to him. The book was open in the middle, the pages drenched, red ink running and blurring together. Juan pressed the smoking barrel of the M-16 against the Satanist's heaving chest.

"You-you don't know what you've done," the leader squealed. "The Rain Gods will be angered now. You have deprived them of their bounty. They will destroy us all in retaliation! We summoned them—brought them all back with the rains."

"Rain Gods," Juan snorted. "You mean like the fucking mermaid we killed earlier?"

The man's eyes grew alarmed. "You killed the siren? You fool! Don't you realize the consequences?"

Juan spat in his face. "She killed one of our people."

The leader snarled as Juan's spittle ran down his face. "Leviathan is coming now! He wants revenge. You have killed his beloved and halted his sacrifices. You will pay dearly for these transgressions. Leviathan is slow to rise, but when he does, you shall know his anger. It is written in the *Daemonolateria*. Leviathan is coming. He of a thousand tentacles!"

The wounded man began to laugh and turned his face toward the sea. Blood poured from his mouth and nose.

"You worship this thing?" Juan asked. "This Leviathan?"

"Yes."

"And he's coming here?"

"Oh yes. Very soon."

"Well then, I guess you won't be around to meet him."

With the barrel still pressed against the leader's chest, Juan squeezed the trigger.

I flinched and looked away. When I turned back to

them, Juan had rolled the corpse over with his foot. The man's back was a gaping ruin.

Juan ejected his magazine and slid a fresh one into place. "How's it look, Taz?"

"Quiet. I think they must have all been up here."

"Christian, can you walk?"

He nodded weakly and then struggled to his feet. He stumbled towards me, but Ducky caught him.

"Easy, dawg. I got you."

"K-Kevin," Christian stammered, "where's Louis?"

I opened my mouth, closed it, and shook my head. Christian began to sob.

"Let's get out of here," Juan said quietly.

I pulled him aside while Ducky helped Christian limp towards the stairs.

"What's up?" Juan asked.

"I figured you should know. There was—something in the water."

"What kind of a something? Another mermaid?"

"No. I'm not sure what it was. All I saw was a weird green light. And tentacles. Big fucking tentacles. Some of them were the size of tree trunks."

He stared at me and I knew he believed me. At that same moment, the blazing fire suddenly went out. The roof was pitched into darkness.

"Shit," he said. "We'd better get going."

I stumbled as we walked towards the door. I glanced down and saw that I had tripped over the book. Pausing, I knelt down to examine it. The soggy pages were ruined now, unreadable. I wondered if that had something to do with the fire going out.

We entered the dark stairwell.

"What was the priest babbling about?" I asked as we ran down the stairs. "He said they started the rains?"

Taz swept the hallway with his rifle, but it was clear. "They said all kinds of shit. Talking loud and saying nothing."

"Keep moving," Juan said.

Instead of continuing the discussion, I concentrated on conserving my breath.

We made it back to the raft, and untied it as quickly as we could. We pushed off, with Ducky and I rowing again. The night was strangely quiet, except for Christian's stifled cries.

I reached out and touched his shoulder. "I'm sorry about Louis."

"Thanks, Kevin. I mean that. Did he—did he suffer? Was it over quick?"

I thought about Louis's eyes as the tentacle pulled him down into that weird ball of light.

"No," I lied. "It was over quick. He never felt a thing."

Christian smiled sadly. "After all we've been through together, I just can't believe—"

Something jumped out of the water in front of us. A dolphin. It chattered in alarm and then plunged back into the water.

Taz leaned forward. "What the hell was that all about? I thought they were supposed to be friendly and shit."

The ocean suddenly came to life around us. Massive schools of fish plowed through the waves. More frenzied dolphins leapt from the water. In the distance, I spied the black hump of a whale. A flock of seagulls wheeled overhead, screeching in what sounded like fear.

All of them were hurrying away from the area.

"What the fuck's this shit?" Ducky shouted. "The fucking fish gonna attack us now?"

"Something's spooked them." Juan pointed his rifle at the surface. "They're fleeing from something. Row faster!"

We did. He didn't need to tell me. I thrust that makeshift paddle into the water like a knife through butter. My heart raced in my chest.

"Animals can predict earthquakes," Christian pointed out. "Does the same go for fish?"

A triangular fin broke the surface just a few feet away, and I saw the gray, sleek body of a shark beneath it. Taz drew a bead on the shark, but Juan pushed the rifle barrel down.

"Don't shoot."

"It's a fucking shark, Juan! You seen *Jaws*?"

"It's not after us. See? It's swimming away, too. Leaving the area."

We were about halfway back when we heard a great, sonorous bellow—part whale, part subway train—deep and powerful and extremely pissed off, by the sound.

Ducky jumped, and almost dropped his oar. "What the fuck was that?"

"Look!" Christian pointed back the way we'd come.

At first, I didn't understand what I was looking at. The Trade Center building was barely visible, its walls engulfed in a quivering, snaking mass of shadows. Then I realized that the shadows were tentacles. There were hundreds of them, covering the walls and the roof. I followed them down to the ocean's surface, and I screamed.

A great, bulbous head emerged from the water, the size of a hot air balloon. In fact, that's what it reminded me of—a rubber, obsidian balloon—like what you'd see in a Halloween parade. Even from a distance, I could see its huge, teardrop-shaped eyes, glaring at us with a clearly malevolent intelligence.

"Row!" Juan shouted again. It sounded like something inside his throat ripped.

A loud, explosive crash rumbled behind us as the creature began to tear the building apart. Powerful limbs squeezed, cracking the concrete. They coiled around the steel girders, twisting and bending them with monstrous strength.

A corner edge of the building splashed into the water, sending a massive wave surging towards us. It rocked our makeshift raft, threatening to capsize us. We held on, clinging for support. Wave after wave crashed into us, and then the waters subsided again.

Ducky and I rowed as fast as we could. My arms ached by the time we arrived back at our building. The rest of the group stood on the roof, watching in horror as the entire Trade Center crashed into the ocean. Lee tied us off securely and we scrambled off the raft.

We quickly filled the others in on everything that had transpired over at the Trade Center—the graffiti, the Satanists and that weird spell book, the fight, and Louis's death. They'd been watching through the telescope, but the thickening fog obscured much of the battle and they still had questions.

"What the hell is that thing?" Mike shouted.

"Apparently," Juan gasped, trying to catch his breath, "according to the cultists, it's the husband of that mermaid we killed earlier."

"They called it Leviathan," I said.

"Leviathan?" Anna asked. "You mean like in the Bible? The thing that swallowed Jonah?"

"It's a Kraken," Salty said. "I tried to tell you, but nobody believed me."

"Don't start with that shit again," Sarah snapped. "Not now. That's the last thing we need."

Lashawn hugged Ducky and Taz both. Sarah draped a blanket over Christian's shoulders, but it was as wet as everything else, and I doubt it provided him much comfort. Lori ran to me and I hugged her tight, our wet bodies shivering against each other as we watched the destruction. Danielle, James, and Malik cowered against Anna. Danielle began to cry, and a moment later, the boys joined her.

The squid creature's rage echoed across the ocean like thunder. It heaved itself forward and then sank beneath the waves, sending a plume of water thirty feet into the air.

"What's it doing now?" Lashawn asked.

"I think," Juan said, "that it's coming for us."

He was right.

CHAPTER TEN

Believe it or not, for some strange reason, we didn't run or panic. Maybe we couldn't. It was as if we were all suddenly paralyzed. We stood transfixed, fear rooting our feet to the roof as the creature approached our building. Its sleek, black body surfaced again, cutting through the waves, and then submerged. Part of it looked like a squid and part of it looked like a giant snake. I caught a glimpse of an appendage resembling a big, membranous wing, but the spray concealed it before I could verify that's what it was.

The storm intensified. The raindrops stung our exposed flesh, splattering against our faces like bugs on a windshield. Thunder grumbled overhead and blue flashes of lightning seared the weeping sky, turning night to day. The waves crashed against the building, their size and intensity increasing the closer the monster came.

"It's a Kraken," Salty said again. "Just like what I saw before."

"Shut up, old man," Sarah snapped.

Lee sank to his knees in a puddle and began to laugh.

"What the hell is wrong with you?" Taz growled.

"It's fucking Cthulhu, man," Lee cackled. "Just like in the role playing game!"

"What are you talking about?" Juan asked.

"Cthulhu! H. P. Lovecraft's big, ugly squid god? Lives under the sea? Has a head like an octopus? That is not dead which can eternal lie, et cetera, et fucking cetera? Any of that ring a bell with you?"

"Motherfucker done lost it," Taz said. "Ya'll better lock him up somewhere before he hurts somebody."

"What is he talking about?" Mike asked. "Who the hell is Lovecraft?"

"Horror stories," I said. "Lovecraft was a horror writer."

I'd tried reading H. P. Lovecraft once, after watching the movie *Re-Animator*, which was based on one of his stories. I was disappointed to find that the book wasn't nearly as cool as the movie.

Lee continued babbling. "My students studied Lovecraft every October, along with Poe and Bierce and Hawthorne's supernatural stuff. Did you guys know that some people actually believe Lovecraft based his Cthulhu mythos on a real-life entity?"

Sarah raised her hand, as if she were a student in Lee's class. "Can I ask why we're standing out here on the fucking roof discussing early twentieth century pulp fiction while that thing is heading towards us? Shouldn't we be doing something?"

Her question seemed to galvanize us, snapping our indecision.

"Good question," Juan said. "Anna, get the kids downstairs. Lock yourselves in a room and stay there. No matter what you hear, don't come out. Find something to defend yourselves with, just in case. Sarah, Lori, Lashawn, and Mindy—get the rest of the guns and bring them up here, on the double. The rest of you take positions all around this fucking roof. He's sure as hell not getting us without a fight!"

Taz ejected his clip and slid a fresh one into place, then noticed that Lee was still kneeling in the puddle. "The fuck you doing, Lee? Get your ass up! That thing is gonna be on us any minute now."

"It's Cthulhu!" Lee shouted. A droplet of water dripped from his nose. "I'm telling you guys, it's fucking Cthulhu, man! We are so screwed."

"It's not Cthulhu!" I grabbed Lee's shirt and yanked him to his feet. "Cthulhu is a fictional character! Lovecraft made him up!"

"Just like the mermaid, right, Kevin? Was she made up too?"

I shook him hard.

"Lee, listen to me. You're scared. That's understandable, man, because I'm scared too. But you've got to get a grip, dude. That thing is *not* Cthulhu!"

"Well it sure as hell isn't Flipper, now is it?"

Another wave crashed into the building, the crest lapping over the edge of the roof. The creature's head emerged from the surf, and when it roared, I felt the roof shake beneath my feet.

Juan braced his legs against the edge, and raised his rifle. "Kevin, take Lee downstairs. With the state he's in, he's not going to be any help. Give his gun to

Christian, get him to his room and then get back up here!"

"Give me your gun, Lee." I held out my hand.

He met my eyes. His voice was barely a whisper. "It's not going to do you any good. Not against that."

"Maybe not. But give it to me anyway."

He surrendered the weapon and I handed it to Christian, who checked to make sure that it was loaded. Then I helped Lee to his feet and guided him towards the stairwell. He babbled the entire time about squid gods and lost cities. We were halfway through the door when the shooting started. The screaming followed a second later. I led Lee to the bottom of the stairs, and then ran back up. The rain was falling like gravel, thick and hard, but I barely noticed.

Leviathan was upon us.

Dozens of thick tentacles whipped through the fog. Everybody opened fire, but the appendages were hard to hit, moving as fast as they did. Taz blasted a hole in one of them and it retreated, only to have three more immediately take its place. One of them slapped the pistol from Christian's hands, and a third wrenched a radio antenna from its mooring on the roof.

I fumbled for my pistol, but it slipped from my wet hands and skittered across the roof. Scrambling to retrieve it, I ducked just as a muscular tendril slashed through the air above me.

One of the tentacles coiled around Christian's midsection and squeezed. He fired a shot into the appendage, but the creature refused to let go. Christian wailed, his eyes bulging in their sockets as his face turned red, then purple, then black. Dark blood exploded from his nose and mouth, and ran from his ears in thick rivulets, then finally burst from his pores. Mike ran to help him, but three more tentacles seized him, too, wrapping themselves around his legs and waist. He squirmed, clubbing at the appendages with his empty rifle.

Then he began to scream.

The tentacles were lined with rows of suckers—except that they weren't suckers. They were mouths. Tiny little circular mouths, lined with sharp, needlelike teeth.

And they began to feed . . .

The tentacles were eating Mike alive. He shrieked as they gnawed through his wet clothing and burrowed into his flesh. Blood welled out from between the rubbery coils. I remembered the purplish mark on Jimmy's head, the blemish that had looked like a raw hickey, and finally I understood what had happened to my friend. I raced toward Mike, but the tendrils snaked out over the water, taking him with them. The creature waved him about like a rag doll before dropping him into the ocean.

Leviathan's head emerged from the water, dripping seaweed and slime. Up close, those baleful eyes were as big as taxicabs. It roared again and I felt a blast of hot air rush over me. It stank of rotten fish and brine. Salty ran past me and dived into the stairwell. Juan shouted at him to help, clicked empty, and glanced around for assistance. But there was none to be found. Taz and Ducky were involved in their own struggles with the creature, and piles of brass casings littered the roof at their feet.

Then Sarah emerged from the stairwell, armed with two rifles. Seeing Juan's plight, she ran toward him, but Leviathan was quicker.

Juan yanked a white phosphorous grenade from his belt and pulled the pin. At the same instant, another serpentine appendage seized him. The tentacle slithered around his chest, pinning his arms to his side. He was still clutching the grenade. I've thought about it many times, and I'm still not sure if he held on to it out of some suicidal notion, or if he was just so scared that he forgot he was holding it. The tentacle lifted him skyward, and he screamed, his legs kicking helplessly. The mouths began to feed on him, chewing at his flesh and clothing. Then there was a bright flash as the grenade exploded, showering us all with gore—Juan's and the creature's. The stump of the tentacle sank below the waves, spraying ichor in its wake. There was nothing left of Juan, not even enough for the seagulls.

Taz and Ducky's resolve shattered then, and they broke for the stairs.

"Let's get the fuck out of here, yo!" Ducky shouted.

"Word," Taz said. "Come on, Kevin! Sarah! Let's haul ass!"

"We've got to stop it," Sarah insisted.

"We can't," I said. "It's useless. Just run!"

A dozen more tentacles slapped down onto the roof, cracking the surface, and I turned and ran. Sarah fired off a few random shots, and then fled with me. We darted through the doorway and met Lashawn and Mindy halfway down the stairs.

"We've got more guns," Mindy said.

"Forget about the fucking guns," Taz hollered, brushing past them. "Bullets ain't doing shit to that thing! Get the fuck out of my way."

Mindy didn't move. She glanced beyond us, up the stairwell. Her eyes were wide and teary.

"Where's Mike?" she asked.

Before I could answer, she pushed past me. I reached for her, but she slapped my hand away and ran out into the rain. I heard her scream—followed by the terrible sounds of tentacles slithering across the roof. Another appendage wound through the doorway and groped its way down the stairs. The mouths inside the suckers worked silently.

"Let's go!" I shoved them forward. We raced down the steps and regrouped in the lobby. The tentacle didn't follow us.

"I don't think it can reach us here," Sarah panted, breathing heavily. "We should be safe."

Ducky wiped the water from his brow. "Yeah, until it rips the motherfucking roof off this place."

"Which should be any minute now," I said. "Shit. I don't know what else to do, you guys."

"So we just give up?" Sarah asked.

I sighed. "You've seen the size of that thing. How the hell are we supposed to fight it? There's no other way out of the hotel. And we can't swim for it or take the boat. Not with that monster outside. So if you have any bright ideas, now would be a good time."

She didn't answer me, so I continued.

"Listen. Maybe it sounds weird, but I'd like to go find Lori. If we're going to die anyway, I'd like to be with her when it happens."

"I can't believe this." Sarah shook her head. "Have you lost your mind?"

"I hear you, playa," Taz said. "Kevin's right. We might as well go out with a bang."

Sarah continued shaking her head.

Taz grabbed Lashawn's arm. "Come on, baby. Lets go."

She took two steps with him, then turned and looked at Ducky over her shoulder.

"Lashawn . . ." His voice cracked.

She broke free of Taz's grip. "Wait. What about Ducky?"

Taz whirled around. "Ducky? What the fuck? He's my homey, yeah. But shit—we all gonna be dead in ten minutes. I want to spend it with you, baby, not Ducky! You cool with that, right, Ducky?"

"Yeah, dawg," Ducky sighed. "I'm cool with that."

I could hear his heart breaking, and apparently Lashawn could, too. She walked toward him.

"Where the fuck you going, Lashawn?" Taz's face was a mask of confusion.

She flipped her wet hair from her face. "I'm staying here with Ducky."

"Why?" Taz took a step toward her.

"Because I love him, you asshole!"

Taz gaped at them both. Slowly, he raised the assault rifle. His hands were shaking.

Ducky took a step backward, distancing himself from Lashawn.

Taz's voice was ice cold. "You *what?*"

"I love him. We've been knocking boots behind your back for months. I'm sorry that you found out like this, but it's true. If I'm gonna die, I want to be with *both* of you."

"This is not good," Sarah whispered in my ear. "Do something."

The hotel shook as Leviathan continued his assault.

Ducky held up his hands, feigning ignorance. "Yo, Taz, listen. That bitch is crazy! Come on, man. We boys. How long we been boys? We rolling with the same crew and shit. Druid Hill for life. Remember?"

Taz shook his head. "Druid Hill crew my ass, you low motherfucker. You were sleeping with her this whole time. You were knocking boots with my girl!"

Sarah intervened, placing herself between them. She held up a hand. "Think about what you're doing, Taz. This isn't the time. We need to work together right—"

"Get the fuck away from me, bitch." Taz brushed past her.

I grabbed Sarah's arm and pulled her away.

"Come on, baby," Lashawn begged Taz. "Calm down. It don't have to be like—"

He shot her in midsentence. It happened quickly, and for a second, I didn't understand what had just occurred. The rounds punched through her breasts and abdomen, and lodged in the wall behind her. The white plaster turned red. Lashawn looked surprised as she slipped to the floor. Ducky screamed and Taz whirled around, aiming the rifle at his friend.

I stepped in front of Sarah and called Taz's name. My ears were ringing.

"Stay the fuck out of this, Kevin."

"Come on, man," Ducky pleaded, hands held out in

front of him. "Don't do this. The bitch ain't worth it, Taz."

"You *fucked* my girl, punk! Did you think I would just let that shit slide? You were supposed to be my boy."

A tear slid down Taz's face as he squeezed the trigger. Ducky jittered like a marionette as the bullets struck home. He fell to the floor, glassy eyes staring at nothing. I squeezed my trigger a second later, aiming at the center of Taz's shaved head. It blew apart like a rotten pumpkin, splattering the wall with brains and shards of bone.

"Oh God . . ." Sarah gasped.

I pried the assault rifle from Taz's fingers, took a step backward, and then collapsed to my knees. My stomach heaved, and the bile burned my throat as it rose. I crouched there, vomiting until there was nothing left inside of me. I wiped my mouth with the back of my hand.

"You okay?" Sarah asked.

I nodded. "Yeah, I think so. I—I've never killed somebody before."

"What now, Kevin? What are we going to do?"

I slowly rose to my feet. "I've got to find Lori."

"But she could be anywhere."

"I know. That's why I have to find her."

"But what about—"

Above us, the roof shook as the thing outside slammed against it. Cracks spider-webbed across the ceiling. My feet sloshed as I took another step and I looked down to find myself standing in a puddle. Water was beginning to trickle down the stairs from the roof.

"Shit." I closed my eyes and rubbed my temples. In

less than an hour, our ranks had dwindled from eighteen to eight. I figured the rest of us would take about half that time.

It turned out that I was right.

I ran, determined to spend my last moments with the woman I loved.

"Kevin," Sarah called after me.

Not stopping, I shouted over my shoulder, "If you're coming, then move your ass."

She glanced back at the stairway. The trickle had turned into a torrent and the cracks in the wall were widening.

"Wait for me," she said and then followed.

We found Lori in the lobby on the nineteenth floor, cradling Anna's head in her lap. Lee, Danielle, James, and Malik lay nearby. There was blood everywhere—on the walls and the carpet and even the ceiling. A kitchen knife jutted from Lee's throat and his eyes stared sightlessly. None of the kids were moving. They'd been stabbed. As I followed the trail of blood, I noticed that the walls and ceiling on this floor were beginning to crack, too. The building shook beneath our feet as we ran towards them. Plaster fell from the ceiling.

Sarah knelt beside Anna. "Anna? Can you hear me?"

Anna turned her head and coughed; blood leaked out of the corner of her mouth.

I crouched down beside Lori. "Hey, you okay?"

She looked up at me, her face glistening with tears. "Kevin . . ."

I took her hand. "What happened? Who did this?"

"Lee—he found Anna and the kids here in the lobby, while I was looking for more weapons. When I showed up, he was acting crazy, talking about sacrifices and how the Satanists had the right idea. He-he said we had to sacrifice one of the kids. That if we did, that thing outside would let the rest of us live."

Anna coughed again, spraying us with blood.

"Jesus Christ," Sarah said. "He completely lost it."

"What happened next?" I prodded Lori gently.

She wiped her running nose with the back of her hand. "He must have gone to the kitchen first, because he had a knife. Before Anna or I could stop him, he . . ."

She broke off, sobbing. I placed my hand on her shoulder and squeezed.

"He got James and Malik right away. Anna tried to stop him and he stabbed her and then Danielle. I was so scared. I had the guns in my hands and I didn't even think to use them. I guess there wasn't time, anyway. He was stabbing Anna again, so I dropped the guns and jumped on his back. We wrestled, and I got the knife away from him and I-I stabbed him. I stabbed him in the neck. It got stuck and I couldn't pull it back out. But there's so much blood. Why is there so much blood?"

"Sarah, check the kids." I kissed Lori's forehead and brushed the hair from her eyes. I soothed her with assurances that it would all be okay, even though I knew it wouldn't.

I examined Anna while Sarah bent over the kids' bodies. It didn't look good. Anna's insides peeked at me through the wound, pink and glistening.

"How are the kids?" I asked Sarah.

She shook her head, turned away, and began to weep.

Anna smiled at me and tried to speak.

"We've got to put pressure on this," I told her. "You just hang in there, Anna."

"No," she rasped, "that won't do any good. It's too late, Kevin. Too late for us all."

"Bullshit." I tried to smile, but it felt phony. "We'll have you fixed up in a jiffy."

"He killed my babies." She raised one trembling hand and pointed at Lee. "He killed my babies. Why? He seemed like such a nice man. . . ."

"I don't know."

Her eyes suddenly seemed far away.

"Look," she sounded surprised. "Is that the sun? It's so bright."

She exhaled, her chest collapsing. She did not breathe in again.

I reached out and closed her eyes with two fingers. Then I bent over and kissed her on the head. Her skin was wet.

"Good-bye, Anna."

After endless days of rain, she'd seen the sun again. I figured we'd see it, too, before the night was done.

Taking Lori by the hand, I pulled her to her feet. The building trembled again and there was a loud crash on the floor below us. The hallway swayed under our feet. Lori grabbed onto me to keep from toppling over.

"What's happening?" she screamed.

"It's that thing. Leviathan. It's destroying the building. Water's coming in from the top."

"The lower levels are flooding, too," Lori said. "Mindy and I saw it when were looking for guns. Where is she, anyway?"

I shook my head. "It got her. And the others, too."

"All of them?" she gasped.

"Except for me, you, Sarah, and maybe Salty. Have you seen him anywhere?"

"Salty? No. Just . . ." She pointed back to the bodies in the lobby.

Sarah got to her feet. "I'm going to find him. He might be hurt."

"Okay," I said. "I'm going to stay here with Lori. Be careful."

"Good luck." She started down the hall.

"You too," I called after her. Then she was gone.

Another tremor struck, bouncing me off the wall. Chunks of plaster rained down on us. Deep inside the walls, something groaned.

Lori wiped her eyes. "Kevin, will you hold me?"

"Yeah." I swallowed. "I'd like that very much."

"We're not going to make it, are we?"

I started to lie to her, but I couldn't. Not anymore.

"No," I said, "we're not going to make it, Lori. Not with that thing outside. It would kill us as soon as we tried to escape. We're trapped."

"Let's go to your room, then. I want to smell the pine tree in your garden while you hold me, and I want to fall asleep before it happens. I can fall asleep in your arms and not wake up."

"Okay. That sounds good." Personally, I wondered how the hell we'd be able to fall asleep while a monster ripped the roof off the building, but I didn't ask.

We made it back to my room while the creature tore the building apart around us. We lay down on the bed, not bothering to remove our wet clothes and boots, and our bodies entwined. Legs, groins, chests, and arms—we were as close to each other as two human beings could be. The rain hammered at the skylight, rattling it in its frame, but I ignored the noise, concentrating solely on Lori. I wondered how we'd go. I hoped that the water would flood our level and engulf us. Drowning was better than being crushed under the wreckage—or suffering the same fate as those on the roof. I thought about Mike being eaten alive by the tentacles and silently vowed that Lori wouldn't meet the same fate. I'd kill her myself, if I had to, before I'd let that happen.

"Can you smell the pine?" she murmured.

"Yes. It smells good. Not much else grew in that garden, but the tree did okay. Maybe I wasn't such a bad gardener after all."

She nodded against my chest and closed her eyes.

I closed mine as well. It wasn't bad. Not bad at all. It felt good. Right. Leviathan's rage was nothing more than background noise, faint and distant.

"I love you, Lori."

"I love you, too."

This was a good way to die, surrounded by the warmth of someone you loved.

So when there was a knock at the door, you can understand why I was pissed. Lori gasped in surprise and I jumped as well. Something heavy crashed into the ocean with a loud splash as the second knock came.

"A tentacle?" Lori asked.

"Can't be," I whispered. "I don't think they can reach that far, and I don't think it knows how to knock."

"Salty? Or Sarah, maybe?"

"It has to be. Who else?"

A third knock, more insistent.

Lori sat up. "We can't just leave them out there, Kevin."

"No, I guess we can't."

I got up, sloshed to the door, and opened it on the fourth knock. Salty grinned at me, appearing embarrassed. Sarah stood behind him. Both of them looked small and afraid.

"We're sorry, Kevin," Salty said. "But we just didn't want to be alone."

"It's okay," I told them. "Come on—"

Behind me, the skylight exploded, showering the bed and the garden with shards of broken glass and rain. Lori screamed. I turned in time to see the tentacle lift her from the bed and yank her through the hole.

"Lori!"

I ran towards her, and jumped up on the garden table. I reached for her, and she reached back, but it was too late. The image is burned into my mind, her arms outstretched, her face frozen in terror. With a final scream—a scream cut short by the creature's squeeze—she was gone. Leviathan pulled her out into the night. Rain poured through the gaping hole where the skylight had been. I collapsed underneath it, sinking to the floor, shrieking and clenching sods of dirt from the garden in my fists. Broken glass cut my hands and my blood mixed with the mud.

Then, the hole in the ceiling grew dark again. I sensed it even before Salty and Sarah cried out in alarm. I looked up and stared straight into that huge, malevolent, yellow eye. Leviathan stared back at me.

I shook my bloody fists. "Give her back!"

"Kevin," Sarah shouted. "Get away from there!"

I stayed where I was, rooted to the garden, staring into Leviathan's eye.

It blinked once, and then, with one last fading cry, it was gone, vanishing into the rainy night.

Revenge. During the raid, the Satanists told us that the mermaid was Leviathan's bride. I'd killed its lover, so now it had killed mine in return. Call it the laws of nature or the circle of fucking life.

Blood streamed from my clenched fists. I lifted my face to the skies and the rain showered me. The droplets rolled off my cheeks and into the garden. They were seeds. Rain seeds. My own tears joined them, and I wept like the sky. I had finally learned how to cry.

Kneeling there in my garden, I rained.

PART III

THE WORM TURNS

Upward did the waters prevail;
and the mountains were covered.
And all flesh died that moved upon the earth,
every beast and every man.
And every creeping thing . . .

—Genesis
Chapter 7, Verses 20 and 21

CHAPTER ELEVEN

I'm back again. That took a lot out of me, writing down Kevin's story exactly the way he told it to us. Reminds me of the character in H. G. Wells's *War of the Worlds*. Halfway through the book, the protagonist told his brother's story—about what happened to him in London and what the Martians did there. Of course, that was fiction and this isn't. But the reader got a glimpse of what was happening elsewhere from it.

I reckon you've gotten a glimpse of what was happening up north. Now you know everything that I know.

So there's that.

I drifted off for a while after I'd finished relating Kevin's tale, and I just woke up again. My hand hurts worse than ever. My fingers are swollen and there's pain shooting up my wrist. Everything below my waist is still numb, though, and that's a blessing.

My broken leg is swollen up to about three times its normal size. It's black-gray and greasy looking, like a sausage that's been left out in the sun too long. It stinks, too. I can't feel it, and I reckon that's good, because it sure looks painful.

Despite the pain, I'm hungry. Hungry and thirsty. And the nicotine cravings are still there, too.

Something's poking me on the inside, and I think it might be a rib. The purple bruise on my stomach is getting darker and I'm still spitting up blood. There seems to be more of it now. I woke up in a pool of it.

Not good. Not at all.

I've got to finish this. Finish before it's too late. I'm in the home stretch now. The last part. Once I'm done, I'll put this notebook up somewhere safe. Hopefully, it will stay dry. If I had a bottle that was big enough, I'd roll the notebook up and stick it inside. That would be funny. Just like the note in a bottle that a shipwrecked man tosses out into the sea.

S.O.S.!!! Save me!!!

Actually, now that I think about it, that's not funny at all. Because I don't think anyone is going to save me. There's no cavalry riding to my rescue. There's no ship on my horizon.

God, I need a dip.

And I'm rambling again. Ain't gonna finish this at all if I keep that up.

So . . .

Carl and I were silent for a long time after Kevin finished telling us his story. Our coffee had grown cold and so had the house. I shivered and rolled the sleeves of my flannel shirt down to stay warm. Daylight, or the gray light that passed for it, was fading fast, and the fog grew thicker, pressing against the kitchen windows like a solid white wall. Sarah had joined us in the kitchen halfway through the story and she was quiet as well.

Finally, I stirred. I reached for both of their hands, took them in my own, and said softly, "I'm very sorry for what both of you have lost."

"Thanks," Kevin said. "That means a lot. It's hard thinking about it."

Sarah gave my hand a gentle squeeze and said nothing.

Carl cleared his throat, scooted his chair back, and returned to his post at the window in the kitchen door—the door that led out onto the earthworm covered carport.

"How about some more coffee?" I offered.

"Awesome." Kevin sat back and cracked his neck joints. "A cup of coffee would really hit the spot."

Sarah nodded. "Yeah, I could use some, too. Want me to get it?"

"No," I said. "You sit right back in that chair. I'm not so old that I can't fix a cup of coffee for my guests."

With his index finger, Carl drew a smiley face in the condensation on the window. Then he added two little antennae.

"Anything moving out there?" Kevin asked him.

"Nope, but I can't see more than a few feet on account of this fog. Can't even make out the carport. It's as thick as Rose's potato soup out there."

The thought of Rose's potato soup made my stomach grumble. I filled the kettle with bottled water and then put it on top of the kerosene heater to boil. I had decided long ago to dispense with my resolve to conserve kerosene. The way things were going, we probably wouldn't be around much longer anyway and the conservation wouldn't matter. While we waited for the kettle to whistle, I got out a bag of potato chips, some beef jerky, and what was left of the stew, and served them up.

"Sorry," I said. "It's not exactly a meal fit for a king."

"It's better than anything we've had in a long while," Sarah said around a mouthful of cold stew. "These vegetables are great. I wasn't hungry earlier when we ate, but now I'm starved."

I scratched my whiskered throat and watched them eat. "Earlier, you mentioned something you called 'the White Fuzz.' You said it grew on people?"

Kevin nodded. "That's right. Horrible stuff. Completely consumes you until there's nothing left."

"I think I saw something like that down yonder in the hollow." I pointed out the window. "Yesterday morning, when I was out looking for teaberry leaves. A pale white fungus. Never saw anything like it before."

Sarah's tone was one of concern. "You didn't touch it, did you?"

"No. I didn't like the looks of it, so I left it alone. But I saw it growing on a deer, too, and he looked sickly. It was growing up his legs and hindquarters. Kind of like mold or moss."

Kevin wiped his mouth with his shirt sleeve. "That's the White Fuzz, alright. Good thing you didn't touch it, or you'd be covered by now. The stuff works fast. Consumes its host."

Carl turned away from the window. "Do you know what it is? Where it came from?"

The two young people shook their heads.

"It's just one more consequence of the rain," Sarah said. "Like the worms and everything else."

The kettle started to whistle, and I pulled it off the heater and filled their mugs. Kevin took a sip and smacked his lips in satisfaction. I got up and fetched the sugar. Then I turned on some music. The soft sounds of Ferlin Husky's "Wings of a Dove" filled the house.

"So what happened next?" Carl asked. "Did Leviathan come back? And how did you folks get from Baltimore to here?"

"Carl," I said, "maybe they're tired of talking about it. Can't it wait till tomorrow?"

"Well, I reckon."

"Curiosity killed the cat," I reminded him.

"Yeah, but satisfaction brought him back."

"We can tell you the rest," Kevin said. "That's okay. It happened, you know? As incredible as it all sounds, it really happened. Not talking about it won't make that any less so. It's like they say in that old Led Zepplin song. 'Upon us all a little rain must fall.' But I would like to wash up first, if that's okay?"

"Sure." I blew on my coffee to cool it. "I laid a towel and washcloth out for you in the bathroom. You'll find them next to the sink. The washbasin is full of clean water, and there's a bar of soap next to it."

"But I want to know what happened," Carl said. "Listen, you can't wash up now. This is like a Saturday matinee cliffhanger!"

"For crying out loud, Carl," I spat, disgusted with him. "You're worse than a little kid."

"Sarah, you want to take over?" Kevin asked.

She brushed her long, blond hair from her eyes. "Yeah. I'm okay to talk about it now. Those worms outside just brought it all back for a while."

I showed Kevin to the bathroom and when I came back, Ferlin Husky had been replaced with B.J. Thomas's "Another Somebody Done Somebody Wrong Song." B.J. wailed that he missed his baby. I missed mine, too, and I was starting to crave a dip again as well.

Sarah hummed along with the tune. "My mother used to listen to this when I was little."

"Was she a country music fan?" I asked.

She shrugged. "I don't know. I guess so. I don't remember much about her, really. She died when I was eight years old."

She pushed her empty bowl away, drained her mug of coffee, and relieved Carl at the window. Carl sat down at the table.

Sarah stared out into the fog for a moment, gathering her thoughts, and then she began.

"After the creature, Leviathan, as Kevin insists on calling it, took Lori, it disappeared. We didn't see it again. But we were still in trouble. Leviathan had destroyed most of the hotel during its assault, and the upper levels were flooding fast. The water was rising, and within a few hours, the nineteenth floor was underwater, and it was spilling into the twentieth. Plus, it was still trickling down from the roof, through the cracks in the ceiling and the walls. We could feel the building shake every time a strong wave hit it. We had to get out. It was either that or stay there and let the whole thing fall down around us.

"Kevin was in bad shape. He just sat there in the garden, and we couldn't get him to move. He just kept humming 'Raindrops Keep Falling on My Head.' When he talked, all he'd say was that he was waiting for Lori to come back, over and over. He'd really cut his hands up bad on the glass, and he was losing blood. But eventually we got him to understand the situation and he snapped out of it. The monster had destroyed the raft, but since Salty and I had watched Lee build it, we had a pretty good idea of how to make another one. I guess we could have swam for it, found another building that was safe, but after what we'd just been through, none of us wanted to swim in that water, not knowing what was lurking beneath the surface.

"For the next hour, Salty and I gathered materials and put another raft together while Kevin bandaged his hands and half-heartedly salvaged supplies. By the time we cast off from the roof, the water had flooded the twentieth floor and was rising to the top of the hotel. We weren't even a mile away when one entire corner of the building sheered off and collapsed into the ocean."

"It's a good thing you made it out," Carl said. "Sounds like it was just in the nick of time, too."

"Yeah, it was. But we weren't out of the woods. Not by a long shot. The current pulled us out to sea, away from the city. We drifted for two days and we didn't have paddles or a sail or anything to guide us. We couldn't even be sure of which direction the raft was drifting. The rain blotted out the sun and moon and the stars, so we couldn't navigate using those. I think we drifted southeast and then farther south, before coming back in over where land used to be. The tides tossed us around. The whole time, we worried about running into more mermaids, or what we'd do if Leviathan decided it was still hungry and came back for more. Luckily, we didn't see anything other than seagulls and a few schools of fish. A shark passed pretty close at one point, but we scared it away by shouting at it. And we saw an albatross, which Salty said was a good omen."

Carl interrupted her. "Do you really think that squid thing was Leviathan from the Bible?"

"Kevin sure did," Sarah said, shrugging. "It's as good a name as any, I guess. To be honest, Mr. Seaton, I never really believed in God or the Bible. I'm still not sure I do, completely. Despite what I said earlier, about God breaking His promise, I don't believe that what's happening outside is some sort of divine judgment. The rains are just the consequences of an environmental collapse; an apocalypse that we put into motion with the start of the industrial revolution. We're humans. We fuck things up. That's what we do, and that's all we ever did."

"And that's where we disagree," said Kevin, stepping back into the kitchen. He smelled like soap, and his skin was red from scrubbing. His hair was still damp, but he looked like he felt better. "Sarah and I have argued about this at length. The greenhouse effect doesn't explain what's happening, and scientists had pretty much said so before the news stations stopped broadcasting. It doesn't explain things like the White Fuzz or these creatures, either."

Carl leaned back in his chair. "So what does explain it?"

Sarah rolled her eyes. "Kevin thinks this whole situation, everything that's happening, was caused by black magic."

"Well think about it," he insisted. "During the raid, the Satanists had a spell book, the *Daemonolateria*—whatever the hell that means—and supposedly they used it to summon up that squid thing. If they could do that, then doesn't it make sense that they cast other spells too? It makes sense that they cast some sort of spell to cause all of this. Their leader told us as much, during the raid. How else do you explain the weather? One day, it starts raining all over the world, all at the same time. The Sahara, the Alps, London, Paris, New York, Baghdad—even in fucking Antarctica. That's just not natural. Almost overnight, the entire world starts flooding. Storm surges stronger than anything a normal hurricane could generate wipe out most of the world's coastal cities. Tsunamis eradicate entire islands—millions and millions of people dead in a matter of days. Not weeks, but *days*. Does that seem scientifically plausible to you? And what about the mermaid?"

"We still don't know that's what it really was," Sarah said. "They say that manatees look like—"

"Oh, for Christ's sake, Sarah! A fucking manatee? Come on. You saw it just like I did. You were there. It controlled you for a second, too, the same as the rest of us. Pull your head out of your ass! If it wasn't a mermaid that killed Nate, then what was it?"

253

She didn't have an answer for him. Instead, she turned away and stared out into the mist.

"Forget about the mermaid for a minute," Kevin continued. "What about everything else we've seen? What about those worms outside? You believe in those, don't you?"

"I'm afraid to believe," Sarah whispered. "Because I'm afraid of what that will mean."

Now, it was Kevin's turn to stay silent.

"Well," I said, trying to ease the tension, "I do believe in the good book, and I've let the Lord guide me all of my life—especially now. But I don't think the rain or those worms out there or anything else that's happened is a form of divine judgment. God just doesn't work that way."

Kevin scoffed, his laughter short and sharp. "Hello? Sodom and Gomorrah? The great flood? Any of that ring a bell with you, man?"

"Sure," I said. "Maybe He did in the Old Testament, but not anymore. That's why He gave the world His son. But look, I don't want to preach or get into a theological discussion here. This ain't the time or place for that, and we're all pretty tired."

"Sorry." Kevin held up his hands in apology. "You're right. But if this isn't a manmade ecological disaster, God's final judgment, or some form of black magic holocaust, then what is it?"

"I don't know about the rain," I said. "But I do think that those worms are natural."

Kevin sighed. "Then where did they come from, Teddy? Why haven't we encountered them before?"

THE CONQUEROR WORMS

I took a sip of coffee and fought back another nicotine craving. "I'm no expert, but I've read about scientists finding worms in some awfully strange places. At the bottom of the Marianas Trench, feeding on whale bones, and even inside of volcanoes. Who knows what lies at the center of our planet? They discover new species every year. Maybe we didn't know about them before, but these particular worms have probably been around for a lot longer than we have. Maybe they've been hiding deep below the surface. Now, conditions have finally forced our two species to encounter each other for the first time."

"But there would have been some kind of fossil record," Sarah said. "Something to let us know they were here."

I shrugged. "Maybe. Maybe not. But they're here now. And I don't even reckon we've seen the really big ones yet."

Carl stiffened, his soup spoon hovering halfway to his mouth. "What do you mean, Teddy? That thing at the crash site was big as a bus."

"You saw that mess out there on my carport. All those night crawlers? At first, I assumed the rain had driven them to the surface like that. Now, I think it might have been their big brothers that forced them topside instead. Animals behave strangely before an earthquake or a tsunami. Maybe this is something like that. Maybe they were fleeing the larger ones. And if those big worms we encountered today pushed the little worms above ground, then what do you suppose is forcing the bigger ones up now?"

"Something like Leviathan?" Kevin asked.

I nodded. "Exactly. There are more things in heaven and earth than are dreamt of in your philosophy."

Sarah looked surprised. "I didn't take you for a Shakespeare fan, Teddy. You've read *Hamlet*?"

"Only three times. I prefer *The Tempest* and *A Midsummer Night's Dream*, myself. I was always partial to Puck. He was a funny one."

"Damn nonsense," Carl said. He sat his spoon down and stared at his half-full bowl of stew. "So, if you're right, Teddy, and there's an even bigger worm somewhere out there, then how do we fight it?"

"I don't know," I admitted. "But I reckon we ought to start planning for it now. The Bible says Leviathan was big enough to swallow Jonah whole, and from what you've told us, I'd say that's so. Just like the worm that swallowed Salty and Earl today. But as huge as that thing was, there's bound to be something bigger on the way. And I don't want to be here when it shows up. The problem is, I don't know where we can go. We're on top of the mountain. Everything below us is flooded. Only place higher than here is the ranger station up on Bald Knob, and we don't know what the situation is there. It could be worse than here. Those worms could be all over the place—or worse than the ones here."

The others didn't have any ideas, either. Carl picked his teeth, Sarah looked at her broken nails, and Kevin stared at the coffee mug in his hands, the one with WORLD'S GREATEST GRANDPA emblazoned on it, that the kids had gotten me for Father's Day five years ago.

After a moment, I asked Sarah to continue with her

story, if only to take our minds off the present situation for a little while.

"Well, like I said, we drifted on the raft for two days. None of us slept very much, and the salt in the air started to blister our skin and lips. We were cold and wet and miserable, and we didn't have anything to keep the rain off of us except for our raincoats, and all three of us got sick. Salty developed a really nasty cough, deep down inside his chest. Kevin and I started to worry that it might be pneumonia. He started running a fever. Became delirious, babbling about Krakens and sea gods and something he called the soul cages. He said they existed at the bottom of the sea, and held the souls of sailors who'd died. He begged us not to let him end up in one. Then, on the third day, Cornwell found us."

"That's the fella who was piloting the chopper?" I asked, remembering how the seatbelt had cut him into three pieces.

"Yeah. He was a traffic reporter for a television station in Pittsburgh. He'd been flying from place to place, wherever he could find fuel and dry land, mostly. Most helicopters need to refuel every two hours, but his was specially equipped to stay in the air during media emergencies. It held enough fuel for a five-hour flight, and he had maps of every fueling station along the East Coast."

"Is there much dry land left?" Carl asked.

"Mountaintop islands like this," Sarah said. "But that's about it."

I tried picturing our mountain as an island, seen from above, and found that I couldn't.

Sarah continued. "Cornwell's brother, Simon, was with him. They were looking for fuel when they spotted us in the water. By then, we'd drifted far from any recognizable landmark, but there were still occasional rooftops or antennae sticking up from the ocean. We paddled over to a water tower and climbed on top, and they managed to get the helicopter in close enough to pick us up."

Kevin grinned. "Remember how Salty was scared of the rotors? He thought they'd cut our heads off."

"He crouched down as low as he could go," Sarah smiled, remembering, "and scrambled onboard. Turns out he was afraid of flying. I think he would have been happier to stay on the raft. But him and Cornwell hit it off, and pretty soon he got over it. We wasted a lot of fuel, just flying around and looking for survivors, but Cornwell had the luck of the devil, because he kept finding refueling stations that were still above water. Eventually, we decided to try for Norfolk, Virginia. Obviously, the city wasn't there anymore. It's gone, along with the rest of the coastline. But Salty figured that all of those ships docked in Norfolk and Little Creek and Yorktown would have to go out to sea when the water started rising. Otherwise, they'd have been bashed against the piers. Now that the wave threat was over, he thought they'd still be in the area. Salty said that if we could find an LPD or an LPH that was still seaworthy, we could land on their flight deck. Maybe even a big carrier, like the *Coral Sea* or the *Ronald Reagan*. I guess Cornwell wasn't the best navigator, because we ended up way off course. Instead of being over Maryland and Virginia, we ended up in West Virginia. We were almost out of fuel and supplies when we found a dry spot on top of Cass Mountain."

"That's where the Greenbank Observatory is," Carl said. "We've gone hunting up there a few times. Teddy's from there, originally."

Sarah arched her eyebrows in surprise. "Really?"

"I was born in Greenbank," I told them. "Lived there all my childhood, in a little Jenny Lynd type house with a lean-to kitchen. Of course, it's not there anymore. The old home place burned down years ago, and Greenbank's a lot bigger place these days. But it's nice to know that the town survived the flood and is still there."

Sarah scowled. "No offense to your birthplace, but I wish it wasn't there. We got stuck at the observatory for two weeks. There's this weird cult that has taken over there. They call themselves the B'nai Elohim. I think that means 'divine beings' in Hebrew. At least, that's what their leader said. I thought we'd left the crazies behind us, but I was wrong. They're everywhere these days. The B'nai Elohim weren't like the Satanists back in Baltimore. They didn't worship sea monsters. But they were just as crazy."

"How so?" Carl asked.

"They believed that an alien race of superintelligent geneticists from outer space created humans by fooling around with primate DNA. And they insisted that flying saucers were going to land at Greenbank and rescue them and that we could go along for the ride. They said that this had happened on earth once before and that an alien named Noah rescued everybody in his spaceship."

I shook my head in disbelief.

"They didn't try to hurt us," Sarah continued. "Not at first, anyway. We knew they were whacked, crazy I mean, but we needed food and fuel and they had it and were willing to share. There was awful stuff going on. Incest and possibly child abuse, though we couldn't confirm it. But we stayed, desperate circumstances and all that. Then three of the men tried to . . ."

She sighed, clasping Rose's sweater around her.

I tried to soothe her. "Listen, you don't have to talk about it if you don't want to."

"No, it's okay." She took a deep breath. "Three of them tried to rape me. They came into my room in the middle of the night, and when I woke up, they were leaning over me. They had my arms and legs pinned to the bed and all three of were naked. I don't remember their faces, but I can still hear their voices." She paused. "Their voices are burned into my mind. One of them had a really hairy back and he had a tattoo of a snake. A king cobra. Isn't it weird? I don't remember what they looked like, but I remember that. I managed to get loose and I broke one of their noses and fractured the arm of another. But they had guns and mine was sitting in the corner of the room, out of reach. It might as well have been back in Baltimore. And I screamed for help. Simon and Kevin came to help me."

"Simon?" Carl asked.

"Cornwell's brother," she reminded him. "They busted into the room, and the men shot Simon while Kevin got me away from them. There was nothing we could do. They shot him in the stomach, and the blood was pouring out. He put his hands over the wound, and the blood started bubbling between the cracks of his fingers."

She shuddered with the memory.

"Simon told us to go on—that he'd hold them off. But then he was dead, just like that, and the men were jumping over his body. Kevin killed all three of them as they were chasing us. We found Salty and Cornwell, and made it to the chopper, but just barely. Salty shot one of the guards, and we took off."

Carl asked, "While ya'll were on Cass Mountain, you didn't see anything like those worms outside?"

"Not at all," Kevin said. "That's why I thought maybe all the weirdness was just confined to the ocean. Obviously, it's not."

"We left the observatory," Sarah continued. "We didn't have much fuel, but Cornwell had been studying a tourist map during our stay. He figured we could land at some place called Bald Knob, if it was still above water, hole up in the Ranger tower, and figure out what to do next. But right before we reached Bald Knob, we crashed in your backyard instead."

"Courtesy of crazy old Earl Harper," I muttered. "May he rot in pieces."

"Rose wouldn't want you to speak ill of the dead," Carl said, "but then again, she didn't have no love for Earl, either."

"Who was he, anyway?" Kevin asked.

"Earl?" I whistled through my false teeth, leaned back in the chair, and drained my coffee. "Earl was a local. What you'd call a good old boy, except that there wasn't anything good about him. He lived over yonder in that shack his whole life, except for a brief stint in the Marines. He got kicked out about two months after boot camp. Never did find out for certain what he did, but I've heard he kept threatening suicide and that he even cut his wrists a few times; little, superficial cuts that didn't amount to anything. Basically, he just wanted attention.

"Anyway, Carl and I had a friend named Hobie Crowley. Hobie smoked all his life and got lung cancer about ten years ago. He didn't have much family, so he checked into the V.A. hospital over in Beckley. Died there, too, and now he's buried up at Arlington. While he was in the hospital, Hobie met a fella who had served with Earl in the army, and Hobie told us about it when Carl and I went to visit. According to this guy, Earl's unit got tired of his fake suicide attempts. He was disrupting things, and all of them were paying the price for his foolishness. Their master sergeant told them to handle it for themselves, so that's what they decided to do. One night in the barracks, they all got a hold of Earl, dragged him into the showers and cut his wrists for real. He was back here soon after that, living with his parents until they died and staying on over there ever since.

"He lived off welfare mostly, just like half the rest of this state's population. See, there's just not much work in West Virginia, unless you can farm or fix cars. That's what Earl did. He fixed junked cars and sold them for beer money, poached a deer or two or five to put grub on the table. He was your standard redneck hillbilly. Except that Earl was crazy, too."

"If he was so crazy, how'd he live this long?" Kevin

asked. "I'm surprised somebody didn't try to help him, have him committed. Or else put him out of his misery for good."

"Oh, folks have tried."

"They did?" Kevin snorted. "Not hard enough, then."

"Rose and I, and Carl, and most of the other folks in Punkin' Center tried to help Earl at one time or another. But we gave up. It was like feeding a stray dog. You're nice to him until he bites your hand, and then you don't feed him anymore. The sheriff was out at Earl's place off and on for the last ten years or so, straightening him out on one thing or another. The Secret Service even paid him a visit one time."

Kevin sat up straight. "For what? Was he one of these militia nuts or something? The Sons of the Constitution? Did he post something threatening online?"

"No, nothing like that," I chuckled, "though it wouldn't have surprised me. I know that Earl thought Timothy McVeigh got a raw deal; thought he was a real patriot. And Earl wouldn't have known how to use a computer if his life had depended on it."

"Well what was the Secret Service checking him out for?"

"Monica Lewinsky, believe it or not."

"Monica Lewinsky?" Sarah's brow crinkled. "The girl that banged President Clinton in the Oval Office?"

"The same. During that whole big stink, when Ken Starr was investigating the White House and all of that, Earl became convinced that Bill Clinton was the Antichrist. Said he even had the Bible verses to prove it. Now mind you, before President Clinton, Earl swore up and down that it was Gorbachev. Remember that birthmark on top of Gorbachev's head? Earl thought that wine stain hid the number of the beast."

"Six-six-six," Kevin whispered.

"Wasn't there a movie about that?" Sarah asked. "*The Omen*?"

"Maybe," I said. "Never much cared for those horror movies. I was big on John Wayne, and Laurel and Hardy. And a few of—"

Something splattered against the window with a wet thump and Sarah skittered away from the door. It was a wad of slime, clear and viscous. It clung to the glass like phlegm and slowly started to dribble down the pane.

All four of us stared at the slime, and then at each other. In the silence, we heard that now familiar hissing sound—the whistling of a worm, and somewhere close by, too. Kevin and I both ran to the window, but the fog concealed everything.

"Do you see any worms?" Kevin whispered.

"Nope." My heart hammered in my chest. I turned to Sarah. "Did you see anything come up to the window?"

"No, there was nothing. Just the rain and the fog."

"Then they can spit, apparently," Kevin mused. "Maybe that slime is like acid or poison or something."

I shook my head. "No, I've touched some it, had it on my fingers, and it didn't do anything to me."

"Sure smelled awful, though," Carl added, making a face. "Stank to high heaven."

"That it did," I agreed. "Like fish and chlorine, put in a blender and mixed together."

We listened for a while longer, but the noise didn't

repeat itself and there were no more spit attacks. I took Sarah's place at the door and continued with my story.

"Anyway, Earl reckoned that Bill Clinton was the Antichrist, and before him, Gorbachev. He figured the birthmark on Gorbachev's forehead was hiding a six-six-six. And before that, it was Henry Kissinger and Ronald Reagan. His troubles with the Secret Service started in the middle of the Clinton impeachment hearings. One night, Earl showed up drunk down at the VFW post in Lewisburg, claiming that if Clinton weren't stopped, God would destroy America for its wickedness. That got him some applause from the hard-line Rush Limbaugh junkies that do their drinking in there, but not much else. So then Earl wrote an angry letter to Clinton and mailed it off to the White House. He even included his return address. I don't know for sure what he said, but I guess he made some threats and I guess they took it seriously, because one sunny morning in April, two black SUVs came cruising through Renick, crossed over the Greenbrier River, and started up the mountain to Punkin' Center. We all got on the horn with each other as they passed by, because everybody knew who they were. You can tell, if only by the official government plates on the back of the cars. They cruised up the dirt road out yonder and eight federal agents knocked on Earl's door, paying him a less than friendly visit. I guess that eventually they decided he wasn't a threat, because nothing else ever happened. For a while after that, Earl calmed down, but soon, he was back to normal. He started up again when Gore and Bush ended up in court over the election, and some folks called the Secret Service, but they must have determined he was harmless. Just a lot of hot air."

"Boy," Sarah said, "did they miss the call on that one or what?"

"They sure did." Carl nodded. "Earl got away with talking crazy like that, but I have to fill out a damn stack of forms and wait three days every time I buy a new hunting rifle for deer season. There's no justice in this world."

I grinned at Sarah and Kevin. "Don't mind Carl. He's just mad because they wouldn't renew his hunting license last year, on account of his eyesight."

"That's because they're a pack of idiots." He frowned. "Ain't nothing wrong with my eyes, and I can see fine to shoot."

"I hope so," I said. "Because something tells me there'll be plenty of shooting before this thing is done."

Carl's face grew sullen and grim. I'd never seen him look older than he did at that moment. Or more frightened.

The conversation was sporadic after that, and we remained on topics other than the weather and what the rains had brought with them. I needed a dip bad, and I had to fight to stay awake. I was exhausted, that type of weariness that creeps into your bones and makes your eyes itch. The coffee wasn't doing anything to help me, either. My daughter, Tracy, had given me some coffee and chicory that she picked up while on vacation in New Orleans. I hadn't touched the stuff, because it made me jittery, and the doctor had told me to stay off of it. But I seemed to recall that it had more caffeine than regular instant coffee did, and wondered if I could rig up some way to brew it on top of the heater. Doctor's orders be damned. And I was already jittery. The can was down in the cellar's pantry.

I grabbed the halogen flashlight, clicked it on, and opened the door that led downstairs to the cellar. Darkness greeted me, along with a familiar smell. That wet, fishy stench was in my basement now, although more muted than it had been outside.

I swallowed and suddenly Sarah was there behind me with the pistol in hand.

"Need any help?" she asked.

"Sure," I said, a bit too eagerly. "But let's be careful. You smell it too, don't you?"

She nodded. "You think they're inside the house?"

"Not yet. But I reckon they're close."

We started down, and my joints creaked along with the old wooden stairs.

An inch of water covered the concrete floor, and pretty much everything that hadn't been sitting up on pallets was now ruined. Forgetting that Sarah was with me, I cursed, and then blushed when she giggled.

I walked around, shining the light into corners and surveying the damage. A three-inch crack had appeared in one cinder block wall. The fissure ran the entire length of the wall, floor to ceiling. The floor was cracked, too, and the washing machine leaned to one side. I noticed that the concrete had begun to sink beneath it.

Sarah chuckled. "I hope you have flood insurance."

"Reckon they'll pay up?" I tried to play along, though my heart wasn't in it. The damage was new, and hadn't been here the day before. With the amount of water that was seeping in, I'd have my very own indoor swimming pool within a matter of days. The loss of some of the personal items that had been stored downstairs was hard to take as well—boxes of toys from when the kids were young, old photo albums, and holiday decorations. All of it was waterlogged and damaged. The word processor that the kids had given me was still safe, but the particle-board desk it sat on was starting to puff up. That fake wood stuff soaks up water like a sponge.

"You okay, Teddy?"

"Yeah, I'm all right. Just makes me mad, is all. Some of this stuff was junk, but a lot of it was irreplaceable. Wish we'd had an attic here, rather than a basement."

Other than the cracks in the floor and the water, I didn't see any damage. The basement still seemed relatively sturdy. We made our way over to the root cellar, which was separated from the rest of the cellar by plywood and panel walls and a sturdy wooden door. The floor inside the root cellar was just dirt and I had a bad moment as we opened the door. I was expecting to shine the light on an earthworm, sticking up from a hole in the floor. But it was clear, and we stepped inside.

"What do we need, anyway?" Sarah asked.

"There's a can of chicory coffee down here. I just wanted to grab that. It's got more caffeine in it than the stuff we've been drinking."

"You needed me to help you carry a can of coffee?"

"No," I admitted, lowering my voice. "I needed you

to come along because I'm a scared old man who wasn't sure what he'd find down here."

Sarah smiled and gave my hand a squeeze. "That's okay, Teddy. Don't be embarrassed. I'm scared too."

"It wasn't just that. You make for a lot prettier company than Carl or Kevin do. So I let you come along."

She laughed, and the basement seemed to brighten with the sound. "I like you, Teddy. You remind me of my grandfather."

I smiled. "Then he must have been a marvelous man. And like I said already, you remind me a lot of my granddaughter. She'd have liked you."

"It feels good to be here. After all Kevin and I have seen, this feels . . . normal."

"Well, I'm awfully glad you folks are here, too. I mean, I'm sorry about the circumstances, and about what happened to your friends. But you don't know how grateful I am to be around people again. I was so lonely. Thought I might be the last man on earth."

I cleared my throat before she could reply, and tried to change the subject. I shined the flashlight beam over the rows and rows of jars. Rose had canned every autumn since we'd been married, and during the Y2K craze, she'd canned even more, convinced that civilization was going to collapse and we'd run short on food.

"Your wife's handiwork?" Sarah asked.

"Oh, yes. Rose loved to can. I always had to have a garden, just so she could can vegetables every fall. Reckon we might as well take some food back up with us."

I grabbed mason jars full of green beans, beets,

strawberries, peas, collard greens, corn, and squash, all grown in our garden, and applesauce made from the fruit grown on the tree in our backyard—the tree that the rains had now uprooted. The cans I'd taken from Dave and Nancy Simmons's place were still upstairs, and I figured these would supplement them well. I found the coffee and chicory, too, and put everything in a cardboard box. Sarah reached down into the potato bin and pulled out a few big ones that hadn't rotted yet and then grabbed a jar off the shelf and looked at me in a mixture of puzzlement and disgust.

"Is this what I think it is?"

"Deer meat." I nodded. "From a six-point buck I got last year. You should have seen how long it took Carl and me to drag it out of the woods. Don't know if you noticed, but we're not exactly spring chickens."

"I'll bet you were tired," she said, and as if to stress her point, she yawned.

"You can go on back upstairs if you want. I'll finish things down here."

"I don't mind. I can wait."

I grabbed a few more items, and then we waded through the ankle deep water and made our way back up the stairs. The flashlight beam started to falter, and I reminded myself to change the batteries. Wouldn't do to be without light if those things attacked us during the night.

Could they get in? I wondered. They could certainly tunnel well enough; Carl and I had seen proof of that. But could they dig through a concrete floor? I thought about what we'd found at Dave and Nancy's house, remembering the destruction and that bright red smear of blood on the wall. Then I recalled Steve Porter's hunting cabin and Carl's own missing house. Yes, I decided, they could indeed tunnel through concrete—or at least, dig around it enough so that a building collapsed into the ground.

How did you protect yourself against something like that? The answer was that you didn't. There was no way.

So I tried to put it out of my mind.

When Sarah and I got back to the kitchen, Carl had assumed watch duties again and was telling Kevin about how he'd gotten poison ivy over every inch of his body after he lay down in a patch of it with Beverly Thompson back when we were teenagers. Both of them were laughing, and Kevin had tears streaming down his face as he clutched his stomach. The sound of it chased my fears away.

I fashioned a crude filtering system out of paper towels and used it to brew the chicory. It was nasty stuff, sort of like drinking hot tar mixed with cat piss, but Kevin and Sarah seemed to enjoy it. Carl took one sip, made a face, and left his mug untouched.

We agreed that it was pretty much pointless to stand at the window and keep watch. The darkness outside was overwhelming, and we couldn't see more than a few feet beyond the carport. The little worms were still there and I couldn't believe my eyes when I saw their growing numbers. They were two feet deep in most places now, the pile so high that the ones on the edges of the carport spilled out into the wet grass. The ones around my truck came up over the tires, and were working on covering the bumper.

"If things ever get back to normal," I laughed, "I'm going to gather those things up and open a bait and tackle shop down by the river."

"Not me," Carl said. "After what we saw today, I'm never baiting a hook again."

I wondered again where they were all coming from and what could be chasing them to the top. Was I right in my hypothesis? Was it something worse than what we'd already seen?

We moved into the living room and talked for a bit more, but the yawns were contagious and soon we were all rubbing our eyes. Exhausted, we agreed that we seemed to be relatively safe for the moment and decided to discuss our escape plans in detail in the morning, and try to come up with some other options. Then we all retired for the night. Carl took one bedroom and Sarah took the other. Kevin sprawled out on the couch and I fixed him up comfy with some extra blankets and pillows. We posted a watch, just in case.

Carl drew the first shift, which was uneventful. I relieved him at midnight. I didn't want to disturb Kevin, so I sat in the kitchen doing my crossword puzzle in the soft light of the kerosene lantern. I was still stuck on a three-letter word for peccadillo, something with an "i" in the middle, when I heard the soft whisper of flannel behind me.

"Sin," Sarah said over my shoulder. "S-I-N. Three letter word for peccadillo."

"Well I'll be," I whispered, grinning in the lantern's glow. "I would have never figured that out for myself. Been trying for days. I'm mighty glad you folks dropped in."

We both laughed quietly, and then a troubled shadow passed over her face. She stared out the window, in the direction of the crash site. We couldn't see the wreckage. It was too dark. But it was there, just the same.

"I'm sorry," I said. "That was a bad joke. I didn't mean 'dropped' of course."

"No, don't apologize. It's okay."

In the living room, Kevin stirred uneasily on the couch. He called out for Lori and then turned his head and went back to sleep.

"Poor guy," I muttered. "He'll live with that for the rest of his life."

Sarah nodded.

We sat in silence for a few minutes, listening to the rain because there was nothing else to listen to, except for the occasional snore from Carl, drifting down the hallway like a ghost.

"Why don't you go back to bed," Sarah said gently. "I'll take watch for awhile."

"Oh, that's all right," I replied. "I haven't been sleeping too good anyway. It's the nicotine withdrawal. Gives me nightmares."

"I can't sleep, either. I dreamed about Salty and Cornwell and the crash."

"Well, I reckon we can keep each other company then."

"It's quiet," Sarah said. "You'd think the sound of the rain would lull us to sleep, but it doesn't."

"Nothing friendly or comforting about that rain," I agreed. "It's unnatural."

"So you definitely agree with Kevin's theory?"

"I've been thinking about it some more since dinner.

I agree that these events weren't the result of global warming or some other ecological disaster. As for the spell book he mentioned, it could be, I guess. There's weird stuff in this world. We've all seen it. Goes back to prehistory. People in the Bible practiced black magic. I don't pretend to understand everything in our universe, but I know there are things that science can't explain. Call it paranormal or supernatural or whatever, but it exists. My own mother had a book called *The Long, Lost Friend*. Lots of folks in the Appalachian Mountains had a copy back in the old days. It was a spell book, but mostly harmless stuff—how to cure warts and deworm your cattle and protect yourself from the evil eye—things like that. Folks back then, even God-fearing Christians, swore by it. All I know is the stuff worked. I remember one time, when I was little, we were all out chopping wood. My granddaddy cut his leg with the ax and my grandmother put her hands over the wound, said a few words out of the book, followed them with a prayer, and the bleeding stopped—just like that. So it did work. You don't see it much these days, because now everything is explained and cured by science. Maybe that's why we're in the mess we're in now—because of our reliance on science. Maybe we lost touch with something else. Our spiritual side. The part that still believes in—and needs—magic."

Sarah stared at me with a bemused look. "Why Teddy, I didn't know you were a philosopher, too."

I laughed quietly. "Only one in Punkin' Center, unless you count young Ernie Whitt or Old Man Haubner down in Renick—and he ain't been the same since his horse kicked him in the head."

"And where are they now?" she asked. "Ernie and Haubner?"

I shrugged. "Gone off with the National Guard. Dead, maybe. I don't know. During your travels from Baltimore to here, did you see any signs that our government was helping folks? FEMA settlements or tent cities or anything like that?"

"No. There was nothing. There's not a lot of dry ground left, at least in the places we flew over. Like I said earlier, just the mountaintops. Everything is flooded."

"And it's still raining," I said. "Guess it's just a matter of time before the waters reach us."

"Unless the worms do first."

"Well, I don't think much else will happen tonight, but just in case, you ought to get some sleep."

"You need it more than I do," she said. "Why don't you go to bed? Let me take over?"

"No. If I go to bed now, I'll just lay there having a nicotine fit."

She laughed softly. "I thought Salty had been bad when it came to needing a cigarette."

I stopped breathing. During his story, Kevin had mentioned that Salty was a smoker, but I'd forgotten all about it.

Could there be cigarettes outside?

"I reckon he ran out of them, too." I was on the edge of my seat, waiting for her response.

"Salty? Oh no. We raided a gas station in Woodstock that was still above water, and he hauled out as many cartons as he could carry."

"Huh. Good for him. He thought ahead. Wish I'd done that." I kept up the small talk and tried not to give myself away, to reveal what I was thinking. Because what I was thinking wasn't just crazy. It was downright suicidal.

And I was going to attempt it anyway.

I waited a few minutes and then I said, "Begging your pardon, Sarah, but I've got to go to the bathroom."

"Out there?"

"Well, just out onto the back porch. Don't want to use the carport, on account of all those worms on it. But the back porch is close enough to the house. It should be safe."

"Couldn't you just pee in the sink or something?"

"At my age? Shoot, I'd be lucky if I could aim it that high. Besides, that's just downright unsanitary."

"Well," she said reluctantly, "just be careful. I'll wait here and stand guard."

"Okay. Be back in a bit. This might take me a few minutes. And no peeking. It doesn't always work as quick as it did when I was younger. I think he gets stage fright sometimes. Especially if there's a pretty young woman staring at him from the window."

She giggled. "I'll watch through the window pointing out at your carport. How's that?"

"Much better."

I put on my rain gear and walked to the back door. The fog was thick and I couldn't see more than a few feet away from the house. I listened, but the only sound was the rain. I checked the rifle and made sure a round was chambered.

Taking a deep breath, I stepped out onto the porch and closed the door behind me. It wasn't just black outside. It was obsidian. With no power or lights, and with the stars and the moon blocked out by the perpetual haze, the darkness was a solid thing—a living creature. It seemed to cling to me. Combined with the fog, it made sight almost impossible. I'd forgotten the flashlight on purpose, because I didn't want Sarah to know what I was doing—and because I didn't want to attract the attention of anything lurking out there in the night. Now I wished for the flashlight, for a lighter, for anything to push the darkness back.

"Teddy Garnett," I said to myself under my breath, "you are a damned old fool, and you're about to get yourself killed."

I stepped off the porch and my boots sank into the mud with a squelching sound.

"Well, I'm tired of being old and I always was a fool."

I started for the crash site.

"And I don't have much of a life left anyway."

The raindrops echoed in my ears.

CHAPTER TWELVE

I glanced back at the house to make sure that Sarah wasn't watching me from the window, but I could barely see it, even from a few feet away. The heavy fog and the darkness had swallowed up the house as if it had never been there. I tried to breathe, but the lump in my throat was too big. I don't know that I've ever been more scared in my life than I was at that moment, but it was too late now. The plan was already in motion.

Forcing myself to calm down, I crept through the mud and made a direct line for where I thought the tool shed should be. My plan was to duck behind it, hiding myself from view of the kitchen window (just in case Sarah could still see what I was up to, even through the mist). Then I would cut across the yard to the field.

I'd only gone maybe another twenty or thirty feet when I realized that I didn't have a clue where I was or what direction I was heading. As impossible as it sounds, I was lost in my own backyard. I'd lived here for a good part of my adult life, built the house and shed with my own hands, mowed the lawn thousands of times—but now it was an alien landscape. I glanced around in confusion, looking for something familiar, some recognizable landmark. But there was nothing. The darkness and the rain had swallowed it all, and the ground was torn up from the worms.

Pressing on, I listened for some sign that the worms were nearby, but all I heard was the rain, beating against my hat and slamming into the ground. It seemed to grow stronger with every breath, as if feeding off my fear. I wandered in the darkness—wet, cold, and afraid.

The insistent craving for nicotine grew worse with each step I took, now that the possibility of actually getting some existed. The addiction had overridden every ounce of common sense and instinct for self-preservation that I possessed, and the only thing that mattered now was getting to that helicopter wreckage and finding Salty's leftover cigarettes. I wondered what I'd do if I got there and couldn't find them, or worse, if they were destroyed in the crash. I briefly considered turning around and heading back to the house, but then I pushed the thought from my mind. I'd come too far already and my body was humming from the promise of the tobacco to come. If I had to, I'd hunt down the worm that ate Salty and cut it open and fish his last pack from its belly.

The worst part is that I knew just how unreasonable and stupid I was being, but I didn't care. The cravings were controlling me now, and I was helpless—completely under their whim. I slopped through the mud, hoping that I was going in the right direction. The wet rifle was cold in my hands and my fingers grew numb.

Suddenly, I heard a noise to my left, the sound of something striking against metal. I froze and my body's demand for nicotine vanished, replaced with a cold, paralyzing feeling of dread. I stood there waiting for the sound to be repeated again, waiting to hear that telltale worm hiss, but neither came. I tried to judge where I was and what the noise could have been. If my calculations were correct, then the carport was to my left. Maybe the metallic noise was something brushing up against the truck. But I couldn't be sure. If it was, then I was heading in the right direction, but had placed myself between the shed and the house, rather than going behind the shed.

Could it have been one of those cow-sized worms, sneaking up on the house, or worse yet, creeping along behind me? I didn't know.

Rather than standing there in the darkness trying to figure it out, I kept going. Soon enough, the ground beneath my feet changed from muddy yard to muddy field. It was rockier, more uneven, and I knew that I was going in the right direction. I paused, sniffing the air, and caught a faint hint of oil and burned metal. I smelled something else, too—that familiar fishy odor.

I was close to the crash site, but so were the creatures. Which meant they were also close to me.

There was no sound, no hint of movement, but I could feel them just the same.

I went even more carefully now, and each footstep seemed to take an eternity. The stench from the wreckage grew stronger as I got closer to it. My pulse quickened and a headache bloomed behind my eyes. I could taste phantom tobacco on my tongue, and the mixture of anticipation and fear threatened to overwhelm my senses.

Not that I had any sense left. I was convinced of that now. Common sense had been thrown right out the window the moment I'd decided upon this hare-brained scheme.

As I proceeded, I found myself wondering how the worms hunted. Was it sight or smell, or did they sense our vibrations through the earth? I thought back to the first one I'd seen, the one that had eaten the bird. It had leaped from the ground. The one in the shed had been concealed beneath the floor, but had it known we were there before Carl started stabbing it? The creatures that had come slithering out of the woods were above ground, so that seemed to indicate that they had seen Carl. But then the big one, the granddaddy of them all, had come straight up out of the earth, tunneling towards us from below. How had he known we were there? Maybe he heard the gunshots and the helicopter crash, or sensed us walking above him? Or, was it possible that the other worms communicated with him somehow, maybe through some kind of telepathy, and let him know that lunch was served?

And why did they eat us, anyway? Their smaller cousins ate dirt, if I remembered correctly. They drew their nourishment directly from the soil, absorbing the nutrients and minerals and expelling what they didn't need. Why couldn't these big ones do the same and just leave us alone? Lord knew there was plenty of dirt around, now that the floods were killing off all the vegetation. Why couldn't they just eat that?

Once again, I found myself thinking that, while I may have been the smartest man in Punkin' Center, West Virginia, I sure didn't know a whole lot about worms.

My heel came down on a shard of metal, and then I stumbled over another piece. I'd found the crash site. More wreckage loomed out of the mist, twisted into sinister shapes by the darkness. The rain pelted it all, clanging softly off the steel and fiberglass. The feeling of being watched increased, and the little hairs on the back of my neck stood up. The ammonia stench grew stronger.

I heard a weird sound then, trickling water, like there was a stream nearby. But that didn't make sense. The closest creek was down at the bottom of the hollow, almost a mile away—well past the place where I'd searched for teaberry leaves. Still, I looked down at the ground, and sure enough, there was a stream of running water at my feet. I wondered how that was possible, since I was standing in a relatively flat field.

I took a few more steps and then I could see the debris scattered all around me, pieces of the helicopter and personal belongings that had been tossed out by the impact: food, empty water bottles and soda cans, a cracked wristwatch, scorched clothing, a ripped tent, broken survival gear. I spotted the cockpit seat, but it was empty. The worms had eaten all three portions of Cornwell, even his scraps and guts. Even his blood was gone, washed away by the rain.

THE CONQUEROR WORMS

The sound of running water grew stronger now, and the current licked at my heels. Debris washed by me. I still couldn't see where the stream was going, but the flow increased and I started to get a bad feeling.

Then the ground suddenly gave way beneath my feet.

I teetered on the edge of a great hole, the one left behind by the worm that had eaten Salty earlier in the day. The water was pouring down into the chasm, and the mud along the sides of the hole collapsed underneath me. My arms pinwheeled helplessly. I started to slide and took a step backward, plunging the rifle stock into the ground to stop my fall. I took one faltering step backward, then another. More mud slipped into the hole. A plastic water bottle floated by and disappeared over the edge.

Hyperventilating, I cursed myself again for being such a stupid, weak old man, driven by his need for a chemical fix. I'd almost fallen into that hole and there was no telling how far down it went. I could have been killed, or worse yet, I could have hit bottom and broken my hip or some other bone. I imagined what it would be like to lie there at the bottom of the crevice, shivering from the cold and the pain and unable to move or see. Would the walls have collapsed on me—smothering or crushing me to death—or would I have stayed alive long enough to hear something slithering towards me in the darkness while I lay there helpless and paralyzed?

This quest was idiotic, and I knew that now. I was thinking clearly again and all of my nicotine dreams had fled, replaced with a healthy dose of pure terror. I decided to turn around and head straight back to the house. Sarah would be getting worried by now. I'd been gone for far too long. I couldn't risk her coming out into the night to look for me.

I started back in what I thought was the direction I came from, and that's when I spotted it—a carton of cigarettes, lying half submerged in the mud.

Instantly, I forgot all about dying, all about the worms and their burrows. My fears vanished. This idea hadn't been stupid or pointless. It had all been worth it after all!

I knelt down in the stream, sat my rifle aside, and pulled the carton from the mud. The cardboard fell apart in my fingers, but the cigarette packs themselves were sealed in cellophane. I held my breath as they fell out.

Oh please be dry! Please be dry! That's all I'm asking . . .

I picked up a pack and it turned to mush in my hands. The water had soaked through the cellophane, making them useless. I tried another pack, but it was ruined, too.

Without thinking, I said, "Damn it!"

Something hissed in the darkness.

Instantly, the fish stench became overwhelming. I froze, peering into the mist, not wanting to see it but looking just the same. The creature hissed again from somewhere to my right and I heard it wriggling through the mud. My hands began to tremble and the last soggy pack slipped from my fingers and floated away in the current.

The worm snorted, sounding like a bull getting ready to charge.

Please Lord, I prayed in silence. *Please, Lord, get me out of this. I've lived a good, long life, and I'm willing to come be with you and Rose and the rest of my family whenever you see fit to take me, but don't let me die like this. Not this way. Don't let me die inside the belly of one of these things. That's no way to go. I promise you I will never pollute my body with this crap again. Even if I ever do find some, I won't let a dip pass my lips, if you'll just send that thing away. It can't end like this. What's the point, God?*

"Teddy?" Sarah's voice echoed in the distance. The fog seemed to distort it. "Are you okay? You've been out here for ten minutes."

The worm snorted again, and began to splash around in the mud. My hand crept slowly towards my rifle.

"Teddy? Teddy, are you out here?"

It started slithering away from me. I still couldn't see it, but I could hear it as clear as day.

"Teddy, where are you? Answer me!"

The worm moved faster now, making a beeline for Sarah's voice. Here was proof that they hunted at least by sound.

So I let it know exactly where I was.

"Sarah! Get back inside the house! They're coming!"

My voice sounded small and weak, and the fog seemed to mute my words. I wasn't sure if Sarah heard me or not, but the worm certainly did. It hissed angrily, and two more answered it from either side of me. The ground trembled with their approach.

"Sarah, run!"

Jumping to my feet, I seized the rifle and ran. I ran like I hadn't run since I was in my twenties. I ran like a rabbit being chased by a pack of beagles. I didn't look back, and even if I had, I wouldn't have been able to see much in the darkness, anyway. But all around me were sloshing sounds as the worms gave chase.

The cold air wheezed through my lungs, burning my throat. My knees and calves groaned in protest. I'd been pushing my body hard the last few days and now it was letting me know that it was unhappy with the situation. My muscles rebelled and a fresh burst of pain spiraled through my limbs.

I slipped in the muck, fought to keep my footing, and lost precious seconds, allowing one of the creatures to gain on me. It lunged out of the darkness on my left, covering the distance between us in seconds. Its pale body was obscenely swollen and coated with glistening slime. I skidded to a halt. As the thing bore down on me and opened its maw, I raised the rifle and fired. The blast lit up the night for a second, but then the light was gone, along with what was left of my night vision. The shot ripped into the quivering, rubbery flesh, and stinking fluid gushed from the wound. The worm writhed, from what I guess was pain. Its entire body contorted with spasms.

Without waiting to determine just how much damage I'd done, I set the rifle stock against my shoulder and fired again. Convulsing and enraged, the worm spat at me. A wad of warm phlegm landed on my shoulder, and the stench made me gag. I worked the bolt and got off a third round. Its back end lashed towards me, showering me with mud. I dodged around the convulsing monster and continued running.

My boots churned through the mud. Sweat broke out on my forehead and my breathing hitched as pain radiated throughout my chest. Behind me, I could hear more worms giving chase. I coughed and tasted warm, salty blood in the back of my throat.

I realized then that I wasn't going to make it. The knowledge settled over me with a strange, almost calm sense of certainty. Either the worms would catch me or I'd drop dead of a heart attack—or just plain old-aged fatigue. I halted again, pointed the rifle barrel behind me, aiming blind in the darkness, and squeezed the trigger. Then I dashed away again.

I stumbled and my foot came down hard, sinking into the ground. Ice cold, muddy water flooded my boot. I tried to move, but I was stuck. It felt like my boot was embedded in a slab of freshly poured concrete.

Something barreled down on me from behind. I cast a frightened look over my shoulder and screamed. Three more bus-sized worms were slithering towards me. I wrenched my foot free and began running with one boot and one muddy sock.

Then, like a beacon in the night, a flashlight beam speared through the darkness.

"Drop!" Sarah shouted, and I did.

Flashlight in one hand and her pistol in the other, Sarah opened fire, pausing only long enough to draw a bead after the weapon pulled to the side with each shot. Brass jackets rained into the mud at her feet. The worms squealed behind me, but I didn't turn to look.

"Now run," she called. "This way!"

Pushing myself to my feet, I loped towards her. Sarah put an arm around my waist and I tossed mine over her shoulder. She half guided, half dragged me back to the yard. I felt the wet sidewalk beneath my foot.

"Wh-what about the worms?" I gasped.

"They're gone," she said. "Damn things squirmed away as soon as I started shooting. I don't know if I killed them or not, but I bet they think twice before trying to have us as a midnight snack again."

"Not those," I wheezed. "The—the ones on the carport."

"We'll have to wade through them."

"No." I stood up on my own and held a finger to my lips. "I heard something there when I came outside. Something banged against the truck. It could be another of the big kind. Let's go around back instead."

She nodded and we cut through the yard to the back porch. Once we were safely inside and verified that the worms were indeed not giving chase, Sarah wheeled on me.

"What the fuck were you doing, Teddy? You could have been killed. You almost were!"

"Sshhh," I cautioned her. "No need to wake up Carl and Kevin."

She shook her head. "I can't believe they slept through the shooting."

As if in confirmation, Kevin grunted in his sleep, called out for Lori, and then turned over on the couch.

"What were you doing out there?" she asked again, lowering her voice this time. "Why were you so far from the house?"

"I told you, I had to pee. I guess I just got turned around in the dark."

"Bullshit, Teddy. You were in the field."

My shoulders slumped. "I was looking for Salty's cigarettes. I wasn't thinking clearly."

"I'll say. Jesus Christ . . ."

We both slipped out of our wet coats, and I took my muddy sock off as well. Then I sat down next to the heater and warmed myself. Sarah stood over me, scowling.

"You really scared me out there. That was an incredibly stupid thing to do."

"I know," I admitted. "But at least we learned something tonight."

"What? That you're literally willing to die for a cigarette? I didn't need to know that."

"No, I'm not talking about that."

"Well, what else did we learn, professor?"

"That bullets are effective against those things."

"I don't know." Sarah peeked in on Kevin and then sat down next to me. "I hit them, yes, but I don't think I hurt them very much. If I remember correctly, worms have segmented bodies. You can cut part of them off and the severed portions will still function. If anything, we just scared them off."

"Well, that's better than nothing. Hopefully they're gone for the night and things won't get worse."

"I don't—"

Sarah was interrupted by a dull thump from out on the carport, something bumping against metal. The same sound I'd heard earlier. Then it was repeated.

We both froze. She stared at me, her eyes wide. She reached for the pistol.

"My truck," I whispered, and grabbed the shotgun. "I parked it at the edge of the carport when Carl and I came back yesterday. When I checked it earlier, the worms were up over the tires."

"So?"

"That sound was something striking metal, and the truck is the only metal thing out there. That's the sound I was telling you about."

We kept listening. Silence, followed by another thud, and then a harsh, raspy voice.

"And God said to Noah, 'The end of all flesh is before me; for the earth is filled with violence through them; and I will destroy them with the earth.'"

We gaped at one another.

It was Earl Harper. The crazy bastard was alive, and having an old-fashioned revival meeting right outside my house.

"That's in the Bible!" he shouted. "Genesis six, verses thirteen to seventeen. That cunt of a wife of yours wasn't the only one around here who knew her scripture, Garnett! Bet you didn't think I was paying attention at Bible study, did you?"

"Is that who I think it is?" Sarah asked.

"Yeah." I nodded. "It's Earl."

"What are we going to do?" Sarah whispered.

Silencing her, I got up and crept across the floor, gripping the rifle as tightly as I could.

"Garnett! You awake in there? Answer me, you son of a bitch!"

Carefully, I peeked out through the window in the

door. There was no sign of Earl, and the carport was deserted. The worms were still there, two feet thick in most spots. The old picnic table and my truck were islands in a sea of wiggling, churning, elongated bodies. But there was no Earl.

"And behold," he continued preaching, "I do bring a flood of waters upon the earth and everything that is in the earth shall die! That's from the good book too. Old Earl Harper knows his Bible!"

It sounded like he was standing right outside. I pressed my face against the cold, damp glass and stared, but I still couldn't see him. Earl's voice was muffled, like he was underground, but close by. Something thumped against the truck again and I froze.

Then, the worms around the truck began to move, slowly rising like there was a helium balloon trapped beneath them. They swelled upward and then started to fall off, sliding back down to the pile of their brethren. As they slid away, they revealed Earl.

He had hidden underneath them. He'd concealed himself beneath their bodies.

When the big worm was chasing us all, he must have made it as far as the carport and burrowed underneath the night crawlers, lying beneath them and waiting until he was sure it was gone or that our guard was down.

Earl stood up and brushed the remaining worms from his shoulders and head and arms. Then he saw me gaping at him through the window and he grinned—a smile that seemed to split his face wide open, flashing yellow teeth and curling his lips back into a grimace. Cheshire Earl.

"I am their priest," he shrieked. "I speak for the

worms! Come and listen to their gospel. Listen to the true Word. The gospel of Behemoth!"

Sarah said, "Oh, shit."

I took a deep breath. "This night just went from bad to worse."

But I had no idea just how bad it would get before it was over.

No idea at all . . .

CHAPTER THIRTEEN

Sarah pressed up against me, trying to see over my shoulder. When she caught sight of Earl and the worms dropping from his body, she gave a muffled cry. Earl began to laugh.

In the living room, Kevin finally woke up. He called out in the darkness. "Teddy? Sarah? What time is it? What's going on?"

"We've got trouble," I yelled. "Go wake Carl up and let him know that Earl's back. Tell him to bring his gun."

"Say what?" He rolled off the couch and sprang to his feet, rubbing the sleep from his eyes.

"Listen to me," I shouted. "Just go!"

I turned back to Earl. He was wading towards the door and I swear to God the worms were moving out of his way, clearing a path for him, like Moses parting the Red Sea.

"These are God's creatures," Earl hissed through clenched teeth. He bent over, picked up a handful of worms, and then let them slip through his fingers.

"They talked to me while I laid here. All day and all night long, they told me things. Told me their secrets, Garnett. You wouldn't believe the things they know about. The worms know what lies at the heart of the maze—'cause that's what it is at the center of the earth, a big maze. They crawled into my ears and they whispered to me inside my brain. They told me of the things that live under the ground. The things that should not be. He who shall not be named."

I made sure the door was dead-bolted and then I checked the rifle, verifying that there was a round in the chamber. The barrel was still warm from the previous shots.

"Earl," I called through the door, "I'm only going to say this once. Go home! Get off my carport and leave my property. There's something wrong with you. You need help, and I'm sorry that I can't help you. But I swear to God, if you take another step, I'll shoot you dead."

He stopped and cocked his head to one side. That sneering grin never left his face.

"That's not very neighborly of you, Garnett. Not very neighborly at all."

"Neither is shooting down a chopper full of people." I held the rifle up to the window so that he could see I meant business. "Now get out of here. I mean it. Go on home, Earl. I'm not telling you again. Don't make me do it. I *will* kill you if I have to."

His smile faded.

The worms underneath the doorstep parted, clearing a path for him.

And then Earl charged.

Sarah screamed, "Teddy!"

"Get back, Sarah!"

Swallowing hard, I rammed the barrel of the gun through the window. Broken glass showered down onto the worms below. It was hard to aim, since I was holding the weapon lower than normal, but I pointed the rifle at Earl and squeezed the trigger. The rifle kicked and the shot went wild. The flash lit up the carport and the yard. For a second, I caught sight of the big worms, out there in the darkness. They seemed to be waiting.

Before I could fire again, Earl was at the door. He reached out and grabbed the smoking barrel. His face twisted with rage and he babbled nonsense words.

"Gyyagin vardar Oh! Opi. Ia Verminis! Ia Kat! Ia de Meeble unt Purturabo!"

Sarah frowned. "What the hell is he saying? It's gibberish."

"Ia Siggusim! Guyangar devolos! Verminis Kandara! Behemoth!"

Earl knocked the barrel away from himself just as I squeezed the trigger again. The rifle jerked in my hands, its roar filling the house. Carl and Kevin ran into the kitchen. Carl shouted something, but I couldn't hear him because my ears were ringing. I turned to call for help and the rifle went limp in my hands.

I looked through the hole in the window. Earl was gone again, but he hadn't gone far. As the ringing in my ears faded, I heard him laughing in the rain. He ran through the darkness, his feet squelching loudly in the mud. The big worms had disappeared as well.

"Teddy," Carl shouted, "what in the world is going on?"

"Earl's alive," I gasped, stepping away from the open window. "He hid beneath those worms on the carport, and whatever was left of his sanity is gone. The big worms are out there, too."

"He might as well be dead then. They'll eat him, won't they?"

I shook my head. "I don't think so. They seem to be waiting for something—almost like they're working with him."

"That's crazy," Sarah gasped.

"No, it's not," Kevin said. "The Satanists back in Baltimore were working with Leviathan and the mermaid. Maybe something like that is happening here."

I sighed, and rubbed my tired eyes. "At this point, I'm willing to believe anything, no matter how far-fetched."

"Well," Carl growled. "If the damn things won't kill Earl for us, then let's shoot him ourselves."

Rifle in hand, he started for the door.

"No." I stopped him as he put his hand on the doorknob. "None of us are going outside."

Carl pulled away from my grasp. "Damn it, Teddy! Why not?"

"Because it's not safe anymore, and not just from Earl or the worms. The ground is starting to cave in. You can't see where you're going out there, between the darkness and the fog. You walk around in the dark, and if a worm doesn't swallow you, a sinkhole will. There's a big one out in the field."

"What are you talking about?" Kevin asked. "How do you know this?"

"While you guys were asleep," Sarah told him, "Teddy decided to step out for a pack of smokes. He almost didn't make it back."

Carl let go of the doorknob and sank into a chair at the kitchen table. He rubbed his red eyes and sighed. "You went outside? I reckon you really did need a dip."

"Maybe," I said. "But not anymore. I'm officially cold turkey."

"I've heard that before," Carl said.

I shrugged. "You can believe it this time."

"I recognized some of the words that Earl was shouting," Kevin said. "Ob and Meeble and Kandara. Maybe a few of the others, as well. They were some of the graffiti we saw inside the Satanists' building, during the raid to rescue Christian and Louis. I think they're names or something."

"Names of what?" Sarah asked.

"I don't know. Demons, maybe?"

"Oh, come on, Kevin. Why—"

"I think he's right," I interrupted her. "I don't know how or when Earl Harper became a magus—to be honest, I'd be surprised if he could even read—but that gibberish sounded a whole lot like some kind of spell. Like they do in the movies."

Nobody responded.

Finally, Carl tottered to his feet. "Don't reckon it's too smart for us to be standing around jawing if Earl's still out there and on the loose. We'd better stay awake the rest of the night, and keep a careful watch."

"You're right," I said. "Kevin, you stay here. Carl,

you take the big picture window in the living room. Sarah and I will each take a bedroom window on opposite sides of the house."

"What do we do if he tries to get in?" Kevin asked.

"Shoot him," Carl said. "And if he gets up, then shoot him again."

We each took our positions. I stood in my darkened bedroom and stared out into the rainy night. There was no sign of Earl or the worms and nothing moved in the darkness. The house was quiet. Occasionally, I'd hear a rustle from across the hall as Sarah moved, or Carl sneezing in the living room, but that was it.

I was exhausted, both physically and mentally, so I sat down on the edge of the bed, careful to make sure that I could still see out the window. I yawned. My head felt thick and my eyes itched. The headache still pounded in my temples and my body cried out for nicotine. It was hard to concentrate and my mind drifted. I thought about Rose and our kids and grandchildren. I thought about my days in the Air Force, and of the war, and the places I'd seen and the things I'd done. I thought about my brothers and sisters, and my parents, and of my own childhood. I remembered sunny days—days without a cloud in the sky. Days without rain.

I awoke to the sound of breaking glass, and cursed myself for falling asleep. I sat up on the bed just as Earl crawled through the window.

"Now you'll see, Garnett. Now you'll all fucking see. Behemoth is coming!"

His hand clenched the broken windowpane and a triangular shard of glass sliced into his palm. Earl laughed as the blood dripped between his fingers. A gust of wind blew the rain in behind him, and something else—the all-too-familiar stench of the worms.

Elsewhere, I heard the others shouting. Their footsteps pounded down the hall towards my room. I reached for the rifle, but I couldn't find it in the darkness.

Glass crunched under Earl's feet. He glided toward the bed, wet hair plastered to his scalp, yellow teeth glinting in the darkness. He raised his bloody hands, and in them was the machete I had stored in the shed. He must have broken inside and stolen it.

"We've got unfinished business, Garnett. Seaton and the others, the United Nations folks, are for Behemoth to eat, but you—you were promised to me."

Someone hammered on the bedroom door. I heard voices shouting my name.

"Earl—"

"Save it, fucker. I'm gonna slit you open and gut you like a fish and pull out your insides. I'm going to show you the black stuff inside your belly, and then I'm gonna make you eat it."

The door crashed open and suddenly there was thunder inside the bedroom. Something exploded, and the flash temporarily blinded me. My ears rang and the air stank of cordite. A splash of red appeared on Earl's chest, just above his heart. Sarah fired another round, and Earl toppled to the floor. Carl and Kevin rushed into the room behind her.

Carl gave me a hand getting off the bed. "You okay?"

"I'm fine," I coughed, and prodded Earl's body with my foot. He lay still. The hole in his chest leaked blood, and there was a matching hole in his stomach.

"Is he dead?" Carl asked.

"I reckon so," I said, and kicked him hard in the ribs, just to make sure. Earl didn't move.

Sarah, Kevin, and Carl crowded over his body. Rain poured in through the broken window and the drapes fluttered in the breeze.

"Damn," Sarah said. "I was aiming for his heart."

Carl whistled. "That's still some nice shooting. Only missed it by an inch or so. Remind me to never piss you off, girl."

"What happened?" Kevin asked.

My shoulders sank and I hung my head, ashamed. "I fell asleep and then Earl broke in. I couldn't find my rifle in time."

The bedroom suddenly seemed to spin. I leaned against the dresser to steady myself.

"What was he babbling about?" Carl asked. "Same bullshit as before?"

I nodded. "Something about Behemoth. Apparently, ya'll were going to be its main course tonight."

"There's that name again," Kevin said. "You starting to believe now, Sarah?"

She frowned. "Can we not discuss it right now, please?"

The dresser trembled against my back.

Sarah moved to the window and looked outside.

"See anything?" Carl asked.

"Nothing. There's no sign of the worms. I don't smell them, either."

Kevin moved to her side. "Could they be gone?"

My legs wobbled and I swayed on my feet. Then I noticed that the others were swaying back and forth, too.

Kevin frowned. "What the fuck?"

On the dresser, the pictures began to rattle. Rose's framed embroidery, the one she'd made during our first year of marriage, fell off the wall and crashed to the floor. I heard things breaking elsewhere in the house.

Carl braced himself against the wall. "It's an earthquake for sure this time! Hold on!"

"No," I told him, "it's something else."

At that moment, Earl groaned and opened his eyes.

"Garnett," he croaked. "He's coming. Now you'll see . . ."

"Shut up, Earl."

I kicked him again. This time my boot landed right in his groin, just to illustrate my point, and I almost lost my balance in the process. Earl grunted and the air whooshed out of him. More blood bubbled from the hole in his chest. The house continued to shake.

"Look," Sarah shouted, pointing out the window. "What's that? Out there beyond the clothesline?"

I turned to where she was pointing and my heart seemed to stop. My skin felt cold.

The thing that should not be . . .

It hurtled toward the house, a legless, eyeless thing, five times larger than the one we'd encountered before. Its body was milk-white and so pale in some places that it was almost translucent. Slime dripped from the creature's body, leaving a glistening trail in its wake. It barreled across the yard and rolled over the shed in one segmented wriggle, squashing the building flat.

"What is it?" Sarah screamed again.

"Hell," I said simply.

"Behemoth," Kevin whispered. "It's fucking Behemoth. Leviathan's big brother."

Sarah backed away from the window; Earl opened his eyes again.

"Now you'll see, you bastards," Earl cackled, blood spraying from his lips. He sat up, grunting with the effort. "This is the hour of *His* coming. *Behemoth!* Verminis! The servant of He Who Shall Not Be Named. He is the brother of Leviathan, the son of that old serpent! The Worm from beyond space. The Star-Eater. Behemoth the Great!"

"Shut the hell up, Earl!" Carl shouted. He raised his rifle, drawing a bead on the madman, but the ground shook again and his aim wavered. "Ain't you supposed to be dead?"

I didn't wonder about Earl's miraculous resurrection. I just stared, absolutely transfixed by the monstrous thing bearing down on us.

The worm was colossal, but even that doesn't begin to describe it. I told you before that I'm no writer. I don't even know where to begin when it comes to describing that thing. To be honest, I'm not even sure it *was* a worm. The quivering, jiggling mounds of segmented flesh were leathery and thick, like rawhide.

For a second, I thought back to when the kids had been little. One summer, Rose and I had taken them to Washington, D.C. for vacation, and we visited the Museum of Natural History. I remembered the feeling of awe that had gripped me as we stood under the life-sized replica of a blue whale that hung suspended from the ceiling, and how we'd marveled that such a giant creature could exist on the earth.

The thing slithering towards the house could have easily swallowed that blue whale whole. It was that big. It blocked out the cloudy night sky as it neared the house. The creature opened its mouth and hissed; the sound was like a bomb blast. I felt the pressure on my eardrums.

"Get the fuck back!" Kevin shouted.

"Move out of the way," Carl told him, still pointing his rifle at Earl.

"Forget about the hillbilly," Kevin snapped. "We've got bigger issues!"

With an incredibly powerful lurch, the monster launched its front segments into the air. It stayed there for a moment, suspended above the house. Then it plummeted downward and plowed into the dirt, sending a massive plume of soil and rock into the air. With a shock, I realized that it was burrowing its way beneath the house. Its gargantuan bulk tunneled into the ground, disappearing from view. I couldn't see it, but that didn't matter. It was easy enough to track.

We could feel the creature's approach beneath our feet. The vibrations sounded like a jackhammer.

Groaning, Earl slowly lurched to his feet. With frightening strength, he shoved Kevin out of the way, knocking him onto the bed. Earl struck Carl's rifle aside, and Carl took a step backward. Earl's filth-covered hands clutched at Carl's throat and Carl's eyes bulged in their sockets.

"I am born again," he snarled.

Without even aiming to avoid hitting Carl, Sarah raised her pistol and pointed it at Earl. "Let him go!"

"Back off, bitch," Earl wheezed, "or I'll squeeze

his goddamn eyes right out of his head." Blood streamed down his chest and back, and bubbled from his lips. I wondered how it was even possible that he was standing.

Kevin tumbled off the bed, searching for his gun in the darkness. I finally spotted mine, lying half under the bed where it had fallen when I fell asleep. I bent over to snatch it up and a particularly violent tremor rocked the house. As I rose, my head banged into Kevin's stomach. Kevin fell backward with a squawk, landing on the mattress again.

"I said let him go," Sarah warned. "Now!"

Carl and Earl spun in a circle, their hands wrapped around each other's throats. They toppled to the floor, and Earl rolled on top of Carl's body, sitting astride his chest. Carl's face was turning purple and the tiny blood vessels in his eyes were rupturing, turning them bloodshot.

I raised my rifle and tried to get a clear shot, but there was too much going on; so instead, I crossed the room, intent on ripping Earl from my best friend's body.

"Behemoth's gonna eat you all," Earl said. "Wait and see! No sense in running. There's nowhere to hide."

Carl's tongue protruded from his mouth.

I stared through the crosshairs, and that's when I noticed it. The veins in Earl's forearms bulged, and something squirmed inside them, just beneath the skin. Something long—like a worm.

Moving quickly, Sarah crossed the floor and struck Earl on the back of the head with the pistol butt. Earl's grip stayed firm. She swung again and there was a sickening crunch. Dime-sized drops of blood flew across the room, splattering against the wall. The house shook as she hit him a third time, and Earl's grip loosened. His hands slipped from Carl's throat and he fell over, sprawling onto the floor.

Carl sat up weakly and shook his head. He coughed, and I noticed red welts around his neck in the shape of Earl's fingers. I knelt beside him while Sarah checked Earl's pulse.

"You okay?" I asked Carl.

He squinted, his eyes shut in pain. "C-cant . . . catch . . . m-my . . . breath . . . H-hurts . . ."

The tremors increased. Pictures and knickknacks crashed to the floor. Somewhere below us, the foundation groaned.

"Carl, can you stand up?"

"It h-hurts . . ."

"Earl's dead," Sarah told us. She stood up and spit on his body. "That's for Salty and Cornwell, you son of a bitch."

"You sure he's dead this time?" I asked.

She nodded. "I can't find a pulse."

I considered telling the others what I'd seen burrowing around beneath Earl's flesh, but decided against it. There was no time.

"Come on," I urged Carl. "You've got to stand up. I know it hurts, but we've got to go."

The floorboards buckled and all across the house windows shattered in their sills. The dresser slid several inches across the rug.

"What are we going to do?" Kevin shouted. "It's right underneath us!"

"Grab Carl's arm," I told him. "Let's try to make it to my truck."

"But the rest of the worms are still out there."

I held on to Carl. "That don't matter now, Kevin. Sarah proved that they ain't bulletproof. The truck's our only chance."

We helped Carl to his feet. He coughed again, tried to swallow, and winced. The claw marks on his throat were raw and red; angry looking welts that stood out against his pale white skin.

"And when we get to your truck?" Sarah asked, wiping Earl's blood from the pistol butt.

"Try for Bald Knob, I guess. Pray that things are better there."

"That thing can swallow your truck in one bite," Kevin argued. "This is pointless."

I let go of Carl and jabbed my finger into Kevin's chest. "Do you have any better ideas, boy?"

Kevin shook his head. "No."

"Then shut your mouth. I'll be damned if I'm gonna wait around here while that thing eats the house out from underneath us."

"Hey—"

Sarah cut him off. "Let's go."

She stepped out into the hallway. Another tremor shook the house and she bounced against the wall.

Another bout of coughing seized Carl, and he doubled over, grasping his throat.

"Just . . . leave . . . me . . ."

"Don't even start with that," I said. "We're going to be okay."

306

THE CONQUEROR WORMS

Behind us, the dresser toppled over and the floorboards began to snap like twigs.

Sarah urged us on. "Come on. The whole damn house is caving in."

We made it to the kitchen. While Kevin kept Carl propped up, I ran to the hutch and grabbed my truck keys off the top of it. Just as I did, the entire house seemed to jump up into the air. There was a horrible, deafening rumble from downstairs, followed by the sounds of snapping timber and crumbling masonry. Something—either the basement floor or one of the retaining walls—collapsed. All of us were thrown to the floor. Above me, I heard tiles sliding off the roof.

Then, Behemoth roared. It sounded like a steam train was charging through the basement. The noise filled our ears, filled the house itself. It drowned out the rain.

"Holy shit," Kevin gasped, picking himself back up. "He's right underneath us!"

"Everybody out," I said. "We're out of time."

"You can say that again," Earl rasped, stumbling into the kitchen. Blood streamed from his split scalp, staining the collar of his shirt.

Kevin looked at Sarah as she clambered to her feet.

"I thought you said he was dead," Kevin shouted.

She stumbled. "He didn't have a fucking pulse!"

"Let he who believes in me have eternal life," Earl wheezed, and took another step forward. This time, it was unmistakable. Long, thin forms moved beneath his skin, traveling through his bare arms and climbing up his neck and face.

Sarah choked. "Oh my God . . ."

Carl and I raised our rifles at the same time.

"Go ahead," Earl cackled. A worm fell from his open mouth. "Shoot me again, you bastards."

Before we could, the house bucked in its frame again and then tilted to one side. Carl and Sarah were both knocked to the floor again, and Sarah's pistol went off. Kevin crashed into the refrigerator. The kitchen table and the hutch both slid towards me, slamming me into the wall and pinning my legs. An excruciating jolt of pain ran through my entire body, from my toes all the way up my spine. I screamed, and black spots swam before my eyes. I fought to keep from vomiting as another surge of pain coursed through my body. My left leg began to shriek, from the thigh down. I knew right then that it was broken.

Above us, the roof split open, revealing the dark sky. The rain poured through the snapped timbers and the wind howled, buffeting us all. The temperature in the kitchen immediately dropped.

Beneath our feet, Behemoth roared.

Earl staggered backward into the living room and Carl crawled after him. The two of them grappled and rolled onto the couch, which had also begun to slide across the floor. Carl's fingers sought the bullet hole in Earl's chest, and he shoved one inside. Shrieking, Earl snatched up a heavy glass ashtray from the coffee table and brought it swiping down on Carl's forehead. I heard the sickening crunch from where I was pinned in the kitchen, even over the cries of the creature. The ashtray shattered.

The house slid another foot, swaying like a boat at

sea. The couch crashed into the recliner and Earl jumped free, abandoning Carl and wheeling on the rest of us. He still clutched a dripping shard of the ashtray in his hand.

Lying in a prone position, Sarah aimed and fired. The shot went wild.

The thing beneath our feet hissed like an industrial furnace ready to blow.

Sarah fired a second shot, catching Earl in the shoulder. He jerked backward and then grinned. Sarah pulled the trigger again as he flung the shard of glass at her. The third bullet plowed into Earl's thigh. Another quake shook the house and Earl charged Sarah, leaping into the air despite his wounds. It was almost like he was possessed.

Gritting my teeth against the pain, I fought to stay conscious, while Kevin ran to help Sarah. Earl's teeth sank into her wrist and her blood welled around his lips. Sarah shrieked, dropping the gun onto the tilting floor. The house rolled again, rattling the foundation. Kevin slid away from them, his hands grasping uselessly.

The tremor shook the hutch, and both it and the table slammed into me again. This time, something snapped—I heard a wet sound inside my chest. I cried out in agony, struggling to free both myself and the rifle. Every tiny movement was excruciating.

The floor splintered beneath Kevin and his lower half dropped through the hole. He clutched the broken timbers, holding on for dear life.

"Oh Jesus," he screamed. "I can see it! It's in the basement!"

With her free hand, Sarah dug her fingernails into

Earl's face, slashing at his nose and cheek. Skin peeled away, leaving red racing stripes. Worms burrowed beneath the wounds. Earl tried to scramble away, but Sarah rammed her elbow into the bullet wound in his shoulder.

"Not this time, you son of a bitch," she snarled. "This time, I'll make sure you don't get back up."

Carl rolled off the couch, dazed and bleeding.

"My God is hungry," Earl rasped, and then punched Sarah in the face—once, twice, three times in rapid succession. Sarah's shoulders sagged and blood streamed from her nose. Then, twisting her hair in his fist, Earl forced her head down and marched her past me across the rolling floor. Her body was limp and she put up no resistance. They were heading towards the basement.

I don't know how he kept moving, how he stayed alive. Earl was in bad shape; a bloody, shot-up mess. But somehow, he refused to die. Perhaps whatever was crawling around inside his body had reanimated him. Taken control. Maybe there really was something to the black magic gibberish he'd been spouting before, or maybe he was just being bullheaded. I don't know. I can only tell you that it was almost as frightening as the monster digging up through my basement floor.

Earl and Sarah reached the door. He gave her hair another twist, and she squealed.

"Sarah!" Kevin screamed, trying to free himself from the hole.

The rain pattered against the kitchen tiles.

"Carl," I shouted. "Get up! My leg's busted and I can't get loose! You've got to help Sarah and Kevin!"

Carl shook his head, trying to clear it. He wiped the blood from his eyes and tottered to his feet.

"Come on, Carl," I urged. "Move!"

Earl flung the basement door open and Sarah screamed. At the same time, Kevin freed himself from the hole.

I don't know if it came from the open door or the chasm in the kitchen floor, but the stench was overpowering. It immediately filled the house, choking me with its ammonialike stench. My eyes and nose burned.

But as bad as the creature's smell was, the sound— *my God*—the sound was worse. That same forceful exhaling of air that I had heard the other worms make, now magnified tenfold. It pushed against my eardrums, making my head throb.

Sarah teetered at the top of the basement steps. "Let me go, god damn you!"

"My pleasure, bitch!" Earl pushed her forward. Her shriek was cut short, lost beneath the cry of the great worm.

Kevin crept unsteadily past me as the floor began to shimmy again. Enraged, he threw himself at Earl and they both pitched forward into the cellar.

Carl made it across the floor to where I was pinned. Grunting with exertion, the two of us managed to push the table and the hutch aside. My leg and side throbbed when I moved, sending a fresh burst of pain that made further movement impossible.

"Where's it hurt?" Carl asked me.

"My leg's broke," I panted, "and I might have busted

a rib, too. I'm not sure. But don't worry about me. Kevin and Sarah fell into the basement. Help them."

But Carl wouldn't listen. He lurched away, looking for something.

"Carl, what are you doing?"

"Finding something you can use for a crutch. Now hush. Just rest."

I glanced around the kitchen in confusion, staring at the wreckage of my former life with Rose. Amazingly, the only thing that didn't seem to have been destroyed was the kerosene heater. It had slid a few inches, but remained upright. The kettle had fallen to the floor and rolled away, but the heater itself stood firm.

"Carl, just forget about it!"

He didn't answer, and passed from my sight.

I dragged myself forward to the doorway—each inch that I crawled was excruciating. Sweat broke out on my forehead and under my armpits, and my body began to tremble. The creature's stink grew stronger— overpowering my senses as I drew closer. Finally, I reached the basement stairs and peeked over the edge, afraid for what I would find.

I screamed.

The cellar floor was gone, replaced by a giant, slavering mouth—at least twenty-feet wide. It sounds crazy, but that's the only way to describe it. The entire floor had vanished and Behemoth's mouth occupied the space where it had been. A small outcropping of concrete at the bottom of the stairway was all that re- mained. Kevin and Earl struggled on this tiny alcove, while Sarah lay bleeding on the stairs. Below them, the worm pulsed and quivered hungrily, the massive throat convulsing. Its mouth was lined with lamprey-like tentacles, each one tipped with another tinier mouth of its own. These smaller mouths opened, even thinner tendrils emerging from them. Then, rising from the center of Behemoth's throat, rose a stalklike tongue composed of more worms, blind and wriggling. All of the tentacle-worms chirped greedily, sensing the prey above them.

"I found this—my God . . . ," Carl gasped behind me. Blood still dripped from the ugly-looking gash on his forehead. He held a baseball bat in one hand, which I guess he'd thought I could use for a crutch.

He gaped at the creature below us. Then, without another word, he turned and fled.

"Carl!" I was shocked and dismayed. I'd known Carl for most of my adult life, and never once had I known him to be a coward.

Earl shoved Kevin toward the edge of the pit. Kevin punched him in the temple. Snarling, Earl punched him back. Kevin dodged the blow, brought his knee up into Earl's crotch and then grabbed the madman by his neck and waistband. With a single, mighty heave, he threw Earl over the side.

Behemoth roared, as did the small worms inside his mouth.

Earl screamed, twisting in midair. The worm-tongues stretched forward in eager anticipation. Pale slime dripped from their mouths. Earl latched on to a jutting piece of floor support and clung to it, dangling over the stinking maw. The earthworms inside of him wriggled from his gunshot wounds and burst through his arms and cheeks. One uncoiled from his ear and plummeted down into the pit.

"I—I worship you," he cried out. "Lord, please!"

"Kevin," I shouted as best I could, weak from the pain in my leg. "Sarah! Let's go."

Sarah didn't move.

My leg was starting to swell, and when I coughed blood leaked from the corner of my mouth. Then my ears began to ring and my face felt flushed. I knew enough to recognize that I was going into shock.

"Hurry," I gasped.

Kevin stood at the edge of the concrete and stared down at Earl.

Earl's fingers slipped on the concrete and he struggled to hold on. "What are you looking at, boy? Give me a hand."

"You shot down our helicopter," Kevin said. "You killed our friends."

Earl's arms trembled and his face turned white. More earthworms dug their way out of his flesh. "Y-yeah, but I'm—"

Kevin stomped on his fingers. Hard. Hard enough to make me wince, despite my own pain, and despite everything that Earl had done. Screeching, Earl lost his grip and fell. His scream lasted only as long as his descent—about two seconds.

Then, the worm-tongues inside Behemoth's throat began to feed. At the same time, the throat muscles contracted and Earl was drawn farther inside.

Kevin picked up Sarah and plodded up the swaying staircase.

Beneath him, Behemoth swallowed Earl with a noxious, gaseous belch. Then the mouth opened again and the tentacles began to slither upward, feeling their way across the bottom stair.

"Please, hurry," I coughed, and more blood trickled from my mouth. Each cough brought a sharp, stabbing pain in my side.

Suddenly, I sensed movement behind me and saw Kevin's eyes grow wide. I turned around and there was Carl, wearing a pair of oven mitts and lugging the still hot kerosene heater.

"I thought you ran off," I told him, smiling weakly.

"Not hardly." His bloody expression was one of wounded pride. "Why would you think something like that, Teddy? After all we've been through? I didn't run off. I just went and cooked something up."

I coughed blood and nodded at the kerosene heater. "Isn't that a bit hot?"

He nodded, struggling to hold the heater upright. "Yeah, and it's burning a hole through these here oven mitts. This thing got one of those automatic safety shut off switches?"

"No," I groaned, as Sarah and Kevin stumbled out of the tilting stairwell.

"Good," Carl said. "Then get out of my way."

Kevin gently sat Sarah down. "Can you stand?" he asked her.

"Yeah." She nodded, and then caught sight of my leg and the blood leaking from my lips. "Teddy, what happened?"

"I'll be okay." I smiled, trying to reassure her. "Been through worse back during the war."

Kevin stood up. "We've got to get you guys out of here. Mr. Seaton, what are you doing with that kerosene heater?"

Carl nodded towards the basement stairs. "Reckon we'll see if that big ugly bastard likes hot food."

Wincing, I dug into my pants pocket and tossed Kevin the keys to my truck. I was thankful that I'd put them there before the table and hutch had pinned me against the wall. Otherwise, they'd be lost now, scattered by the rolling floor.

Kevin caught them with one hand. "What now?"

"I want you to go start my truck. I don't know if Earl messed with it or not, but we need to find out. Take Sarah with you."

"But what about you guys?" Kevin asked.

"Don't you worry about us," Carl said. "We'll be right behind you."

"We've got to help you out of here, Teddy," Sarah argued. "And Carl—you've probably got a concussion. Your head is really bleeding."

"I'm fine. Just a scratch." He sat the heater down.

"It's not a scratch," she said. "And neither one of you is fine!"

"You just go with Kevin," I shouted back. "See if my truck starts. If it does, then get out of here. Go to the end of my lane, hang a right, and just keep on going till you run out of road. When that happens, you'll be at Bald Knob, where the big forest ranger tower is. You can't miss it."

"Wait a minute," Kevin spoke up, startled. "That doesn't make sense at all. We sure as hell aren't leaving you guys behind!"

"You're not," I said. "Once we've taken care of ol' Behemoth, we'll follow along behind you in Carl's truck. We'll all meet up at Bald Knob."

Kevin frowned. "Have you lost your mind?"

"Listen. Carl and me—we're old. Even if we make it through this, we don't have much time left in this world." I glanced down at my leg, and then back up to them. "Somebody needs to kill this thing, or try to at least. There's no sense in sacrificing all of us, if things don't go well. Now I'm tired of arguing. There's no time."

Sarah touched my shoulder. "But—"

"Go," I said, and then broke into another coughing fit.

"Don't worry," Carl said, and picked up the heater again. "We'll be along soon as we kill it."

"Is that going to work?" Kevin asked, skeptically.

Carl nodded. "I reckon so. At the very least, it'll give him a nasty case of indigestion."

"What if there are more of those creatures outside?" Sarah asked. "How will we get past them?"

"We'll just have to take that chance," Kevin said, jangling the keys.

"Now go," I told them. "Please?"

Kevin tugged on her arm. Below us, Behemoth roared. I could hear the tentacle things sliding on the stairs, inching higher. The house began to shake again.

Sarah turned back to Carl and I. "You promise you'll meet us at Bald Knob?"

I nodded. "We promise."

"If we're able," Carl added.

They stumbled out the kitchen door, pausing to wade through the pile of worms on the carport. Sarah gave us one last backward glance and then they were gone.

I looked up at Carl. "You really think that heater will hurt it?"

"It's worth a try. Bullets sure ain't doing much."

"Well, then nail that thing and drag me the hell out of here."

He nodded grimly and stepped up to the edge of the stairway. "Take a deep breath, you big ugly bastard, cause the next one is gonna burn!"

Behemoth hissed in response.

"Don't miss," I coughed.

"You ever known me to miss?"

"Plenty of times."

He snickered, and then we both laughed. It hurt me to do so, but there was no helping it.

"You're a good man, Teddy Garnett."

"You too, Carl Seaton. You too."

"Bombs away!" Carl turned back to the stairs, raised the kerosene heater up to chest level, and then flung it down the stairs, just as another tremor shook the house. He lost his balance and grabbed for the door frame, but the oven mitts on his hands slipped off the wood. Carl teetered on the edge, and then, with a quick, startled yelp, he was gone.

It happened that quickly.

One moment he was there. The next he was gone, tumbling down after the kerosene heater.

He didn't even scream.

"Carl? *Carl!*"

I scrambled to the edge of the stairs, ignoring the pain in my body. There was no sign of the heater. Or Carl. And Behemoth's mouth was closed, swallowing. Its entire body quivered.

Carl was gone. My best friend in the whole world—my only friend left in the world—was gone. He hadn't died at home in his bed, surrounded by loved ones and friends, or peacefully in his sleep, or even in a faraway veteran's hospital. He'd died inside this creature's stomach.

I closed my eyes.

And then the worm turned.

And screamed . . .

Bullets may not have hurt it, but a blazing hot kerosene heater upended down its throat sure as heck did. The blast of air that barreled out of the monster's throat slammed into me with enough force to ruffle my wet hair, and then swept throughout the remains of the kitchen. My ears popped from the unexpected force of it. The air stank of fishy ammonia and burning flesh, and I could hear the creature's throat sizzling. Behemoth squalled again, retching as the burning kerosene went to work deep within its bowels. The worm's body twisted, racked with earthshaking convulsions as it retreated back down the tunnel, leaving an empty, gaping hole in its place. Chunks of concrete and dirt flowed into the vacant space.

Then the house fell silent. I could hear the clock ticking in the living room (amazingly, it had survived the shaking), and the rain pouring in through the damaged roof and pattering across the tiles and broken furniture.

I hugged myself, shivering in the cold, damp air, and wished to die.

The next sound was impossible to describe, and there's just no way I can do it justice. A massive, concussive *belch* thundered up from far below. It was followed by a rushing noise as dark, dank water spouted up the tunnel and flooded into what remained of my basement. It stank—a sour, spoiled reek that turned my stomach. I gagged and turned my face away. The black liquid rushed halfway up the staircase before slowing, and when I looked back I gagged again, vomiting blood. There were things floating in that digestive stew—a half-eaten deer carcass, the hindquarters of a black bear, a car tire and license plate, soda pop bottles, building timbers, masonry and bricks, the skeletal remains of a human arm, and a plastic trash can.

And the kerosene heater.

And Carl.

Then pieces of the worm itself started to float up: shredded, blackened hunks of pale, blubbery flesh.

And more of Carl. His head bobbed in the soup, and I noticed a sucker mark on his cheek—just like the one Kevin had found on his friend Jimmy.

I leaned back against the wall and pushed the door shut on its crooked frame. It wouldn't close all the way, and I hammered at it feebly, feeling weak and old and small and afraid. I heard the waters below, bubbling and churning and not stopping.

Just like the rain.

Then I closed my eyes and stopped listening.

CHAPTER FOURTEEN

That was last night. Now it's late in the afternoon again, or at least what passes for afternoon these days; that dull, gray haze. I've been writing all night long and straight through the morning, cramming words into this little spiral-bound notebook. My busted leg is swelled up like a balloon, and it really doesn't even look like a leg anymore. I cut my pants open a few minutes ago and what I saw made me queasy. The skin of my thigh is shiny and greasy and stretched like a sausage casing. Like I said earlier, I can't feel anything below my waist and that's a blessing.

I keep saying I won't look down there anymore, but then I do. Morbid curiosity, I guess.

At least there's no White Fuzz growing on me yet. Of course, maybe that would be a blessing at this point. I still don't know what it is or how it works, but perhaps it would be quicker than lying here suffering.

I'm dying. Or will be soon, if help doesn't come. I need a miracle, but those seem to be in short supply these days.

I'm going to die at home—cold, wet, and alone. Not in my bed and surrounded by friends and family, but lying on the floor in a puddle of water. All by myself. Not how I pictured it.

But I finished this, and that's all that matters. I'm done with my tale, my record. My story. Don't know if it matters or not. Who's left to find it? Still, it's here. I'll put it someplace safe. Somewhere dry. And maybe, just maybe, someone will find it, and read it, and know that I once lived. They'll know of Teddy Garnett and what he saw, what he felt and thought, and what kind of man he was. That's the only kind of immortality we have down here; we live on in the memories of those who come after. The other kind of eternal life, the kind my Rose enjoys, exists on the other side, and is unattainable for those left behind—those left alive. We can't enjoy it until we die.

With great effort and patience, and several spells of almost blacking out from the pain, I did manage to drag myself over to the kitchen door, so that I could see outside. The carport was still covered in wriggling bodies, but Behemoth's attack on the house had left the cement outside cracked and broken. The picnic table was knocked over and my Taurus was a crumpled hulk of steel and fiberglass.

Carl's truck lay on its passenger side and the plump end of a canoe-sized earthworm protruded from the driver's side window. The tail wagged up and down, like it was waving at me.

I waved back. And then I laughed. It was either that or cry.

My truck is gone, so I guess that Kevin and Sarah

got away safely. All that's left is two tire tracks full of flattened worms. While I watched, the ruts filled back in with rainwater and night crawlers.

I keep listening, hoping to hear the sound of a truck engine coming down the lane, praying for the sound of tires crunching through the wet gravel. But all I hear is the rain.

Where could they be?

According to my calculations, it would have taken Sarah and Kevin an hour to reach Bald Knob, or maybe an hour and a half, depending on the road conditions. Unless the road was completely washed out or covered with fallen trees. But if that were the case, they'd have turned around and come back, wouldn't they?

Sure they would. Kevin and Sarah were good kids. They wouldn't abandon us. They wouldn't leave two old men like Carl and me here to die. Not like this. They knew I was hurt. Hurt bad. They wouldn't just leave me here. They'd come back. When Carl and I didn't show up by dawn, they'd have come looking for us.

Which means that something must have happened to them.

Maybe they got caught in a mudslide, or maybe they ran off the road or something. My truck's got a pretty good four-wheel drive system, but would Kevin and Sarah have known how to operate it? They were city folk, after all. Could be they're stranded out there somewhere and the truck's got a busted axle.

Or maybe the worms got them. I hate to consider the possibility, but I'd be a fool not to. Are there more of them out there in the mountains, burrowing through the earth? Other than the one inside Carl's truck, I haven't seen any of the big worms. Could be they chased off after Kevin and Sarah. Or maybe Behemoth scared them away.

Or else the worms are up to something. Something that I haven't yet figured out.

Maybe they're just waiting for me to fall asleep.

The house keeps sliding downward, creaking and shuddering every few minutes. Every time it sways, I feel like Captain Ahab, clinging to the mast of my ship. But instead of a white whale, I fought a white worm.

If I have to—if the house starts to cave in completely, I can roll myself out onto what's left of the carport. But I'll wait until the very last moment before I do that. I don't want to lie among those worms.

I'm scared.

I'm afraid of what they might tell me. Would they crawl into my ears and burrow through my brain, whispering their secrets to me the way they did to Earl? What would they have to say? Would they teach me of their legends? Would they tell me what lies at the center of the earth, at the heart of the labyrinth?

Would they preach to me about their earthworm gods?

The water is starting to seep out from under the basement door now, and it's still pouring through the holes in the roof. There's about six inches on the floor and it keeps rising. Won't take long for the house to flood completely.

My lower half is wet, but I'm not going to look. Can't really feel the wetness anyway, so why does it matter?

I wonder if heaven is warm and dry. I sure hope so.

I couldn't find my crossword puzzle book, but I

found Rose's Bible amid the wreckage, and I've been reading it off and on, in between writing in this notebook and falling asleep and gritting my teeth from the sheer pain. I opened the Bible, seeking some comfort, and I read about the Great Flood. I read about how, after the waters had settled, God sent a dove back to Noah on the ark. The dove had an olive branch in its mouth, and that was a good sign. A sign from God, telling Noah that the rains were over and the waters were receding. Then Noah knew that he could come out onto dry land again.

That was the first Bible story I ever heard and it was always one of my favorites. I always believed it and I'd like to believe it now. But I can't. God help me, for the first time in my eighty-plus years on this planet, I just can't.

So I'm lying here, waiting. Waiting to see what happens next. That's how this ends, because that's life. Our stories, our real-life tales, seldom have a perfect ending. Things go on, even after we're gone, and when we die, we don't get to see what happens next.

There's nothing left to say. This is the end of my tale.

I'm waiting for Kevin and Sarah to come back and rescue me.

Or I'm waiting to be reunited with Rose again. I'm waiting to die.

Whichever happens first.

But most of all, I'm waiting for the rain to stop and for the clouds to part and the sun to shine again.

I saw something earlier. It wasn't a worm or a monster or a deer with white fungus growing on it.

It was a crow. First bird I've seen since the robin—a

big, blue-black crow with beady eyes and a sharp, pointed beak, its feathers wet and slick with rain. It perched on the fallen picnic table, swooped down onto the carport, plucked up an earthworm from the cracked cement, and gobbled it down like a strand of spaghetti. Then it flew back up to the table and sat, watching me through the door and the holes in the wall.

It just now flew away. Its black wings sliced through the rain and a long worm dangled from its beak.

The rain didn't slow it down.

The Ancient Mariner saw an albatross and Noah saw a dove. Those were their signs. They were good signs. They brought luck and fortune—and dry land.

Me? I saw a crow eating a worm.

I wonder if that's a sign, and if so, what kind?

I need a dip. Some nicotine would make this easier. . . .